To Kelly,

Thanks for all of y[illegible]
support & help —
Much appreciated

Alan Stone

ADOPTION

CHRISTOPHER STONE

AuthorHouse™
1663 Liberty Drive
Bloomington, IN 47403
www.authorhouse.com
Phone: 1 (800) 839-8640

Published by AuthorHouse 05/29/2015

ISBN: 978-1-5049-1390-4 (sc)
ISBN: 978-1-5049-1391-1 (hc)
ISBN: 978-1-5049-1392-8 (e)

Library of Congress Control Number: 2015908249

Print information available on the last page.

To my wife Peggy, for putting up with me and the many hours she spent reading and finding things to do while I wrote this story.

To Dr. Catharine Wingate Levine who passed just prior to this story's printing. Her beautiful spirit will be missed.

PROLOGUE

Dave Johnson and Rick McKinna were enjoying an unscheduled day off from their junior high school in Sutton, Massachusetts. A Nor'easter had dropped eleven inches of white, powdery snow the night before, and they were going to take full advantage of every minute of their snow day. They pulled their toboggans through dense brush and small trees at the edge of Meadow Pond. They needed to cross the pond to go sliding down Dead Man's Hill at Vandanaker's dairy farm on the opposite shore. Dead Man's Hill sloped down at almost 60 degrees and was considered the prime sledding spot in the neighborhood. It would only take fifteen minutes to cross the pond, but first they had to jump down the embankment after pushing through the leafless, gray brush standing guard at the pond's edge. Rick was first to come out through the last of the branches that scraped his cheeks and poked at his bright, red, knitted, wool hat. The scrapes from those icy, wooden fingers burned his skin as he reached up to wipe away particles of bark and ice left behind.

"Crap," he said out loud. His hat had gotten snarled and pulled from his head, now hanging from a branch in the air about three inches out of reach.

"Freakin son of a toad's ass!" he yelled as he lost his footing reaching for it.

Dave reached out to grab him before he fell onto the ice, but lost his footing, too. Rick took the brunt of the fall, air rushing out of his lungs loudly as his back hit the ice.

"Jesus, Rick, you tryin' to kill us both? I almost busted my friggin' head open on the toboggan!" Dave said, rolling onto his side in an attempt to get up.

Rolling toward the shoreline his eyes caught sight of a shadowed figure sticking out from a dark undercut in the pond's embankment. At first he wasn't sure his eyes could possibly be looking at what was registering in his brain. Although wrapped up tightly in a heavy, insulated, snowsuit, he felt a coldness running through his body from the inside out not the outside in. He wanted to look away, but he couldn't turn his head. It was frozen in place like the winter ice he was lying on.

"Rick! Rick!" He heard himself say, but the words were not coming out of his mouth.

He could hear them in his head, but in his head they remained. His brain became electrified as uncontrolled fear took over his conscious thoughts. He wasn't old enough to comprehend what he was looking at. In one part of his mind he knew it was a woman's head and arm sticking out of the dirt, snow and brush. He also knew the woman was dead. But, in another part of his mind, he was screaming uncontrollably while focusing on her eyes and lips, or rather, where her eyes and lips should have been.

Pushing himself away, wildly flailing his arms and legs, Dave moved further and further away from the shoreline. He looked like a beetle stuck on its back as he let out a low pitched moan moving past Rick who stood brushing snow off his suit while looking across to the other side of the pond. It wasn't until Dave moved past him on the ice that Rick realized something had gone drastically wrong with their sledding adventure.

"What the hell are ya doin'?" Rick yelled. "What the hell's gotten into you?" he asked turning to pick up the rope of the toboggan. That was when Rick saw the woman's face staring at him through two, black, blood-dried holes - dirt-stained teeth smiling, lipless, in dead, cold silence.

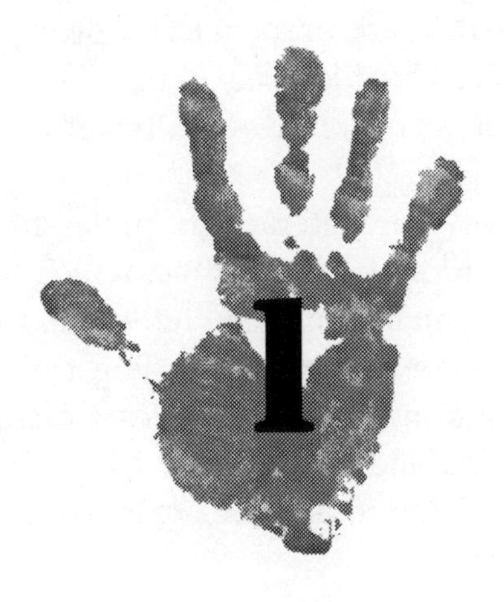

The smell of bacon frying in the old, iron skillet caught my attention. Peggy always used the iron skillet saying it added a generational flavor to whatever she was cooking at the time. Her grandmother scrambled many farm-fresh eggs and fried butter-soaked pirogues for Peggy when she was growing up. She would not think of parting with the old relic. I pictured her standing in the kitchen wearing her loose, grey, pajama bottoms and Becker Jr. College sweatshirt. I was somewhere between waking up and wanting to roll over and ignore my taste buds, which had already sounded the alarm in my stomach, when the all too familiar buzz of my cell phone went off on the night stand next to our bed. I opened my eyes just enough to watch the phone vibrate across the top of the night stand, reaching out to grab it just before it dove off onto the floor. I hate cell phones because you can never get away from them, and when you are the chief of police in a small New England town, you might as well have one sewn onto your ear.

"Chief Kosciak. What can I do for you?" I said, rolling onto my back, looking up at the round, brownish stain on the ceiling overhead. Peggy and I don't know what the stain is. It just appeared one night and was about the diameter of a baseball, just big enough to bother us when we opened our eyes every morning. I joked with Peggy the morning it appeared, telling her I would fix it as soon as I had the time, knowing that I was actually telling her the stain would be there for a couple of years, or longer. She promptly called me an ass, rolling over with a chuckle at my blatant honesty.

"Chief, you better get over to Steve Johnson's house right away," Derek Larson said.

Derek was a five year veteran on our eight member police force. He worked third shift all the time, which the other officers greatly appreciated. During the day, he worked part-time doing carpentry and was known for his amazing finish work. He did mostly restoration jobs on some of the oldest Colonial homes found in our area of New England.

"What's up, Derek? You sound like an alien spaceship just landed on the town common."

I heard him take a deep breath and exhale into the phone. I knew whatever he was calling me about was a lot more serious than the usual weekend bar fight at our local tavern. Derek was never without words and didn't rattle easily, so I could tell he was leading up to something very important.

"Chief, I think we may have found Christine Sawyer."

"What do you mean THINK we may have found Christine?" I asked.

I knew by his choice of words that whomever they found and wherever they found her, it would not be good news. Christine Sawyer went missing eight weeks ago. She was a sophomore attending a local college who disappeared while on her way home from a campus party. She left the party in her father's car around 1 AM on a Saturday morning. She never made it the three miles to her home from the college. The car was discovered a few days later in Purgatory State Park. The car, found by a couple of hikers, was driven off the road into the woods a quarter of a mile. There was no sign of a struggle, and it looked as though the car was completely detailed inside and out before being abandoned. Whoever had abandoned the car did not leave a trace of evidence for us to follow. The state crime lab did not find as much as a carpet fiber out of place. Search parties and blood hounds combed every inch of the park for two weeks, coming up empty-handed.

I assigned two of my full-time officers to investigate any leads or hunches that might help us locate Christine, but so far, we were at a dead end. The Massachusetts, State Police, also investigating her disappearance, were as frustrated as we were with the lack of evidence. I talked with her parents on the phone daily, promising them that I would not give up looking for their daughter until she was found. Now, it seemed, we may have found Christine, and I hoped if it was her, we would find some clue to start unraveling the mystery of her disappearance.

Derek continued, "Steve's son, Dave, and the McKinna kid found a woman's body half buried in an embankment over at Meadow Pond this morning. Steve said on the phone that the boys are very shaken up and scared to death. The woman may have been tortured and mutilated. The boys said the woman's eyes and lips were missing."

I was already sitting up on the edge of our four-poster bed by the time Derek mentioned the mutilation. Christine Sawyer, no one for that matter, deserved to suffer this type of death. I knew I would have to call in outside help in order to process the area where the body was found. Our police force was not equipped to run a full forensic study with the level of detail this type of investigation would require. We would do an initial overview of the crime scene, but the Staties would have to pick it apart snow flake by snow flake. My mind was already full of priorities: things I needed to do in the next few hours to increase our chances of finding clues, clues essential to our determining what happened to this girl and to the apprehension of her killer.

"Derek. Call Dr. Cavanagh and have him meet me at Steve's house in 30 minutes. Tell him what happened, and please tell him the boys may need some medical attention. Tell him I'll need him to go with me to Meadow Pond after we question the boys, to see if we are able to confirm that the dead woman is, in fact, Christine Sawyer. I'll call you when I'm on my way to Steve's. Have Todd and Kim go out and secure the crime scene until I arrive."

I thought about the bacon and eggs I would not have time to eat, and then felt guilty that the thought even crossed my mind. The sound of footsteps in the hallway outside the bedroom door made me turn to look. Peggy walked in a few seconds later and immediately knew by the look on my face, that she would be eating breakfast alone.

Peggy and I met eight years ago when I stopped at her yard sale on a cool, October morning. We didn't know each other before that day, even though we grew up within a couple of miles of one another. I can still see her sitting in a green and white, fold-up lawn chair in her driveway. She sat watching as I drove up in my Ford Explorer, while her daughter Libby collected money for the families of the 911 attack. We chatted while I ruffled through the boxes scattered around the driveway. After our initial "how-do-you-do" and some "break-the-ice" conversation, I ended up going to the local doughnut shop to get us coffee and plain doughnuts. The rest was history. Never did buy anything, but Peggy wrapped up some of the obviously junkier items from the sale and gave them to me on our first Christmas together. This was definitely a sign of things to come!

"Do you have time for a cup of coffee before you leave or should I make you a cup to go?" she asked.

I surmised she already knew the answer.

"You only slept a few hours. Good thing it was only a raccoon that broke into the hardware store last night. If it was some drug crazed felon, you might still be chasing himaround the streets of town yelling, "Stop! This is the chief of police! Stop; or I'll throwmy jelly doughnut at you!" She started to chuckle, but saw that I was not smiling at herjoke. "What is it baby? What's wrong?" she said putting her hand on my shoulder.

"They think they may have found Christine Sawyer's body over at Meadow pond. I have to get over to Steve Johnson's house and talk to his son and Ricky McKinna. They found the body this morning."

"Oh! My God! How are they doing?"

"I don't have the particulars yet, but Todd said they are pretty shaken up, and by the boy's description of the body, she may have been tortured. I'm meeting Doc Cavanagh over there in a few minutes. We'll go over to the pond right after we check on the boys. I'll take that coffee to go."

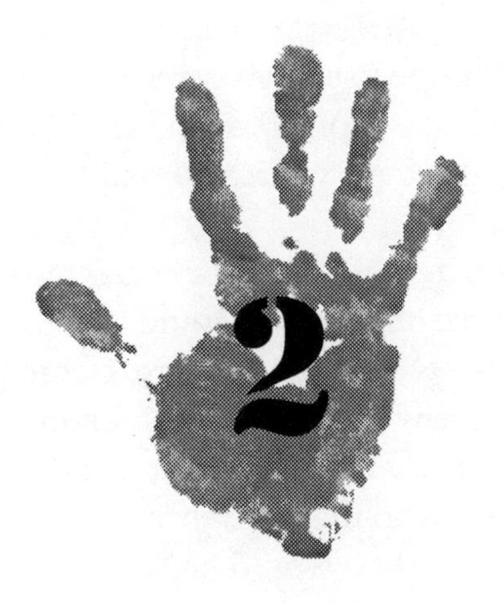

The drive over to the Johnson's house only took about 15 minutes. They lived in a pre-Civil War Cape dating back to the late seventeen hundreds. Steve and his wife Kelly kept the property looking as it did when it was first built. The front step was a square piece of granite with an iron foot scraper embedded into the stone. Flower boxes hung below the tall, front windows and were filled with evergreens and red berries the birds would eat during the winter months. The roof line overhung the house by a foot and a half and the snow in the gutters stood out like a neon sign against the barn-red paint on the clapboards. The house was pleasing to look at and was probably warm and cozy inside next to the pellet stove you could see burning at night as you drove by.

I spotted Doc Cavanaugh's Jeep-Cherokee parked out in front of the house as I pulled onto Prentice Road. Doc opened the door and stood beside the Jeep as I pulled up, stopping behind him. Doc was in his late sixties, very rotund and sported a full head of white hair - the consummate country doctor. One look in my rear view mirror reminded me that I did not suffer from an overabundance of hair like he did and that is why I always kept it cropped very short. Peggy wants me to shave it bald, but I keep telling her I am not Yul Brenner or Bruce Willis. They were born with the right looks for being completely bald. I tell her I am more a cross between a

Rottweiler and a hairless Mexican, Chihuahua. I'm cute and cuddly, just don't piss me off.

"Chief Kosciak. Haven't seen you since you pulled me over for driving erratically the day I spilled my morning coffee onto my lap. Bet you thought you'd caught yourself a real felon." he chuckled as he shook my hand.

"Doc, I've told you a hundred times to call me Ron. You brought Libby into this world, so I figure we should be on a first name basis."

"Well, Ron. Tell me what we have here. Derek told me you may have found Christine Sawyer and that the Johnson boy and one of his friends found the body buried over at Meadow Pond."

"We're not sure yet who the woman is at the pond, but the boys are hysterical and I thought it would be best to check on them first; then ask some questions if they are able to tell us what happened. I sent two officers over to the crime scene to hold down the fort until we can get there. We can go over to the pond when we finish up here."

The front door opened as we reached the granite step. Kelly Johnson stood holding the doorknob looking as though the knob was the only thing holding her up. She was in her mid-thirties with long, light-brown hair touching her shoulders. In high school, she was one of the prettiest and most sought after girls in the entire school. But, as she stood at the door this morning, she looked like she was 65 - her hair was not combed and she had obviously been crying just a few minutes before our arrival. I knew she was more than worried about her son, who we could now hear crying and moaning inside the house. The cries were not the cries you hear when your child has a cut or a bruise from falling off of a bike. Instead, these cries and moans sounded like someone who was possessed or who suffered long agonizing torture. Davey Johnson sounded almost inhuman as we entered the house following Kelly into the living room.

Steve Johnson sat on the floor of the living room with his legs spread open on the oval braided rug, holding his son against his chest. His face was ashen, his eyes pleading, as he rocked Davey back and forth in a protective, nurturing way. Even though Davey's face was buried deep in his father's sweatshirt, his moaning and crying cut through everyone in the room like sound-system speakers turned up to their highest volume. Doc tried to calm the boy with his usual country doctor charm, but in this case, his words were not getting through. It only took doc a few moments to determine Davey's need for immediate psychiatric care. Having seen the tortured, distorted face at the pond disconnected Davey's mind from the reality of his surroundings. Doc explained to Davey's parents that, in cases of intense shock like this, the rebound could be quick or might take a very long time. He prepared them as best he could for what might be a long haul. Doc opened his cell phone to call the ambulance while I turned to Steve and Kelly.

"Where is Rick McKinna?" I asked. "I thought the boys were together when they found the body."

Kelly motioned me out of the living room and told me Rick's parents came as soon as she called to let them know what had happened to the boys that morning. Although Rick was outwardly upset and crying, he did not withdraw to the place of torment that their son Davey was experiencing. Rick described to the grownups the events at the pond and Kelly recounted his story with as much detail as she could remember.

I walked back into the living room and Doc told me the ambulance would arrive in just a few minutes. I suggested to him that I should go ahead to the crime scene and he could catch up with me when Davey was safely on his way to Milford Hospital about half an hour away. I told him that I would call the McKinna's and find out how Rick was doing. We would make plans to stop and question him on the way back after processing the crime scene. I knew I needed to get out to the pond and start looking for answers, and right now, I had no clue where this murder would take me.

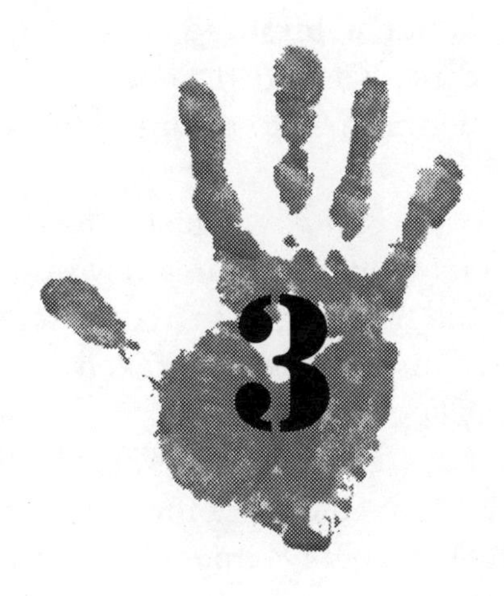

The town furnished me with a four-wheel drive, Explorer. It came with all the bells and whistles of a standard issue police cruiser: a hand-held radio and walkie-talkies that fit into special clips on the dashboard; a GPS system was mounted on the dash; a computer system hooked directly into the NCIS data bases, and its own little arsenal of: a Colt .357 and 12-gauge, pump-action shotgun. Not bad for a little country town. I was ready for everything except a nuclear conflagration.

I called the McKinna's as I drove up route 146 to the turn off at Burdon Street. Meadow Pond was about one mile from the highway. The boys approached the pond by walking across the fields, from the woods, to the pond. Their trek would have taken them 15 to 20 minutes. Driving would take an additional 10 minutes because of stop-lights, stop signs and winding country roads.

The McKinna's told me Rick was still very upset, but, he seemed to be calming down now that he was home. They called their primary care physician and were taking him to the clinic in about an hour. I asked them to give me a call when they returned, and, to be sure to ask their doctor if Rick was mentally strong enough to answer some questions later in the day.

"Chief Kosciak to Todd Bentley: Kosciak to Bentley. Come in."

"Bentley here, Chief. Kim and I are at Meadow Pond. We've taped off an area about a hundred square feet, but haven't approached the area directly where the body is located. We figured you would want to be the first to examine the scene. How long before you get here?"

"I'm on my way over right now. I just left the Johnson's house. Doc Cavanagh will be following me in a few minutes. I'm coming down Burdon Street and will see you in a couple of minutes. Inspect the area outside of the tape for anything that may seem out of place or unusual. Note any footprints leading into or out of the area, besides those of the boys. Look for ANYTHING that looks out of place. Anything at all that catches your eyes. Don't overlook one snow flake. It's a long shot, but we might get lucky. We don't know how long our Jane Doe has been out here. Kosciak out."

I could see the cruiser at the end of the street. Meadow Pond is surrounded by country roads on the north and south sides. The east and west sides of the pond are bordered by brush, woods and fields. The boys came out onto the pond from the west side of the pond which was untouched by builders, farmers or summer campers. The woods stretch about three quarters of a mile from the pond to route 146, a two lane highway running north to New Hampshire and south to Rhode Island.

The tires were making a crunching sound compacting snow as I pulled off of Burdon Street and onto the snow-covered dirt road leading to the pond. The only other tire tracks were those left by Todd's cruiser. I parked my Explorer where the small trees and brush took over and the road ended. It was only a few minutes' walk to the edge of the pond where Todd and Kim met me.

Kim, the only female officer on our police force, worked her way up to the rank of sergeant after only five years. She was very detail oriented with a phenomenal sixth sense when it came to problem solving and investigating crime scenes. She was only five foot six, and worked out in the gym every other day. She was slender, but as strong as any of the male officers on the force. I always sent her on our initial investigations because I knew how thorough she would be. She knew how to handle herself during confrontations with drunks and belligerent, unpredictable suspects. She saved my life one night after I stopped a car with three guys speeding south on route 146.

The car looked like it was riding low to the pavement and I suspected that they were carrying quite a load of drugs in the trunk. I called Kim for back up. She was working the graveyard shift and wasn't too far away. Before she arrived, I got out of my cruiser and approached their vehicle with my right hand on the butt of my revolver. I could tell they were nervous because the passenger in the front seat was slapping the driver on the side of his head screaming obscenities at the top of his lungs. The man in the back seat sat straight up with his head not moving at all. It was his lack of curiosity and lack of movement that put me on my guard. As I neared the trunk of the car I saw Kim's cruiser coming up 146 from the other direction. It would take her only 30 seconds to reach us on our side of the highway. I was looking into the car through the back window and noticed the guy in the back seat move his hands into his lap shifting his weight away from the passenger's door. Instead of walking by the passenger' rear window, I took out my night stick and rapped on it. Ready to hit the window again, I saw the barrel of a sawed-off shot gun move up as the guy in the rear seat moved to the other side of the car. Broken crystals of glass filled the space where I would have stood, mixed with pellets from the blast. I immediately fell back behind the car, drawing my revolver, firing twice through the shattered rear window.

Kim, saw the initial shotgun blast blow out the window, and saw me crouched behind the car returning fire. Without hesitation, she stopped her cruiser in front of their car, jumped out and pointed her Glock at the driver telling him to give it up or she would take him out. The driver pushed open his door, began to get out of the vehicle with his weapon held in his left hand above his head. Kim did not take her attention off of him for one instant. As he brought his pistol to bear down on her, she popped off three quick bursts and the driver fell dead to the ground with three 9mm rounds in the middle of his chest.

The remaining two guys threw their weapons out of the car and placed their hands on top of their heads without being asked. After additional back up arrived, and the two surviving passengers were cuffed and locked in the back of Kim's cruiser, we opened the trunk of their BMW finding five kilos of heroine, six automatic assault weapons and 4 blocks of C-4 explosives. The guys were a four-wheeled battleship with their own drug store. I never forgot Kim saving my life that night and I am glad to remind her every so often.

4

Doc Cavanaugh called me on my cell phone as I saw the first signs of the yellow tape Todd and Kim used to cordon off the crime scene. He told me he would be there in a few minutes as he was just leaving the Johnson's house. I told him I would send Todd up to meet him when he arrived.

Looking over the area leading to the body, I saw the two sets of foot prints left by Dave and Ricky. The path of the toboggan followed one of the boy's footprints and disappeared into the brush. Kim heard me approaching and was walking up from the pond to meet me.

"Chief." she said. "It's pretty bad. I have never seen anything like this. The face is definitely mutilated. The eyes have been gouged out and the lips have been cut away. None of the missing body parts are in the area as far as we can determine. The only footprints outside the taped area right now are from our actual taping and subsequent visual inspection. The right arm, shoulder and head are the only parts of the body visible from the embankment. Someone took their time digging out this hiding place. I'm not sure how the body dislodged and became exposed - maybe an animal or something. If the boys had come by a different route, we may never have found her. I'm pretty sure it is Christine… same hair color and facial features, and seems to be about the same age."

As we walked toward the pond I thought about having to tell the Sawyers their daughter was dead. I could not imagine what it would feel like to have one of my kids disappear without any word, without any trace. I wondered if they had been sitting up night after night unable to go to sleep, feeling guilty and somehow responsible for Christine's disappearance. Now, I would have to bring them the information they feared the most.

Whatever hell they had been living in since her disappearance, it would intensify one hundred fold when they learned that their beautiful daughter was dead...and at the hands of some psycho who had mutilated her and who knows what else. Until now, they had lived with the hope that Christine was alive.

The embankment at the pond's edge was about four to five feet high over the frozen ice of the pond. The snow right above the body was disturbed where the boys came out of the brush and fell onto the ice. The young woman's right arm was sticking straight out towards the ice as if she was beckoning someone to come and find her. Her head was tilted back so that the fullness of her face looked right into my eyes. She was frozen and looked like a mannequin left on the floor in the back storage room of some retail clothing store. Kneeling down, the first thing I noticed was the reddened, bruised circle around her wrist. She was obviously tied up when she was abducted, and my intuition told me she was most likely murdered somewhere else and brought out here to be buried. I surmised the killer buried her here in the early fall not too long after her disappearance. The body was buried too deep into the embankment to have been put there after the ground froze.

Her eyes were torn out of their sockets and her lips cut away, though not surgically. Whoever committed this act of depravity used some sort of knife or instrument that tore the flesh rather than cut the flesh like the precise incision of a scalpel. I did not see the eyes or lips anywhere near the exposed part of the body, and at this point believed the killer probably took them as trophies.

"Chief" I heard Doc's voice through the brush. "How the hell do you expect a guy my size to wander around out here in this maze of scrubs and shrubs. Help me out here will you. If I fall onto the ice it'll break under my weight and you'll be picking me out of the water with a crane!" I helped him down the embankment onto the ice and showed him where the body was located.

"It's difficult to tell how long she has been dead because the cold has preserved her tissues and prevented decomposition. We'll have to wait until we do the autopsy back at the morgue to determine the cause and time of death."

Doc and Kim continued to examine the girl when Kim noticed a discoloration about the size of a quarter on the left side of the girl's neck. The bruise looked odd because of its size and perfectly round shape. Examining the mark closer, she could see some sort of design pattern on the surface of the bruise. Because of the body's position, it was impossible to tell what the design was. We would have to wait until we removed the body from the dirt and brought it out into the light to better see what the design was and if it had any significance related to the murder.

Earlier, on my way to the Johnson's home, I placed a call to Derek at the station to have the medical examiner's van sent to the pond. They were just arriving and were bringing the gurney down to the site as Doc was completing his initial examination.

"Doc, I'll let you and the medical examiner's team finish here. Call me when you get set up at the morgue and I'll stop over to see what you've come up with."

Cavanaugh looked straight into my eyes and said, "Ron. I can tell you right now, I will do whatever is required to get answers from this body. No one should suffer this way. I know I'm just a small town doc, but I will call in every favor from every pathologist I know to help us find the son-of-bitch who did this to Christine."

I patted Doc on the shoulder. He knew I appreciated his commitment. I also knew there would be many long days and frustrating hours spent before we would walk away from this case. I didn't care. All that mattered was finding the killer before he killed again.

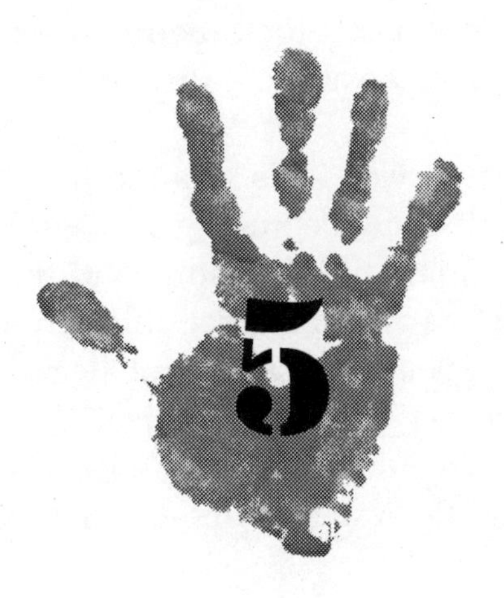

He held the iPod up and advanced the first picture onto the small electronic screen. "Modern technology," he thought as the first picture materialized. Having already looked at the pictures many times this morning, he sat sipping hot coffee brewed with his Keuerig coffee maker. He liked the idea of brewing one cup at a time - always to perfection.

"Just the way I do the things that I do – TO PERFECTION," he thought as he relaxed, lounging in sweat pants and a Grateful Dead T shirt, in the peace of the early morning. There were no sounds to interrupt him while he sipped his hot coffee relishing his work. He and Christine could be alone, undisturbed to enjoy each other's company every morning for the rest of their lives. She was his favorite. He spent more energy and time studying her than the other adoptees, while silently stalking her, hidden in the darkness and shadows. Weeks of precise preparation went into his plans. "Eight weeks since her adoption? God, how time flies when you're having fun," he thought, watching the next picture move onto the small screen while inhaling the vanilla aroma of his hot java, reliving the moments and seconds just before she died.

He liked the next picture best of all. Christine's hair seemed to shine more, and her new look fit her perfectly. The keep sakes in the jar next to him on the end table were a constant reminder of the last person she saw and the last words she uttered just before they consummated her adoption. He took another sip of coffee, closed his eyes and smiled, looking away from the iPod as her picture faded from his mind.

This was the way it was. This was the way it had to be - an unavoidable end and a new beginning. Soon, a new child would be part of his family, just like Christine and the other adoptees. And, just like Christine and the other children, this child would never have to worry about ever being sent away. The child chosen did not know that the leg work was completed. The planning was done down to the last minute detail, and the adoption process would begin very shortly. A small, almost unnoticeable smile began forming on his lips.

"CONTROL, CONTROL, and CONTROL - everything done to PERFECTION," he thought, the smile on his lips vanishing as quickly as it had appeared.

Driving back to the police station from Meadow Pond, I made a quick call to Peggy. She was on her break after escorting the kids in from play time in the school yard. Peggy was the director of a preschool program and loved every one of her fifty-one kids just like they were her own. Every night she told me a story about what one of the kids had said or done during the day which usually made us both laugh out loud. Kids were unpredictable, but at four and five years old, their unpredictability was most often humorous.

I told her about David being brought to the hospital and probably needing some long term care after finding the body. I could sense the mother in her wanting to reach out and hug him to make him feel better. I told her I would probably be late getting home because I needed to catch up with Doc Cavanaugh later in the day to find out the results of Christine's examination.

"Ron. You need to be careful on this one." she said. "My intuition is telling me whoever killed Christine is not your ordinary killer. There is something unnerving about the fact that there was no evidence at all found in the car, and not one person saw or heard anything when she was abducted. Promise me you will watch your back and don't try to go after this killer on your own."

I assured her I would exercise extreme caution during this investigation and that I also felt vibes sending warning signals and raising large, red flags. It wasn't just the lack of evidence that was surprising me, but, that whoever abducted and killed Christine, meticulously detailed the car so thoroughly that even the usual dirt, papers, coins and crumbs found in the little nooks and crannies under the seats were gone. It was the work of a perfectionist who paid great attention to detail. The killer: pre-planned the time and place of the abduction; pre-selected the place to take Christine once she was under his control; the car had been meticulously cleaned and driven out to Purgatory State Park and not one person had seen or heard anything. This entire event was done without any sense of fear or concern on the killer's part. Time was slowly and methodically taken in a cold and calculated manner. This meant the killer was highly intelligent; analytical and organized and therefore, extremely unpredictable and dangerous, as well as extremely confident.

I finished my call with Peggy as I arrived at the police station. She told me she saved the bacon and eggs. She also informed me I was having them for supper. I love her sense of humor… although, I was not sure she was kidding.

As I started up the front steps of the station, I looked over at the visitor's parking lot and was stunned to see Bev and Wayne Sawyer getting out of their car.

"Chief, is it true? Have you found Christine?" Wayne hesitantly asked not really wanting to hear the answer. "A friend called us a little while ago telling us the Johnson boyfound a body out at Meadow Pond this morning. Is it Christine?"

I surmised that someone from the medical examiner's staff, the ER, or a friend of the Johnson's or McKinna's must have called the Sawyers after David was brought in by Ambulance. I was hoping this informant had not heard too much about the condition of Christine's body or, how she was found disfigured and half buried in the embankment.

"Come on in folks. We can talk inside." I said holding the door open for them, wondering to myself just how I was going to tell them about their daughter.

Doc Cavanaugh was ninety-nine percent sure the body of the girl was Christine Sawyer. I would not only have to tell Wayne and Bev their daughter was dead, but also ask them to meet me at the morgue later to make a positive identification. They would have to look at their daughter on a hard, stainless-steel, morgue table and realize exactly what she experienced in the last minutes of her life.

I closed the door to my office as the Sawyers sat in front of my desk. I felt torn as I looked at them holding hands trying to support each other. They were waiting for me to begin speaking and everything outside of my office ceased to exist for the three of us. My office encompassed their entire world for this instant in time. Their world was about to come crashing down on them like an emotional tsunami, engulfing them in its' turbulent and emotional surf.

"The information you were given by the caller is true." I said. "The Johnson and McKinna boys did find a young woman's body out at the pond this morning. The young woman seems to fit Christine's features and age. We have not positively identified the girl as Christine yet… although… Doctor Cavanaugh… does believe its Christine. The doctor will need some time to complete his examination, and then we will need you to come down to the hospital to make a positive identification. I am only sharing this information with you before we know for sure because you came to the police station to ask. We usually would not give out any information until we are absolutely positive. I can only imagine what you must be feeling right now."

Bev Sawyer bent forward in her chair putting her face into her hands. She began to rock slightly back and forth and, although she cried, she did not make a sound. Wayne put his hand onto her shoulder and rubbed very lightly. He looked at me with eyes drained of energy from weeks of agonizing torment and I knew that a part of him would be dead along with his daughter when they identified her later today.

"Chief, can you tell us? Did she suffer?" he asked. "Do you have any idea how long she's been out there? Do you have any idea who might have done this?"

I knew these were the same questions I, or any parent, would be asking if sitting in Wayne's chair. Questions that keep you up at night and haunt you every minute of every day until they are either answered, or they go unanswered until you yourself are buried in the local cemetery. These are questions that perpetuate the nagging, soulful darkness in your heart never allowing you to fully be happy again during your lifetime. Questions that wrap themselves around every thought you have while you wait for answers. Then, if one question is answered, there is still no relief, as another question takes its place.

"Wayne. All I can tell you at this time is that we do believe it is Christine." I replied. "But, there is always the slightest chance we are wrong. I don't want to say for sure until Doc Cavanaugh calls me later today. I know this is a very difficult time for you and Beverly and perhaps there will be some initial closure for you both once Doc calls and asks you to come over to the hospital."

I knew my words were no consolation to them right now. They had been given information by someone who wanted to do the right thing by passing on that information, but without all of the details, the Sawyers were thrust into the turmoil of MAYBES and UNKNOWNS. Whichever way this afternoon went at the hospital, the Sawyers were being pulled back into an emotional black hole that is always part losing a child to violence or tragedy. I hoped Peggy and I would never have to experience anything like this in our lifetimes. Wayne held Bev's shoulders helping her stand to leave my office. Stopping in the office doorway she turned toward me with blank eyes.

"Chief," she said. "I want you to promise me; even if Christine is not the girl you found out there today, that you will not stop looking for the bastard who did this. I do not want another family to have their hearts torn out this way living each day with hopes that they know are really only wishful dreams. Promise me!"

Her last words trailed off against my ears as they turned and left my office. I knew our next meeting would be much worse for them and I wished there was a way to prevent the anguish that would consume them when they identified Christine's body at the morgue.

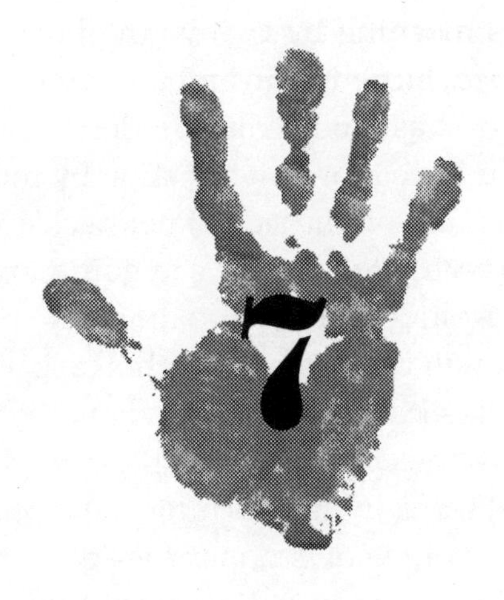

I put in a call to Ken Garber at the State Police facility in Auburn, a town adjacent to Sutton. Ken was the Captain of this unit of Troopers, and held extensive experience dealing with unusual deaths or serial killer type murders. He once solved a ten year old homicide case involving a missing teenage girl while reviewing a Cold Case file after a neighbor sparked his interest in the unsolved crime at a backyard barbecue. While looking through the crime scene photographs, he spotted someone in the crowd standing almost out of sight behind an adjacent building. The figure was shadowy and grainy, but with today's new photographic technology, they were able to refine the image and identify the individual. After a few weeks of investigation and going door to door, Ken located the person of interest, who he was able to link to crime scene photos from additional unsolved homicides committed over a three year period. It was Ken's bloodhound personality I needed to help me get this investigation off of the ground. He would have a lot more pull at the state level than me and, I would not hesitate asking him to collect every favor anyone owed him to increase our chances of catching this killer.

"Hello, Ken. Chief Kosciak, over in Sutton."

"Hey, Ron, how've you been? Long time since I've heard from you. Things must be pretty quiet over there in Sutton. What can I do for you?"

"Ken, we believe we have found Christine Sawyer. Her body was discovered this morning by two young boys out sliding. She was facially disfigured, buried in an embankment at Meadow Pond, and is being autopsied as we speak. We don't know the cause of death yet, but should have more information by the end of the day. There is an unusual mark on the side of her neck about the size of a quarter that we are trying to identify. I'm going to need some help with this one. Our resources are just too limited to perform the kind of investigation that will be required for this case. I'm thinking this is not the first time this killer has abducted and murdered a young woman. When can we meet and put our heads together on this?"

"How about first thing in the morning" he replied. "I will make a few calls and get a couple of Troopers assigned to the case right away. I'll get our crime scene investigators out there this afternoon to start looking over the spot where she was found. Have one of your people call in the location and set up a time. We'll set up the night lights so we can continue through the night. She may have been out there for almost two months, so we may not find too much in the way of evidence. But, there is always the chance the killer may have dropped something that is hidden in the snow or brush. If there is anything there, we will find it. Ron, I know Bev and Wayne Sawyer, so this one is personal for me. Whatever you need, you've got! We need to catch this prick. I'll see you in the morning."

I actually felt better knowing that Ken was now personally involved in this investigation. I also knew Wayne and Beverly Sawyer would be relieved to know Ken was involved. I would make sure to tell them this afternoon at the hospital. Black storm clouds were forming on the horizon and I needed all the help I could get to weather this storm.

I asked the desk officer to call in the location of the crime scene to the State Police, knowing as I drove over to the morgue that the investigation was now in high gear. The next forty-eight hours would be crucial. We had a crime scene to process, an autopsy to complete and we needed to start looking for other missing and/or murdered women in the New England area who may have suffered the same fate as Christine. We needed to do our homework and we needed to do it as quickly as possible.

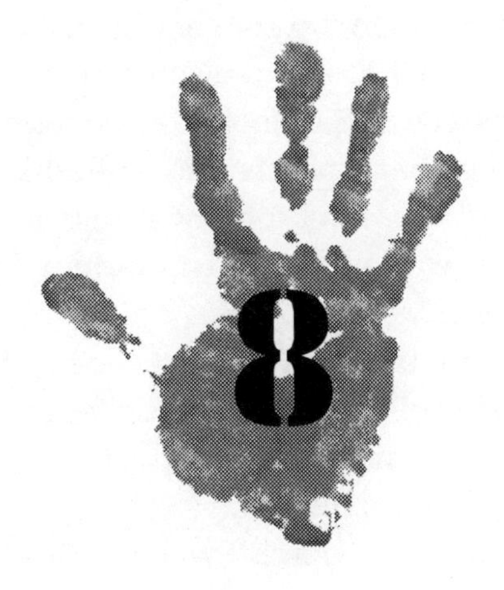

8

"Chief Kosciak. Doc Cavanaugh here. I'm calling to let you know I checked dental records first before starting the autopsy. The dental records of the girl found at Meadow Pond verify that our Jane Doe is Christine Sawyer. Preliminary findings, after the external body exam, show that both her ankles and wrists were bound before she was killed. Our internal exam clearly shows no sign of her being sexually assaulted, which means the killer is not interested in sexual intimacy with the victim. This might be a control issue or an ownership issue instead of a sexual needs type of crime. The killer may be more interested in the courtship rather than the wedding night. Other than taking the eyes and lips as probable trophies, the rest of her body does not seem to have been bruised or mistreated. We still do not know how Christine was killed. We cannot find any external wounds that would have caused her death. We will have more conclusive findings later today when we have completed the internal part of the autopsy.

"Doc, can you determine what the mark is on the side of Christine's neck?" I asked. "The one about the size of a quarter: There was some kind of design within the mark we could not see clearly at the pond this morning."

"We took a picture of it just a few minutes ago. It's being enlarged on the computer screen as we speak. Give me a minute to finish the transfer and I'll bring it up on the screen. Bear with me; I'm not the fastest gun in the West when it comes to digital-image-transferring on a computer. Hmm....It looks like some sort of Gothic design. Like those markings you see tattooed on people's upper arms or backs, with all of the sharp points and knife-like outlines... just much smaller to fit within a circle of, say, a ring, or a small branding device. It looks like it was applied post mortem. I'll give it a close look during the autopsy."

"Doc, I just met with the Sawyers. Someone at the hospital must have told them about Christine's body being found at the lake. They are pretty devastated. I'll need your help later today when I bring them over to identify their daughter."

"Alright Chief, I'll give you a call when we are done and set up for the ID. Call you later."

Doc Cavanaugh walked over to the edge of the autopsy table looking down at Christine Sawyer. His eyes surveyed many disfigured people on this table over the past forty-two years: some from automobile accidents; some from industrial accidents and some the result of homicide, but none were purposely disfigured like Christine. Even an old country doctor like Cavanaugh was shaken to his backbone when he first saw her at the pond. He thought about his own daughter living in San Diego with her husband and three children and said a silent prayer to God that they would always be protected.

Before starting the full post mortem Doc decided to take a second look at the circular mark on Christine's neck. There was no life-like redness or bruising under the skin as there would be if the mark were made while there was blood moving within the tissue. The skin was a little discolored, but basically, it looked like the mark had been put there after Christine died. The killer intentionally put the mark where it would be found. "Bold Son-of-a-Bitch" thought Cavanagh. "I wonder what the significance of this mark is." He would e-mail the photos over to the chief and let the police try to answer that question.

Cavanagh reached over, picking up the scalpel to begin making the "Y" incision on Christine's sternum for the autopsy. As he held the scalpel, there was something about the mark on her neck that gnawed at him. He wasn't sure what it was and stood there for about three or four minutes staring at Christine's neck waiting for some revelation to fall into his brain. He knew there was something he was supposed to be seeing, but for the life of him, he could not yet pin point what that something was.

"What a waste of life." He thought. The scalpel silently incised the skin over Christine's sternum. He would work late tonight to complete the autopsy. The clock said 4:30, and it struck him that lunch time had come and gone. At his age, eating was one of the few luxuries left to look forward to. He thought of himself as a connoisseur of general consumption turning back to the table continuing his work.

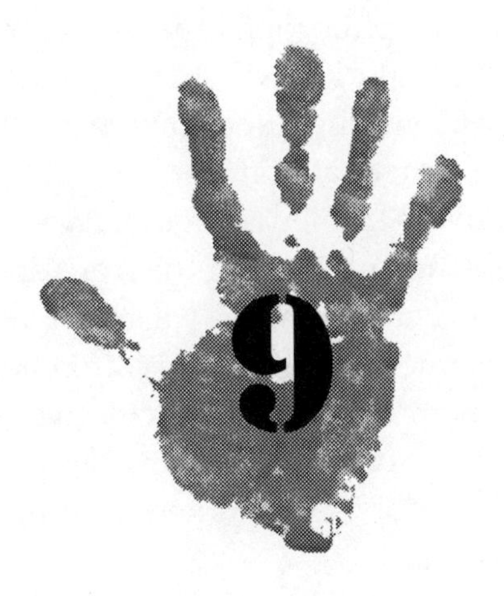

9

I met with Rick McKinna and his parents early in the evening just before supper time. Rick described the details of his and Davey's movements up to and including the time they stumbled across Christine's body at the pond. Although he was still very shaken by the ordeal, he looked to be calming down, I was sure his parents would have him on a very short leash for the next six months. There really was no new information that Rick could add to what we already knew from their previous accounts and the ongoing investigation at the crime scene. It seemed the boys were alone at the pond and no one else was in the area at the time. I was sure this day would be etched into the minds of these two boys for the rest of their lives. I could only hope Davey would recover and be able to go tobogganing down Dead Man's Hill once again someday soon.

Stopping at the house on my way over to the morgue, I saw Peggy's burgundy, Colt van parked in the driveway. This day started out badly, and with the small amount of information we had to go on, I knew things were not going to change much before the end of the day. I would burn my share of mid-night oil tonight at the station.

Walking through the front door, I noted that we always left the front door open when we were not home. This small, country, town-life gave us a false sense of security. You never think a home invasion or murder can happen to you or yours. It is the old, "it will never happen to me", philosophy that we all try to believe. But, in my line of work, I should know better. In today's world, things can happen to anyone, anytime and anywhere. The safest place, unfortunately, was no longer at home!

"Hey. Is that you in the kitchen baby, or have the mice taken over the house?" I said closing and locking the front door.

"Yeah, I'm in the kitchen loading the washing machine. Somebody needs to save your cashmere sweaters and cotton pullovers! I'm tired of seeing you wash them with your work clothes and jeans. Then, when you go to wear one of them, it's shrunken so much you look like a grizzly in a Speedo!" she laughed turning the dial on the machine to start the cycle.

Peggy had a great sense of humor, but in this instance, she was nicely telling me not to do the wash unless I could learn how to do it: that is, put them into her hamper or suffer her wrath! This would insure the proper life cycle of the garments…and me.

"Baby, I won't be home for sup….." I began to say but, Peggy pointed toward the refrigerator and motioned for me to open the door.

"I picked you up a pre-cooked chicken at the market on the way home." she said. "All you have to do is micro-wave it later at the station. Cook it for four minutes on high. I figured you would be working late because of the investigation. I'll leave a couple of lights on tonight so you don't trip and break a leg falling over a coffee table or a chair in the dark when you come home!" She walked over to me, put her arms around my neck, looked up into my eyes and said, "Even if you are a clumsy oaf, you are MY clumsy oaf."

"That's what I love about you." I replied. You are so shy and timid. I don't think I have ever heard you speak your mind."

She slapped my butt, gave me a quick kiss, called me an ass and sat down on one of the kitchen stools looking at me, waiting for me to tell her what was going on. I have learned to be very perceptive and intuitive with Peggy. I can usually tell by her body language just what I am expected to do or say at any given moment. This gift allows me some sort of protection from those times that I am totally incorrect with my assumption!

"Well, there is not much to say at this point," I said. "Ken Garber has assigned some officers to the investigation. Doc Cavanagh is performing the post mortem right now and Jeremy Bickford, the State pathologist, will be coming in to help Doc with the post. I spoke with the Sawyers this morning and have to meet them at the hospital sometime today after the post is completed. Those two people have lived this nightmare for over two months. Hopefully, this part will give them some closure. Although, I fear they will never be able to close the gaping hole in their hearts. I hope, when we catch this son-of-a-bitch, that whoever it is, will resist arrest!"

Peggy stood up, walked over to me and put her arms around me again. She nestled her face against my chest knowing that this case was very personal for me. I could take the traffic stops, B&E's and even bar fights seven days a week, but when a crime involved women or children my tendency was to get very emotionally attached.

"Listen." She said. "Do whatever you have to do. I will be here or over at Libby's visiting the grandkids. Take whatever time you need on this one. Give me a call later tonight just to let me know you are alright." She started to walk away, turned back toward me and asked me the question that had been on her mind right after Christine went missing:

"Hon, do you think Christine's murder is just an isolated incident or do you think whoever has done this has done it before?"

Standing hidden in the night shadows at the end of the alleyway, he watched the entrance to the diner across the street. It was 7:00 pm and the winter, night-time darkness reclaimed hiding spots and crevices exposed during daylight hours. He loved the dark, felt a part of its heartbeat. He belonged to its hidden nature. It concealed things people were afraid to think about.

Joe's is a local "greasy spoon" catering to college kids, only a quarter of a mile from the college campus and actually served one of the best hamburgers and crispy fries he had ever eaten in his life. Tonight, there would be more customers than usual for a Wednesday night, because the basketball game had ended about an hour earlier. He knew she would be here. She was predictable. He always sensed the ones who lived their lives according to a time table. It was almost as if their lives would fall apart and disintegrate if they did one spontaneous thing. This made it very easy to monitor his children before allowing them into his family, made them much more accessible when the time came for their adoption.

Marty had arrived at the diner with her group of friends half an hour ago. He followed them from the campus. They were excited about the basketball victory, never turning around to look at anyone or anything. Like most college aged kids, they were oblivious to their surroundings and wrapped up in their own little worlds. "Worlds revolving only around themselves without much concern for anyone else," he thought, continuing his vigil.

Earlier, when the group entered Joe's, he moved casually across the street walking behind the stores and businesses fronting the street - now closed for the day - watching as they ate their burgers. He watched their mouths move as they talked about their trivial thoughts. It was like watching an old, silent movie where the characters moved and spoke, but there was nothing to be heard. The only thing missing was the piano music that tinked along as the projector hummed in the background.

Marty had first caught his attention when he stopped to buy a coffee at the doughnut shop a few weeks ago. The morning sunlight reflected off of her long, red hair. It shone brilliantly, cascading like a waterfall onto her shoulders, falling down her back another ten to twelve inches creating the appearance of a halo around her face.

"A doughnut and coffee angel." he thought, chuckling to himself as he stepped up to the counter to order his java.

She was alone and sat on one of the stools by the front window watching the cars go by with their hot exhausts smoking into the cold morning air. Her face was perfection in his eyes. He wanted to go over, and sit right down in front of her and to stare at her perfect features. He wanted to look deeply through her to see her future with him as the adoption process started once more. But, he needed to compose himself. Control, control, and control. Control is what kept him hidden, unseen, undetected. Smiling, he stood off to the side of the coffee shop taking small sips to prolong their first meeting.

Over the next few days, he came to the coffee shop each morning at the exact same time to see if she was a creature of habit. Sure enough, she was there each morning, sitting in the same seat, eating the same kind of doughnut, looking out the window day dreaming and watching the passersby. "PERFECT" he had thought as he began to plan their new relationship. One step at a time was the only way to proceed. One piece of information always led to the next piece of information, and he could now start to learn more about her with each passing day.

Once the decision was made to adopt this girl, he began to follow her after she left the coffee shop, adding to her portfolio of behavioral information. Each and every move she made through the course of any given day was essential for him to know in order to act on the day of the adoption. It would take time to learn which campus buildings she frequented and at what times, where she lived, what nights she usually went out, and what nights she stayed in; who were the people she hung with, what times of the day and night was she alone, and what would be the best time and place to adopt his "doughnut angel".

Over the next few weeks, he learned that she lived at home. She was a local and this would mean he needed to be even more diligent about the right time and place for the adoption. Local kids always draw more attention. Everybody knows them. More people are apt to pay attention to a local as opposed to a child from out of town.

However, because she lived in town, he was able to use her street address to learn her name using census records from the town hall.

"Easy as picking an apple from a low hanging branch" he thought smugly, relishing the knowledge of her name. "One piece of information leads to the next piece of information" played over and over in his head. Soon, he would have all the information he needed.

Standing in the shadows outside of Joe's, he knew the adoption would take place soon. Marty would be part of his family by the end of the week. He knew the time and place where she would join him and become one of his children.

The hospital in Milford was small compared to the city hospitals with their life-flight landing pads and sprawling parking lots, their thousand employees walking a never ending maze of corridors and hidden passages. Instead, Milford Hospital had a rural country look to its design and landscaping. The original, main building of the hospital, built in the mid-eighteen hundreds, was still the cornerstone of the facility with wings and additions sprouting out over the years from grants and charitable contributions. The face of the main building was constructed of wooden clapboards preserved meticulously over the century and a half the hospital served the area.

Walking up to the entrance, my mind pictured the days when ambulances were horse-drawn wagons with a canvas stretcher and nurses dressed in a brilliant, white uniforms sitting in the back. A stark difference from the high-tech, motorized, emergency rooms driven by EMT's more skilled today than the doctors themselves were over a hundred years ago.

I took a detour around to the back of the hospital. The door to the morgue was in the rear of the building on basement level. I have often wondered why morgues are always located in basements. I heard the theme song from "The Twilight Zone" playing in my mind. "Great!" I thought, "I'll have the friggin tune in my head all day now!" As I rounded the last blue spruce standing guard beside the door, I saw Jerry Bickford from the State pathologist's office approaching from the opposite direction.

"Good evening, Jerry," I said.

"Good evening, Chief," He replied. "From what the Doc told me over the phone, it sounds like we have a really perverted murderer on our hands. Do you have anything new to go on?"

"I wish we did. I'm hoping like all hell that Doc has found something from his exam that will help us. Glad to see you on this one, though. I appreciate your coming over so quickly. The more expertise we have on this case the better chance we have of nailing this sicko."

I was looking at Jerry standing next to me while we talked. He was good-looking, mid-fifties and also sported a full head of white hair. I wondered what it was with doctors and white hair. I supposed it was similar to the comparison that all small town police chiefs were balding "chrome domes". I chuckled to myself holding the door for Jerry as we entered the basement.

We walked past the requisite gurneys sitting empty on the sides of the corridors in hospital basement, with their used and crumpled sheets hanging off nearly touching standard, grey flooring tiles - silent memories of previous patients. The corridors themselves, dimly lit, added to an unsettled feeling people often experience when they are walking in basements, watching and listening for anything or anyone to jump out from the shadows and darkened doorways. We reached the door to the morgue and looked in through a small, oval, glass porthole. Doc Cavanaugh was standing over the examination table with his back towards the door. I knocked on the glass with the back of my knuckle. He turned, saw me peering in at him and motioned for me to enter.

When he saw Jerry walking in behind me he said, "Jerry, my boy. Am I ever glad to see you!" He caught himself and quickly added: "Ron, I don't mean to infer that I am NOT glad to see you, but you know what I meant. Oh! Shit. I'm glad to see you too." We all had a short laugh and then Doc began: "I have just found something VERY intriguing while performing the thoracic part of the examination. Jerry, get a gown and mask and join me over here.

I want your opinion. I may have just found the proverbial needle in the haystack."

While Jerry put on the green gown and surgical mask, I stood a few feet away looking at Christine lying on the table. People look so different when they are dead. Their skin color changes to a cold, drained, white hue with slight traces and blotches of purple shading. Their eyes no longer shine with the glow of life that was once inside their body. The glint and sparkle of clear, living orbs replaced with grayish clouds no longer allowing the world to enter, or, in Christine's case, black holes of dried blood. There is not the slightest hint of movement within the now vacant shell of flesh and bone. There is no sound, no pulsing energy in veins or arteries. Capillaries on the surface of the skin have no reddened color from blood cells that once flowed from the "Circle of Willis' down to the tip of the big toe. One glance and you know the soul has departed and left its physical luggage behind. Christine Sawyer was no longer of this world. She suffered greatly during the last hours of her life, and now she was beyond the confines of this morgue and unaware of our presence.

"Jerry." Doc started. "When I began my initial exam of Christine a few hours ago, there was something I was looking at that bothered me, but I could not pin point exactly what that something was. It wasn't until I opened Christine's chest and abdomen and began the internal exam that I realized just what it was I had actually overlooked."

Doc moved over to a PC monitor suspended from a wall frame next to the table. On the screen of the monitor were colored graphs and tables displaying foreign looking data! However, as Jerry leaned closer to the screen, I heard a low, vibrating hum begin to resonate from his throat. I watched him review the data a while longer and listened as the hum turned into a "Holy Shit" that reverberated off of the morgue ceiling and walls.

"Doc, you've got to be kidding me!" he blurted out. "What the hell! Do you know what this means? Of course you do, that's why you have it up on the damned screen. I just meant...I mean, it caught me by surprise!"

"Don't worry about it, Jerry," Doc said. "I had the same reaction when I first saw the results of the blood tests. That's when I realized we had the answers to two very important questions. First, how did Christine Sawyer die?"

Doc Cavanaugh had my full attention as he stood silently for a few seconds, as if he was waiting for a drum roll. "Go ahead, Doc. Just do me a favor and speak to me using words I can understand. I am not the best student in the world when it comes to understanding medical jargon."

"Well," Doc started to speak and, at the same time, walked back over to the table, took Christine's face gently in his hands and turned her head so that the right side of her neck was clearly visible. "When I began the initial exam on the outside of the body, I could find no signs of a struggle. There are no cuts, bruises, contusions or any marks that would indicate Christine was able to fight off her attacker for even an instant. The marks on her wrists and ankles show that she was bound after the abduction to keep her subdued. The removal of the eyes and lips are the only external signs of violence on the body. Therefore, I assumed, at the beginning of the exam, that her abductor used some unorthodox means to end her life. I thought perhaps the use of electricity, as it would leave very little external evidence of trauma to the victim. However, I knew there was SOMETHING that kept nagging at me, as if Christine was trying to tell me something. It wasn't until I was performing the internal exam that the results of the blood tests arrived, and seeing Pancuronium on the monitor, my brain finally lit up. Pancuronium is one of three drugs administered during the process of lethal injection. When used by itself, without the other two drugs, the result is muscular paralysis, and, if administered in the correct dosage, will only cause paralysis. The recipient stays conscious throughout the ordeal and is aware of everything that is happening. The recipient can't respond, totally aware, but not able to speak, move or make a sound. Christine was conscious when her eyes and lips were removed. It is my belief, that once he finished with the mutilation and torture, the killer administered the last two drugs that finally stopped her heart and released her from her pain. Once I knew that this was how Christine died, I went back and looked at the mark on her neck. There, hidden in the design pattern of the mark, I found three injection points. The killer injected the drugs into the right, carotid artery."

The look on my face must have given away the disgusted feeling turning my stomach, creating new rage inside my mind and my gut. If Christine's killer had already been in custody, I probably would have driven back to the police station, locked myself his holding cell and torn the killer to bits with my bare hands. I did not want Christine's parents to ever learn what Doc just shared with us. I would do my best to make sure they never did.

"So, Doc", I said, exhaling heavily. "What you are saying is that the person who killed Christine would have to have specialized knowledge about these drugs, how to administer them for a lethal injection, and more importantly, would need to know the right dosage of Pancuronium to use in order to paralyze the victim and keep the victim conscious at the same time."

"That is exactly what he is saying," Jerry interjected.

I kept talking not hearing what Jerry was saying to me. "We could be talking about: a person schooled in medicine or medical treatment; a prison guard or prison employee; someone in law enforcement, or just a person with the intelligence to go on line and investigate these drugs and their use. At least now we have a starting point. We have a place to begin and a direction to go in. Doc, what was the second something you alluded to a few minutes ago?"

Doc Cavanaugh pointed to the mark on Christine's neck and continued, "When I first looked at this mark, I thought it might be a brand used by the killer to show ownership of the victim, arrogance enough to "show" us he is the master of this situation, of this victim, of the police. But, I now believe, he used the branding technique to hide the injection points in order to heighten the drama and make it more difficult for us to determine the "what's and whys" of his thinking. This mark was not put on post mortem like I originally thought when we were examining Christine at the pond. The killer branded her just before she was injected knowing we would look at the brand mark. The killer also knew, at some point, we would find the injection marks. In layman's terms, the son-of-a-bitch is playing with us!"

My thoughts went back to a statement Peggy made earlier as I was leaving the house. Was this person, who was responsible for killing and mutilating Christine Sawyer, also responsible for killing anyone else? Was this an isolated killing made to look like the type of crime a serial killer would commit? Did we, in fact, have a serial killer living in our small community? If so, how long before tortures and kills again?

"Derek Larson to Chief Kosciak, Larson to Kosciak, Come in please." My radio was sounding as I pulled out of the hospital parking lot heading back toward the station.

"Kosciak, here, Derek," I responded.

"Chief, how long will it be before you return to the station?" he asked. "I have some very important information for you regarding the project you assigned me this morning."

"I'll be there in about thirty minutes. I just left the hospital," I answered, noting Derek purposely did not mention what project he was referring to. I wondered at that instant how many other young women might have disappeared, and if they were murdered in the same gruesome manner of Christine Sawyer.

"Put a call into Ken Garber over at the State Police station," I said. "Ask him if he can meet me at the station now instead of tomorrow morning like we discussed. Tell him I have information from Doc Cavanaugh that is extremely important - Kosciak out."

"Received Chief - Will do - Out," he said; the radio going silent.

Thirty minutes later I was parking my Explorer in front of the station. During the drive back from the hospital, I was thinking about the bizarre method the killer used to end Christine's life. Lethal injection showed total premeditation on the killer's part. Whoever this killer was, a lot of time was spent planning and executing that plan. The facial mutilation made me believe the killer was suffering from some sort of mental delusion. The lack of sexual contact with the victim intimated this was not a crime of passion. This was not the case of a raging husband catching his wife sleeping with another man or some jealous boyfriend retaliating after being dumped by his girlfriend for someone else. No, the killer's thoughts were focused on something totally different. The killer was being driven by reasoning inclusive to only his thoughts. Probably a victim of abuse or abuses, a tormented, emotional inferno now raged within this sick and twisted mind. Interpreting the killer's reasoning and understanding would help us solve this puzzle.

"Why kill and mutilate?" I thought.

Ken Garber arrived an hour after Derek placed the call. I was surprised he made it so quickly because it was already 10:00 PM and he was probably home when he received the call from Derek. Ken's about six foot four with a full head of black hair. God, how I hate these guys with hair! His muscular, square frame is well-suited to his Massachusetts State Police uniform. The silver captain's bars on his shoulders glistened as the lights in my office reflected off of them onto the wall, creating two spots of light moving across pictures of Peggy and the girls. His urgent stride told me he was anxious to learn what Doc Cavanaugh discovered during Christine's postmortem. As he entered my office, I began to speak before we even began exchanging any type of greeting.

"Christine was killed by lethal injection. Pancuronium was injected into her carotid artery to paralyze her, and after he removed the eyes and lips, he administered the last two drugs which stopped her heart."

"What the fuck! You mean to tell me she was CONSCIUOS when that bastard mutilated her face? That mother-fucking-son-of-a-bitch! Ron, I...," He said falling silent, turning his head to look out my office window. Ken was obviously emotional about this case. Knowing the family for many years made this difficult for him to separate the personal from the professional. After a moment of silence, he continued, "Did Doc find anything else during the exam that might help us?"

"No," I said. "He found nothing else that would be critical to our investigation. He believes the mark on Christine's neck was used to camouflage the entry points of the needles. Doc also said that there was no sexual abuse involved and no other mutilation done to her body. However, the news Derek shared with me when I got back to the station a little while ago will rattle you right down to the laces on your boots."

Before I could say another word, Ken looked right into my eyes and said, "There is the probability you will find at least four more bodies buried out at Meadow Pond. There have been four girls reported missing in a one hundred mile radius of Sutton, and all of them have disappeared within the last two years. Am I correct?" It was obvious Ken's investigators were reviewing past records just as we were. I would rather have two agencies investigating the same information to reduce the possibility of missing some important piece of information that might be critical to solving this crime.

"Well, I see we are on the same track with this Ken, and you're absolutely right. The first two abductions occurred in Worcester. The next one happened in Northbridge and the last one in Oxford. All young women in their late teens to mid-twenties, each disappearing without a trace and no witnesses. These girls just vanished. Vehicles from two of the abductions were recovered without so much as grain of sand in the carpeting. Is this the same information your guys came up with?" I asked leaning forward in my chair, putting my hands to my face and elbows onto my desktop.

"Pretty damned close Ron. But, to go a little further: none of the victims' families ever received any type of ransom note or phone call regarding their daughters. There was no attempt at all to contact them asking for any sort of ransom. None of the parents, family members, relatives, neighbors or co-workers interviewed have any ideas or suggestions as to why these girls would have gone missing or why they would be targeted and abducted. We know most perps have a motive for their actions. Very seldom do these people act on a whim or spur-of-the-moment impulse. Offenders at this level are directed by thought processes that drive them to perform unspeakable acts, sometimes with no control over their own actions. So, in this case, my gut instinct is telling me the same thing yours is telling you. We may, in fact, have a serial killer on our hands. His body count just went up to five, and he will continue to abduct and kill young women until we stop him!"

Ken and I looked at one another both knowing, without saying a single word, that this case was the type of case every law enforcement officer prays they will never have to work… this type of investigation takes its toll on everyone. The victims, victim's families, law enforcement personnel working the leads and clues, medical personnel and even the spouses and families of all those involved who would suffer during the weeks and months ahead.

Just as Ken was standing up to leave, Derek came charging into my office. His face looked like the proverbial deer in the headlights as he spoke: "The Staties at the crime scene over at Meadow…," he hesitated, caught his breath, and continued in broken, short words. "They…just…found ...another...body!"

13

When I arrived at Meadow Pond, the crime scene buzzed like a bee hive with a dozen or so investigators and officers combing the surrounding brush, small trees and pond's embankment. Although the Staties were in control of the crime scene, Toddand Kim were the ones who actually located the second body. Both looked like the last eighteen hours were starting to catch up with them. They had been searching the embankment about one hundred feet from where the boys first stumbled upon Christine's body earlier in the day. Kim was pulling dead leaves and small branches away from the embankment when she saw the tips of three fingers sticking out of the dirt. She immediately called over to Todd and the two of them cleared away just enough of the soil to expose the entire left hand of the victim. The original crime scene immediately quadrupled in size.

A silent hush hung over everyone like a fog bank blanketing an inlet harbor. The discovery of the second victim, combined with the knowledge that four other young women were known to have disappeared within a one hundred mile radius of Sutton, told us we were standing at the burial site of a serial killer. My mind was racing at the thought of finding four more bodies buried out here. So far, other than the two bodies, no other items or clues had been found that would help our investigation. Whoever our killer was, he or she was as meticulous with the burial of the victims as he or she was with the detailing of Christine's car.

The thought crossed my mind that it would be easier on our small police force if the other victims were found outside of our jurisdiction. This investigation was certain to be an emotional drain on our police force as well as a financial drain on our town. I kept thinking that I should be ashamed of myself for thinking about economics at a time like this, but this was the reality of a small town police force.

Approaching Todd and Kim, I could see they were visibly shaken by the discovery of the second body. Sutton has never experienced multiple murders like those of this event. We have had the usual domestic disputes that sometimes turn very violent, but to my knowledge, there had only been one homicide in the town's history. The husband of the murdered woman left a note saying that his wife was dead because government agents were watching him through his television set. He knew she was part of the conspiracy, so he shot her and then turned the gun on himself taking his own life. Surreal as that murder suicide was, it was not even close to what we were dealing with here.

"Where is the second body?" I asked as Kim looked up to meet my eyes.

"Right over here Chief," she said pointing down the embankment about fifty feet away. "We haven't moved anything else since we exposed the hand. The Staties have kept their distance, too, waiting for you to get here before they dig her out the rest of the way."

Todd was looking out across the ice-covered pond as Kim and I spoke. He turned slowly, looking at me with a knowing sense and said, "There are more victims buried out here aren't there, Chief?"

"Yeah," I spoke softly. "There could be up to four more victims that we know about right now. I just met with Ken Garber at the station, and while we were talking, Derick came into my office and showed us what his investigation turned up. We don't have much to go on right now, so please, keep this under your hats until we can develop a base of information to work from. We don't want any information leaking out to the press that we don't personally release ourselves. Ken agrees and will instruct his staff to keep the lid on this as well. Right now we do not want our killer to know who we have found or what we know, which right now, by t... is damned little and very frustrating. Kim, I want you to tag team the Statie who is in charge here at the scene. I don't care how much OT you have to put in. I want to know what they know, when they know it. Todd, I need you to get back to the station and give Derek a hand going through the information on our other four victims. We need to compare the files on each of these girls and try to find a connection linking them to our killer. Let me know whatever you find, whenever you find it. I don't care if I am eating a god-damned York Peppermint Patty with the President of the United States, you find me and let me know."

Neither Kim nor Todd said a word. They knew me well enough to know I was shifting into my "take no prisoners" mode and would be increasingly more demanding of everyone on our team as the hours and days went on. I walked over to the spot where the second body was buried and saw the exposed hand sticking out of the dirt. It did not look real to me as I stood looking at the ground in direct proximity to the beckoning fingers. A solitary hand, reaching. I felt as if she wanted me to grab her hand and pull her out of this dirt grave back into the world of the living, or perhaps she wanted me to get closer so she could whisper something into my ear to help me trap her tormentor.

Looking over to my right, I could see the opened hole in the dirt embankment - Christine's earthen sarcophagus these past months. As the State Police began removing our second victim, I wondered how long our second Jane Doe had slept silently by the water's edge and how long it would be before we found yet another grave. I took out my cell phone and called Doc Cavanaugh to tell him about our second victim. Because the State Police investigators were already at the scene, I asked Doc to stay at the hospital until we could extricate our newest Jane Doe and transport her there for his initial examination. I also asked Doc if Jerry Bickford was still there, and if so, to please let him know his assistance with the additional post mortem would speed up the process and get the information to both local and state police that much quicker.

"Chief Kosciak," I heard one of the officers, who was part of the team removing our Jane Doe from the winter ground, call out. "We have her pretty much freed up here. Do you want to take a look before we put her into the bag for transport?"

I didn't say anything, but, motioned with a wave of my hand and nod of my head that I did want to look. Walking toward the body I felt a tightness grow in my stomach. The kind of cramp you get when you are anxious and really do not want to do something, but know you have no choice. I did not want to look at another young, beautiful girl lying dead on the ground, the victim of some perverted maniac. But, there she was, about the same age as Christine. I put her at about twenty-two to twenty-five old. Her brownish- blond hair was the same color as Christine's. She was about the same height and weight, but, there was one marked difference between the two girls. Our Jane Doe still had both of her eyes and her lips. Instead, the killer cut off both her ears!

14

The winter moonlight fell across leafless hills, silhouetting fingers of trees reaching toward the sky. Skeletal branches moved slightly with the cold breeze of winter giving them an eerie rhythm. As I was driving back to the station from Meadow Pond, the second young woman was on her way to the morgue. Christine's autopsy would be just finishing up when our Jane Doe arrived. We knew Christine's death was caused by the injection of the three drugs into her carotid artery, and that the circular brand mark on her neck was meant to camouflage the injection points. The brand mark we found on Christine's neck was also found on the neck of our Jane Doe and therefore I was theorizing the killer used the lethal injection procedure on this victim as well. Christine was not sexually assaulted during her ordeal, and if the second victim was not as well, we could be pretty sure that this was not part of our killer's m.o. Though, by removing Christine's eyes and lips and cutting off Jane Doe's ears, the killer was obviously taking trophies as keepsakes. The second autopsy would tell us if the killer worked with any other sort of pattern other than the mutilation. If there was no sexual assault on the second victim, we could be pretty sure the remaining three missing women were also not sexually assaulted. The murder victims and other missing women share the same age bracket and were all enrolled in local colleges. Two were

Caucasian, two were Black, and one Asian. All of this information was beginning to give us a picture of our killer. My only problem now, that this picture came in the form of a jig-saw puzzle with pieces scattered from here to Hades.

Turning onto West Main Street, I decided to stop at the twenty-four hour doughnut shop for a coffee. After losing eight pounds in a month, I was finding it more than difficult to stay away from their sugar-coated, jelly doughnuts. Jelly doughnuts were designed by a very sadistic baker to taunt people like me. Sometimes I gave in to my craving, but lately, I had been holding out steadfastly against devouring one of those little culinary beauties - that is, until tonight.

Opening the door of the Explorer, I saw my brother Paul talking with one of our Highway Department workers. I was not surprised to see him at this late hour because he frequently stopped here on his way home from the weekly poker tournament at the Gray Barn. Paul is a retired history teacher from a neighboring high school and spends his days either playing golf or substitute teaching per diem. Looking over as I approached him in the parking lot, Paul nodded his recognition, ending his conversation and turned walking over toward me.

"Hey there little brother," he said with his usual hint of loving brotherly sarcasm. "How is the family law enforcement officer doing this fine night?"

"I love you too. Good to see you still hanging out at the doughnut shop in your golden years. What are you and Cindy up to?" Cindy was Paul's wife - also a retired teacher.

"Same ol', same ol'. We were up in Peabody yesterday visiting Dan, Alex and the baby. Man, that boy is growing like a corn stock in the July sun. He is only two months old and weighs in at sixteen pounds. Glad I don't have to pay to feed him! What about you and Peggy? Are you guys going to the family get together at Wright's Farm next week?"

Wright's farm is a local restaurant specializing in serving chicken dinners family style. All the chicken, salad, shells and fries you can eat for one price. They have the best French fries in the world (I know this from personal, gastrointestinal experience). Their salad dressing is delicious and is also sold in the local supermarkets.

Each year, around this time, Peggy's dad, his children's families, his brothers and sisters, and all their families, gather at Wrights for an annual get-together. Last year, we reached the largest attendance ever, at seventy-two hungry people eating themselves into oblivion. It is the one time each year where everyone is able to catch up on the "goings on" in each of the families and no one has to do any dishes!

"Yes," I replied. "We wouldn't miss it for the world. Although, we have a new case we are working on, so I think I will only be there for a short while. But you damned well know Mike wouldn't talk to me for a month if I wasn't there to buy him his VO and ginger! Holy shit man, I'm crazy but not stupid!" We both laughed knowing that I was only partly being humorous.

"You working the Sawyer girl's case?" Paul asked.

I looked at him inquisitively, wondering how the hell word of Christine's discovery could have spread so quickly.

"I've heard some people talking around town tonight." He continued, "Word has it that you found her out at Meadow."

"Yeah, we found her buried in an embankment at the pond. Doc Cavanaugh is finishing up the autopsy. It amazes me how fast news travels in a small town. I can't say any more because of the sensitivity of the case. I don't want any more information than necessary getting out to the newspapers. As it is, I'm surprised this much information has already leaked out. By morning, the townspeople will know more than I do." I started to turn away, hesitated and said, "Paul, let me know if you hear anything else out on the street or at the school. Even if you hear something on the 9th tee, give me a call right away."

"Not a problem, little brother," he replied with that older brother's grin on his face again. "See you at Wright's."

Stepping up into my Explorer, I heard Kim's voice on my radio.

"Kim LaFleur to Chief Kosciak, LaFleur to Kosciak."

"Kosciak here; go ahead Kim."

"Chief, can you give me a call on my cell phone? I have something I need to tell you privately."

"Received. I'll call right away. Stand by."

I was trying to talk on the radio and hold my coffee at the same time. Not the easiest thing in the world to do while you are sitting in the cramped front seat of a police vehicle. After struggling to get the coffee cup into the cup holder, I was able to take out my cell phone and call Kim. She answered before the first ring finished.

"Chief," she said, sounding like she was trying to catch her breath. "I didn't want to say anything over the radio just in case someone was on the same frequency listening to our conversation."

"Understood: What do you have for me?"

"Well, you were absolutely right. The Staties have found two more bodies out here at the pond. The count is now up to four! It looks like this is the burial ground for our killer. So far all of the bodies have been found within a couple hundred feet of one another. The last body was found buried about 50 feet inland from the pond's embankment. The Staties have called for more vehicles to transport the women over to the hospital."

"O.K. Stay out there at the scene as long as you can. I know you are coming up on twenty-four straight hours. When you get ready to leave, call into the station and I'll have someone come out there to relieve you. I want one of our team out there at all times. I need to get information as soon as you people do. Kosciak: out."

I sat motionless in the front seat for a few minutes knowing that the remaining girls would also be found buried at the pond. My heart hurt for the parents and families that I would have to contact as each victim was identified. Over the next few days a pallor would begin to fall over this the town. News of this magnitude could not be kept from the public for long, and once they heard the news, they would know there was a serial killer preying on little New England sanctuary. Feeling safe will be a thing of the past, and nothing the police could do would be enough to calm anyone's nerves. Everyone would becoming hyper-vigilant, reporting anything or anyone looking suspicious or out of place. The station phones were bound to ring off the desk tops with leads and tips. The difficult part will be when to really listen to people calling in. You must discern which leads are real and which are false. Hours could be spent following up on a lead called in by someone just looking for the attention. Wasted time, valuable time, crucial time. Time you can never replace.

Pulling onto West Main Street, I decided it was time to check in with Peggy. It was just past midnight, and too late to call. She would be fast asleep by the time I got home. I know I am fortunate to have a wife who understands the demands of a police chief's work. I grew up hearing my father repeat, "my job is seven twenty-four," but the police chief's job is even more than that, and Peggy knew before we were married that I would have two marriages to be responsible for - and sometimes she would be second.

Marty McMaster started her day with the usual flurry of hectic activity a college sophomore late for class would create: running from the bathroom to the bedroom; looking for her comb and blow dryer; putting on eye liner and lipstick and, most importantly, making sure her cell phone was tucked into its place in her small, hand-sewn, beaded pocketbook. Bolting through the kitchen, she grabbed a granola bar, and quickly walked out the back door, across the lawn, and down the sidewalk towards the coffee shop about a half mile down the road. She would have to cut across the small park at the end of their street but other than that shortcut, she would be on sidewalks all the way.

The sun was shining and it was already a heat wave at thirty-three degrees Fahrenheit. There was very little snow on the ground for this time of year, because of the unseasonably higher temperatures since the start of the fall season. Marty would save five minutes by walking through the park. These five minutes were the difference between getting a coffee before her first class at the college began, or having to wait two hours until first break. She did not like the prospect of waiting over two hours for her first cup of coffee. She was used to getting there early enough each morning, having time to sit and enjoy those first sips of hot java, and taking a few minutes to enjoy watching the people walk by in front of the coffee shop window.

Turning off of the sidewalk, Marty started to walk on the brownish, dried, winter grass peeping thru the thin snow covering. She noticed that the ground, although frozen under foot, was still a little wet and spongy due to the temperature having been a few degrees above freezing. "I'm getting dirt all over my sneakers," She thought. "Too late now!" she responded silently to herself as she kept pace across the park.

She did not see anyone else in the park as she made her way up a small incline adjacent to the service road leading to the public restrooms at the center of the park. Just as she was about to reach the apex of the incline, she felt a burning sting in her left thigh. It felt as though a bee had stung her, but, she knew bees hibernated in the winter and tried to ignore the sting which now began to get warmer and burn more intensely. Marty took a few more steps before everything around her started to get blurry and unfocused. Another step and her thoughts began to get confused and disoriented. Before Marty McMaster hit the grass, full faced, she was unconscious.

He waited behind the small outbuilding which housed the restrooms watching to see if any passerby might have seen Marty fall to the ground. "Patience," he said to himself. "Control is the key to survival," he thought pushing a large wheelbarrow toward her limp body lying face down on the wet, cold grass. He quickly wrapped her in dark green plastic placing her limp body into the wheelbarrow. It was a very short distance to the van parked on the service road where he effortlessly transferred her unconscious frame onto a mat on the floor in the back of the vehicle. Once Marty was deposited in the van and he climbed in, they were out of sight, and because the van had no side or rear windows, he could move unobserved as he bound her wrists and ankles using black, plastic, electrical ties. He was now in complete control of his new adoptee. Crouching down next to her he watched her breasts rise and fall slowly beneath her opened winter coat - the quieting effect of the dart he fired into her leg.

She looked even more lovely and soft as he moved his face to within a couple of inches of her lips. He inhaled deeply to pull her fragrance as deep into his lungs as he physically was able. He felt his chest expand to its fullest and knew the adoption process had begun in earnest once again. He wanted as much of her aroma inside of his being as his lungs could hold. He would never leave her like they had left him. He would never stop loving her, never turn his back on her no matter what she said or did. That was the way an adoptive parent was supposed to treat his or her children. They were supposed to show unconditional love regardless of the fact that their adopted child was not birthed from their own loins! "Control - control and control," He thought. "One step at a time will bring you logically to the next step."

Marty would sleep long enough for him to drive her to her new home. Once there, he could transfer her to her bedroom and wait for her to wake up after the effects of the drug wore off. He took another few minutes in the quiet of the van to admire her. Tipping his head very slowly to the left and then to the right, he studied the features of her face and roamed over her body with satisfied eyes. She was young and beautiful. Marty McMaster would make an excellent addition to the family. Besides, the other children were already waiting to welcome her. No one saw the van pull out of the park, turn onto the street and slowly drive away.

16

Marty began to move slowly. Her eyes opening with a slight flutter as the drug wore off. Her thoughts were confused and unclear, but she knew something was not right. She thought she remembered falling at the park, but could not mentally focus on anything - one thought bounced out of the way by another thought. Thoughts were random and did not stay in her conscious mind long enough for her to know exactly what the previous thought had been. She tried to rub her eyes with her hands but, they were not responding the way they should. Both hands moved at the same time, together, in unison. Her hands would not respond separately.

Looking around the room she realized that everything was fuzzy. Nothing was clear. It was like wearing the wrong eyeglasses with a strong prescription. She could see objects, but, everything was distorted. Panic began to overtake her brain. Then, it spread like fire throughout her body, burning into her muscles and bones, making her skin bead with the sweat of fear.

The first sounds Marty made were almost inaudible whimpers. Having heard them many times before, they were like music to his ears. He always enjoyed these first moments watching the new child begin to acclimate herself to his home - this safe environment he provided. He watched Marty become more and more cognizant of her dilemma. The whimpers, now cries of fear, intensified as she began to realize exactly what "bad" thing had happened to her. She remembered walking thru the park on her way to the coffee shop. She remembered the incline, the burning sting in her thigh, and then she could not remember anything until this moment. She recognized plastic electrical ties binding her hands and feet, understanding now why her hands could not move separately. Items in the room began to take on clear shapes and forms as she became more conscious.

The walls of the room were purple with bright yellow trim around the windows and doors. These were same colors as HER bedroom at home. "AT HOME!" she thought. "How could I be in my bedroom at home?" Yet, there was the picture of Willie, her gray-haired sheep dog, sitting on her off-white dressing table. "What the hell?" she thought, as she recognized her lacrosse stick leaning in the corner of the room next to the closet door, with its red stain from the paint gun she accidently fired one night when checking the gun's CO2 cartridge. "How could this be? Why would mom and dad tie me up in my own house? Am I freakin' dreaming?" she thought, as she heard someone move, immediately aware that she was not the only person in her room.

"I hope you will enjoy your room," he said as he stood at the head of the bed just out of Marty's peripheral vision. "I have spent time and energy creating an atmosphere for you to help with your adjustment to your new family. I want you to feel totally welcome here with us. After all, we all deserve to feel safe and secure in our own home."

Marty wanted to look around and see who was talking to her, but she was too afraid to move. Her common sense told her to remain motionless and quiet. Lying absolutely still on the bed, Marty listened as the man continued to speak.

"I visited you in your bedroom a few times over the last few weeks and took some pictures. I made sure I recreated your room down to the very last detail. You will even find I have bought the correct sizes for your bras and panties, jeans, sweat shirts and sneakers. One night, I stood over you watching you sleep for a very long time. You looked so peaceful wrapped up in your comforter with one bare foot hanging off the end of the bed. I noticed you painted your toenails as well as your fingernails. You will find your red polish on the dressing table. You snored just a little bit. I remember smiling and thinking how wonderful it would be listening to you snore in your new home here with us. I almost changed my mind about adopting you that night. You looked so peaceful and serene, but, I knew they would discard you eventually. I knew it was only a matter of time before you would be alone, depressed and wondering what it was you had done to be abandoned and thrown away like leftovers after supper. I don't know how but, I just know when a child is going to need me. It is something that happens. I can't control it, nor do I want to control it. This is the gift I have been endowed with by whatever higher power exists in the world these days. I am the rescuer. I am the consummate parent and guardian. Marty, I have adopted you as my own because I do not want you to suffer the humiliation and degradation you would feel from those people who pretend to be your parents. You need to know and believe that I will ALWAYS be here for you. You are safe now. Here, you never have to fear being alone again. You are part of MY family."

Marty still did not move. She did not look up. But, she knew that he was waiting for some sort of response. Perhaps it was divine intervention, perhaps it was just plain old fashioned luck, but as she was about to speak, a buzzer sounded in an adjacent room. Her abductor's retreat was immediate, leaving the room without saying anything through the door behind the bed. She heard a bolt slide into place, locking it as he left the room.

Marty knew this was not a dream. She would not wake up from this nightmare. She would live in it. She was not naïve person, she knew this was a life or death situation. A person does not break into your house, take pictures of a bedroom, reconstruct that exact room in detail, and abduct you, without being a seriously mentally disconnected and dangerous man. His words were spoken softly, but his tone suggested that if she were to make him angry, he would be capable of doing great harm. She felt the coldness in his words, a coldness permeating his mind and his soul. But, something sincere in his words about becoming part of HIS family suggested, that perhaps, if she played along with his agenda, she might find a way to escape.

"How long have I been here?" she asked herself. The shade on the window was drawn, not allowing any light into the room. It could be the middle of the afternoon or the middle of the night. Marty had no way of knowing.

"I wonder if my mom and dad know I am missing?" was the next thought to cross her mind as she continued to look around at the room she knew so well. He did, in fact, replicate her room right down to the rainbow-colored, elastic, hair-ties in a green, turtle dish on her dressing table. "What was it he said about being thrown away? Why does he think I need to be rescued from my parents? Why does he want me? Who are the "us" he mentioned?" All questions she asked while she waited for his return.

Molly Harrington moved the large UPS box away from the front door of her art store so she could unlock it and open up after closing an hour for lunch. "They must have delivered this package just after I left." She thought. "Excellent. These are the tie-dyed skirts I ordered."

Molly had opened "Molly's ARTS and THINGS" five years earlier, and the store, had earned itself a great reputation within the local and surrounding communities. Molly originally started the store to supply local artists and crafts-people with materials they needed for their specific genre of art. As a painter, you could find anything you needed for oils, water base or acrylic supplies. Molly loved bead work and therefore added displays devoted to beads purchased from all over the world. If you weaved baskets, there was a section specific to all of those articles. Stained-glass supplies glittered in the early afternoon light as Molly put her back pack on top of the counter by the register. In addition to art supplies, Molly displayed her photographic works which sold out almost as quickly as she could develop a new batch. Molly graduated from The New England School of Photography in Boston seven years earlier where she met her partner, and father of their two children, Travis. Together, Molly and Travis ran the store and raised their two children Caroline and Zeak.

Although Molly's prices were a little higher than the larger art and craft stores found in the shopping malls, people still flocked to ARTS and THINGS because Molly was the consummate artist and loved everything and everyone involved in the art world. She was soft spoken, wore very little makeup and dressed pretty much like the 1970's hippies you used to see at the Newport Jazz Festival or on the six o'clock news running from the police after protesting the Viet Nam conflict. One of Molly's goals, was to own a vintage, VW bus with large, colorful flowers painted all over the outside - re-creating an era long lost to social changes.

Clothing of all colors hung in racks at the rear of the store. The tie-dye skirts UPS just delivered would be a nice addition. As Molly held one of the skirts up to inspect it and enjoy the brightly, colored pattern, she heard the door to the store open and close behind her. Thinking it was Travis stopping by with the kids, Molly turned with a ballerina swirl, arms reaching toward the ceiling, on her tip toes, ready to give Caroline and Zeak a big smile and a warm, good afternoon hug.

"Oh!" she said with a startle in her voice. "I thought you were my partner Travis and our children. I didn't mean..."

"That's all right." he said, interrupting her as she stood flat-footed on the floor, a little red faced and embarrassed. Molly noticed right away that the man's voice and words were coldly flat. He was not the usual customer who came in effervescing and bright. Instead, there was an aura of soul-chilling dread making her turn her eyes away from his and look down at the old hardwood, pine floor. "I am looking for a very specific item for one of my children, and I am hoping that you will be able to help me find it. It is a replica of the three monkeys sitting together in line with their hands over their ears, eyes and mouth representing hearing, seeing and speaking no evil. Would you happen to have something like this, or perhaps, know where I could purchase one?"

"I'm sorry, we don't sell anything like that here, but, let me jump on-line and see what I can find for you. It will just take me a second to boot up because I've just arrived myself."

Molly was thankful to turn away from this man and open up her lap top. The distraction took her mind off of the unsettled feeling he was creating in her spirit. She typed in the information and was able to locate a gift shop within a half hour of her store which sold the item the man was looking for. During the four or five minutes it took Molly to locate the item, she realized the man did not move, but stood staring at her as her fingers moved over the keyboard. He never shifted his weight, looked at any other items in the store or looked out the window as people walked by. He just stood completely motionless and stared.

Realizing his grey eyes were extremely focused and boring into her psyche, Molly hurriedly wrote the name and address of the store on a piece of paper, saying, "I've found a store in Worcester that sells an item like the one you are looking for. It retails for twenty-four dollars without the six percent sales tax. It says they have them in stock. I have jotted down the phone number and address for you so that you can call in advance. I hope this will be helpful for you," she said as she hesitatingly held the paper out for him to take from her hand. The thought of him touching her sent a nauseous chill through her body.

"Thank you for taking the time to look this up for me. I do very much appreciate your help," he said as he purposely brushed Molly's fingers, taking the paper in his own.

Molly tried not to show how uncomfortable she was in his presence. But, as he brushed his fingers against hers, he looked into her eyes, a small smile breaking the straightness of his lips, giving away the pleasure he was feeling at that instant. Molly pulled away instinctively backing up a couple of steps as the front door opened, Caroline and Zeak running into the store with Travis close on their heels.

"Mommy! Mommy!" Caroline shouted running up to Molly and grabbing her around her leg. "Daddy bought us a chocolate covered doughnut! Look at Zeak. He has chocolate over his nose!"

Before Molly could say anything else to the man, he vanished. It was as if he never stood there in the first place, as if he never walked out of the store, but just disappeared. Molly watched the front door for a few minutes feeling the darkness he left lingering in the air.

Driving back from Worcester, after purchasing the figurine of the three monkeys from the gift shop, he thought about his brief encounter with Molly. The feeling of absolute control welled up inside of his chest as he remembered how Molly looked down at the floor refusing to look into his eyes, how she'd stepped back after he brushed her long, slender fingers, and the smell of her fear permeating the air between them. Yes, he took a chance looking to purchase the monkeys close to home. But, what of it! No one knew anything. All of his children were safely sheltered out at the pond. No one would bother them out there.

Glancing at the three monkeys sitting on the passenger seat next to him, with their respective hands over ears, eyes and mouth, his mind was thrown back into the dark, cellar closet in his past. He fought mentally to maintain control over the steering wheel of the car, knowing that within the twisted torment of that closet he was powerless. There was no avoiding the memories. They would flood into his thoughts without warning, relentless, without remorse. There was no escaping the memory of the silence, of the solitude and loneliness. And the darkness.

"No, Ma," he said, cowering in the corner of the kitchen with his legs drawn up as close to his chest as he could physically pull them. "No, I'll be good. I promise. I'll be good. I won't take a cookie again without asking! Please! I don't want to go to the cellar. Not again! Please!"

But she did not hear the words he was yelling at her - pleading to her with tears streaming down his eight-year-old face. She only knew he did not ask HER permission to take and eat the chocolate-chip cookie. She also knew he must be punished harshly for not asking. Rightly so, it wasn't his cookie. It was HER cookie. She was the one who worked for it. She was the one who put food on the table every day since that rotten bastard of a husband took up and left her and the kid alone to fend for themselves. She never wanted to adopt him in the first place. She was forced to work as a house cleaner days and then work four nights a week as a kitchen helper washing dishes and cleaning up other people's friggin garbage. All he did was whine and cry. Why they adopted this piss ant she could not remember. He was one large pain in her ass from day one, but, now, he was really pissing her off.

She grabbed him by the upper arm pulling him forcefully into the center of the kitchen floor. Without losing any momentum, she took the roll of duct tape off of the table top and began to tape his wrists together. Once his wrists were taped, she taped his ankles and then his mouth. Totally disabled and unable to stand or walk, she grabbed him by his hair and began pulling him across the kitchen floor toward the cellar door. He screamed into the duct tape and kicked his taped legs in protest to what was happening. This process was not new to him. She threw open the cellar door, and without losing a step, started down the stairs maintaining her firm grip on his hair. He followed through the doorway and felt the first stair fall away under him. He fell downward until the next stair came up to meet him slamming against his small body. Each step bruised the bones and muscles not yet fully developed – a child's bones and muscles. There were twenty-two steps leading down into the cellar, and each left its mark somewhere on his helpless body.

The house was supported by an old, field-stone foundation through which water and dampness entered every time it rained. The air smelled of mildew and was a perfect hiding place for rodents and spiders that lived in the stone-work and wood rafters in this damp, dusky environment. Across the cellar was a closet without a light. It was made of hardwood. The closet door had two locks and a barricade bar across the front. The closet was empty inside. Like the rest of the cellar, the closet floor was just moist, sticky dirt that lived through over a hundred years of occupants' memories.

She stopped just short of the closet, reaching up to a shelf hanging on the cellar wall. Taking down a blind fold and ear protectors, she put them on his ears and around his eyes, blocking out all sound and the dim, cellar light. The ear protectors and blind fold were then wrapped with duct tape just like his arms and legs. She did not want him to loosen them while he sat and thought about his disobedience. Dragging him the last few feet to the closet, she threw him inside like a bag of potatoes against the wall. Slamming and locking the door, she stormed away up the stairs back to the kitchen hurling cuss words into the cellar darkness.

This time, she would leave him alone in the darkness of his damp prison for two days. There would be no food, nor water. Sometimes it was a shorter amount of time. Sometimes it was much, much longer. He knew better than to cry. The more noise he made, the longer he would remain alone in the total darkness of his closet prison.

His van passed in front of the Sutton Police Station before he realized that he did not remember driving back from Worcester. "The benefit of flashbacks," he thought, turning left onto Prentice Road, straight out of town toward his building. Marty would be waiting there for his return. The three monkeys rolled over face down on the front seat as the van hit a pot hole slamming into the front tire with a loud thud.

Marty woke up not knowing what time it was or how long she had slept. The drug responsible for knocking her out was slow to leave her system. She was in a state of half consciousness as she tried to focus, attempting to clear her mind, drifting in and out of sleep like a person recovering from anesthesia after undergoing surgery. There was no saliva in her mouth, and her tongue felt twice its size, making her gag as she rolled onto her side, looking down at the floor praying for a drink of cold water. She did not know if her kidnapper had returned after his initial departure, or if he would return at all. Would he leave her here in this familiar room to starve to death, or was there some other madness he wanted to inflict upon her when he returned? She thought about the word 'adoption' that he had used during his conversation and then gagged again as an unconscious swallow closed the back of her throat, thirsting for relief from this drug-induced drought. Tears of desperation began to move down her cheeks, small rivers of salty moisture she tried to direct into her mouth by twisting her head. She would drink her own urine at this point if that was all that was available. Her tongue was so dry she thought it might crack open when she coughed or gagged again. Her thoughts were broken by the sliding of the bolt lock on the door.

"Shit!" she thought. "What the fuck! Is he going to rape me? Is that what he wants to do with me? Am I going to be some sort of sex toy he uses until he has satiated his madness? When he uses me every way he can think of, will he kill me, and dump my body in some wooded area for the animals to gnaw on until there is nothing left but a few bones and strands of hair mixed in with dead leaves and dried twigs? JESUS! Will somebody please come and take me out of this nightmare! Help ME! Help! Help! Help me! OH, CHRIST, somebody fucking HELP ME!" There was no reply to her inward pleading.

She closed her eyes as the door swung open into the room. Pretending to be asleep, hoping that he would close the door and leave her alone, she listened to his footsteps entering the room. She heard the door close. Then, there was complete silence. She tried to control her breathing mimicking the slow, easy breathing of deep sleep. "Keep your breathing slow and easy," she thought. "Slow and easy - do not move your eyes. Concentrate. Keep your eyes shut. If he knows you are faking, who knows what he'll do." All of these thoughts raced through her brain as she listened intently for the sound of his movement. But there was no sound to be heard. "What is he doing? He must be standing there just staring at me. What the FUCK is he DOING?"

Suddenly, she felt it. Very faintly at first, but heavier as the seconds dragged on ever so slowly, like a long distance runner using a geriatric walker to run a marathon. Without making a sound, he stood by her bedside. Leaning over, he brought his face to within an inch of hers. He began to lightly blow onto her neck and cheek. Blowing very softly in long, extended breaths until he could blow no longer, then, inhaling a new batch of air to start blowing once again, watching for her reaction. She could feel his warm breath entering her nose and shuddered inside knowing that she was breathing in HIS breath. She felt a wave of nausea overcoming her and prayed she would be able to maintain her sleeping ruse, as fear once again began to rise in her mind.

He spoke to her quietly. "Marty. I know you are awake. I can smell the fear streaming out of your pores. I know you must be frightened and wondering what I might do to you, and therefore, I understand why you would want me to think you are asleep. But

I can assure you I mean you no harm. When I spoke before about you being a part of my family, I meant every word. I have rescued you from false parents who would have abandoned you and left you alone to fend for yourself. I know these things. I only want to protect you as I have protected my other adopted children. It is my hope you will give me the opportunity to prove this to you - give me a chance to show my genuine desire to keep you in my family. I would like you to open your eyes and look at me. Do not be afraid. Please, look into my eyes, Marty, and know the truth."

Marty knew instinctively she should not open her eyes and look at her abductor. As soon as she looked into his eyes and saw his face, she was as good as dead. He could not afford to let her go once she could identify him. But there was something hypnotic in his voice. She found herself opening her eyes while every alarm in her body sounded the warning: DO NOT OPEN YOUR EYES! DO NOT LOOK INTO HIS FACE! Her eyes continued to open until she was looking into two, deep, dark eyes staring back at her intently. Now it was too late to retreat. Marty could not close her eyes and pretend she had not looked at him. The die was cast and she would have to play along with him if she were to survive this nightmare.

The room was dimly lit like a house at dusk when the sun goes down, only one or two lights shining through the charcoal grey of the evening. Marty estimated that he stood about six feet tall or a little taller. The full-length, black coat that he wore hid most of his torso and legs, but she knew he was well built and muscular. Squared shoulders and erect posture gave him the appearance of being more statue than human. His movements were almost undetectable and therefore his agility and coordination were probably superior. His face, partially hidden in the shadows of the room, had a lean and angular chin at the jaw line, with straight, thin lips pursed tightly together. His face had a plastic-looking texture, without movement, without blemish - too perfect. For what seemed like an eternity he simply looked down at her lying on the bed. His eyes did not blink or turn away from her. Their eyes locked almost curiously together for this instant in time, absorbing the knowledge of one another. This was what the adoption process was all about. This was the time of acquaintance.

"I need a glass of water." Marty finally said breaking the silence. "My throat is so dry I can't swallow any more. If you want me to be part of your family, this is not the way to start our relationship. I also have to go to the bathroom. I don't know what you drugged me with, but, I have been here for a long time and I feel like I am going to explode. If I don't go pretty soon, I'll pee right here on these sheets." Her words were shaky, but were laced with a confident defiance which he surprisingly admired.

As he started to bend over toward her again, Marty flinched, moving back instinctively to the opposite side of the bed. Her hands and feet were still bound by the plastic ties hindering control of her movements.

"Marty, I am not going to hurt you," he said. "I am going to undo the ties around your ankles so you can walk to the bathroom. Sit still. DO NOT MOVE." These last three words uttered in a low, definite commanding tone she knew he meant.

She felt the ankle ties fall away. Gently grabbing her left arm, he pulled her to a sitting position on the bed. Dizziness overtook her for a few seconds as she became accustomed to sitting up. Marty shook head a few times, helping to clear her mind, as she began to regain some sense of awareness. The fingers of his right hand still firmly held her left arm as she focused - taking deep, long breaths to clear her lungs.

"I will walk with you to the bathroom. You will find a plastic cup on the sink you can use to get yourself some water. Please, do not think about trying to escape. I am going to leave your hands tied and will search you when you have finished, to be sure you have not hidden a toothbrush, comb or some other article in your cloths that you think might make a good weapon, should the opportunity arise. Let me say, my dearest Marty, it is NOT that I do not trust you, but, that, I really do NOT trust you." A small smirk crossed his lips as he enjoyed his impromptu, sarcastic humor.

Marty felt his grip pulling her onto her feet. Her legs were wobbly, but she gained confidence with each step, as he led her over to the door. The hallway was dimly lit and she was actually glad he was holding onto her arm leading the way. She thought these rooms were located in a cellar, but was not quite sure. The building smelled like an old building, with a musty dampness lingering in the background against the walls and floor. By the time they reached the bathroom, Marty was almost frantic to drink a cup of water. Opening the bathroom door, she all but ran over to the sink picking up the cup between her bound hands. She did not wait until the cup was full. Instead, she held it under the faucet only briefly lifting it up quickly to her lips gulping down the first mouthful. The relief was instantaneous, although it took a few more large gulps to clear away the last traces of dryness from her tongue and throat.

Resting her hands on the sink, Marty realized he was still silently standing in the open doorway watching her every movement. Turning her face toward the door, without letting go of the sink, Marty asked, "Are you going to stand there while I go to the bathroom, too? Can't I at least have SOME privacy? It's not like I can go anywhere! I'm in a friggin' bathroom with my hands tied for God's sake!"

Without saying a word, he backed away from the open doorway into the hallway pulling the door closed as the shadows covered him - - his eyes never looking away, he just simply disappeared. After Marty finished peeing, she sat on the toilet in silence for a few moments. She was tired of thinking. The drug had left her exhausted. Although the water quenched her thirst, and the release of pressure in her bladder allowed her more physical comfort, an electricity of nervous emotion was running wildly throughout her body. Calm was a word that did not exist in her vocabulary. She felt like an animal caught in a trap - no physical damage, but, a captive still the same.

Knock. Knock. Knock. Three taps on the door.

"Are you done yet?" he asked. "We need to get back to your room. I have food I need to prepare for you. After you have eaten we need to sit and discuss your adoption. There is much for you to know now that you have come to live with us."

Doc Cavanaugh knew the next few days were going to be exhausting. He wondered, "At sixty-three years of age, with a forty-eight inch waist and high blood pressure, how long can I keep up this pace before I am horizontal on a table next to one of my clients. I'll be the last one to worry about me being dead." He chuckled to himself, snipping the Kelly Clamp closed on the external carotid artery of Jane Doe # 3.

Each of the Jane Doe's autopsied up to this point mimicked the post mortem performed on Christine Sawyer. All of the women were: missing their eyes and lips, or their ears; the drugs used for lethal injection were found in all of their blood tests; the branded, circular mark was found on each neck hiding the injection points, and none of the victims were sexually molested. From this information, Cavanaugh concluded the women probably died at the hands of the same killer.

Looking at lividity and pooled blood on each victim and comparing these findings to the photographs taken of the victims as they were uncovered at the crime scene, and noting the absence of excreted bodily fluids found at the scene, Doc Cavanaugh was able to determine that the women were killed at a different location, and their bodies then transported later for burial at the pond. He noticed large, dark spots of pooled and coagulated blood in areas of the girl's bodies that were not lying on the ground. In fact, almost all of the areas of coagulated blood were located at the highest position of the bodies in the photographs. The law of physics told him the blood would pool in the lowest area of the body, not the highest, if the girls had died at the pond. Therefore, he knew the bodies had been moved to their graves after having been dead for quite some time. The blood, already hardened and coagulated, was unable to filter through muscle and organ tissue when the bodies were placed in their burial positions. Once tests sent to the State Crime Lab in Boston were returned, he would compare all test results and have a more definitive time of death.

Because the bodies were buried in the late fall and frozen through as the temperatures fell below freezing, the usual rectal, and liver temperature probe was useless in determining the time of death for any of the victims – as was testing for rigor mortis after all this time. Rigor would have passed by this time anyway, as it usually passes within forty-eight hours after death.

An interesting clue Cavanaugh noticed at the scene was the fact that none of the victims wore any jewelry -- watches, rings, bracelets or earrings -- or clothing family members said they were wearing at the time of their abduction. Each wore what appeared to be a new outfit, including new sneakers with ankle socks. The killer was making sure to minimizing any opportunity for the medical or police communities to trace these killings back to him should the bodies ever be discovered. New clothing meant it would be more difficult to find any fibers, dried stains, etc., that might have been on any of the victims' original clothing or shoes from the time of the abduction to the time of the killings. The killer could have bought these outfits at any number of stores within a hundred mile radius, leaving it impossible for anyone to trace their purchase back to him.

Cavanaugh wondered why the world spawned evil personalities such as this killer. There did not seem to be any logical reasoning to explain a person's desire to torture and mutilate another human being. But, then, he was just a doctor of medicine and not a philosophical genius out to answer the unanswerable questions of life. Evil has existed in the world since the beginning of time, and he would not be having any epiphany today standing in the morgue performing autopsies on these young women.

Cavanaugh noticed, through the frosted basement windows of the examination room that the street lights were fighting back the nights' darkness outside. Looking up at the generic, medical clock on the wall, he knew it had to be well past supper time. Not only did the clock read 8:57 PM, but his stomach was growling like a lioness prowling the Serengeti Plain, looking for her next meal. A quick smirk crossed his face, as he remembered what his best friend in high school, used to say when he was hungry: "I'm so hungry, I could eat the butt off a Brontosaurus!" Then he would jump into his rusted out, '69 Ford pick-up, drive to the nearest burger joint and order a half a dozen cheeseburgers and a large order of fries. Top that off with a strawberry frappe, and you had the fixin's of a great "FFF"-- Fast Food Feast. Right now though, these memories only served to increase the volume of his growling stomach, as it spoke loudly in protest. He would finish up with Jane Doe #4 in about a half hour and then take a break for a well-deserved meal.

I did not get to bed until after 3am. The first day after the boys found Christine was spent in meetings with FBI and Sate Police authorities. The Feds decided that they would not invest too much manpower because all of the girls found at the pond disappeared within Massachusetts. They did assign one investigator to assist the State Police in case some evidence or information indicated the need for federal intervention - a polite way of saying they would take over the investigation if within the parameters of their jurisdiction. Mountains of information already gathered was being reviewed and re-reviewed. With the discovery of the other girl's bodies at the pond, we now had four times the information to sift through.

Peggy was right to leave some lights on for me. In my present state of exhaustion, I would have done a cartwheel over an end table if I tried to negotiate my way through the living room over to the stairs in the dark. As it was, I missed the first step going up the stairs and almost fell flat on my face. Usually, after work, I sit down in my worn out, leather recliner and sip on a Captain and Coke while I skim through the newspaper. Tonight, I went right up to bed, quietly undressed, and slid under the covers next to Peggy. I laid in the darkness listening to her light, rhythmic breathing. Although I was glad I did not wake her, I would have enjoyed a little conversation, a hug, and a goodnight kiss before I rolled over. My day never seems complete unless we spent time talking or horsing around enjoying down time from the hustle of the day. (Peggy often says I have a strong feminine side.) Tonight would not be a complete day, as I lay in the dark of the room trying to push thoughts of mutilation and murder out of my mind.

The next morning, I felt the back of Peggy's hand moving over the side of my face as she started to wake up. She always sleeps on her side with her arm resting on the top of my pillow, and each morning, I move her hand out of my right eye. Some mornings I am able to roll over and go right back to sleep. This morning I would not have that luxury.

I knew Doc Cavanaugh was up to his neck in autopsies. I hoped Doc had taken a few hours to run home and catch some sleep, but I knew him well enough to know that he probably grabbed a sheet and curled up on his office couch for an hour or two at the most. I wondered if he would be the same person after all of this was over and done. In fact, I wondered if any of us would ever be the same again.

"Hey – Kosciak," I heard Peggy say with morning cotton still in her mouth. "Never heard you come in last night. What time did you get home?"

"Somewhere around 3am, baby. I thought for sure you heard me almost take a gainer up the stairs. I'm not the most graceful person in the world at 3am."

"You're not the most graceful person at any time of the day!"

"Thanks for your vote of confidence," I said patting her butt as I stood trying to find my slippers which always managed to slide under the bed during the night. I have always believed there is a foot fairy who steals single socks while they are in the washing machine or clothes dryer and also hides slippers and shoes under beds and bureaus. You never the find the one, missing sock -- it is never seen again no matter how hard or where you look for it. Using your foot to locate slippers under the bed results in pulling out huge dust kitties on the end of your big toe. This morning was no exception. "Hello? This damned thing isn't a kitty, it's a freakin' mountain lion!" I thought as I looked down at a dust ball covering half my foot.

Finding my slippers on the third attempt, I grabbed my cell phone and walked out of the bedroom heading downstairs to pick up the morning paper -- wherever it might have been thrown today. Our paperboy is not known for his accuracy when throwing the paper up onto the front porch. In fact, some mornings I find the paper in our neighbor's yard or in the bird bath. You would think, being the town's police chief, I would earn a little more respect. However, this morning his aim was right on the money. As I opened the front door the paper was right at my feet. "Will wonders never cease." I thought looking down at the headline on the front page staring up at me in very large, bold, black type.

The instant I read the headline I froze in my tracks. "What the hell!" I blurted out. There, on my front porch, as well as for the other 35,000 customers of our local newspaper, the headline read: "SERIAL KILLER AT LARGE - FIVE BODIES UNEARTHED AT MEADOW POND"

My blood pressure jumped from 140 over 90 up to about 600 over 400. I thought I was going to explode as I stood on my porch, mouth wide open, wondering how this information could leak out so quickly. Who the hell had enough information to call the paper and spill the story? Even I didn't have enough information to discuss this case with the press and I was the goddamned police chief! Picking up the newspaper, I turned back into the house as Peggy came down the stairway.

"Did I hear you using the "F" word again, Kosciak? She asked. "If I heard you upstairs, I know Gordon and Pam heard you next door. If you're not careful they will call the cops on you for using profanity on the front porch, before 7AM, on the Sabbath!" A faint chuckle sounded in her throat as she looked up into my reddened face.

"Can you believe this crap?" I blurted out without paying any attention to what Peggy was saying. "Somebody has already talked to the paper about the serial killer and the four bodies we found out at the pond! The shit is going to hit the fan when everyone reads this. Jesus, baby, I'd like to get my hands on the stupid son-of-a-bitch who did this!"

Peggy knew I was about to go over the edge. The hours had been long; the brutality of the killings was taking its toll, and she knew that I was personally involved. All of these things added up to extreme stress, a trigger temper, and no patience for anyone who did not get on board and work their asses off to find the answers.

"Honey" She said to putting her hand on my chest rubbing lightly in little circles, "You knew this was going to happen. Someone always leaks this type of story for the sensationalism it creates. People want to create this type of upheaval and panic. There is nothing you can do to change what has happened. The story is printed and out on the streets. The only thing you can do is to go out there and do your job. Catch this sicko before he kills some other young girl. Come into the kitchen and have a cup of coffee with me before you have the entire neighborhood up listening to more of your profanities!"

I knew Peggy was right, but that did not help my wanting to kick someone's ass for spilling the beans and creating more problems than we already had. This was not starting out to be a good day! The single largest backlash of this news leak being on the front page was that now the killer would know the murdered girls had been found. Our element of surprise disappeared before we even had the opportunity to start looking for him. He might be out of the country before the next edition hit the newsstands later in the day.

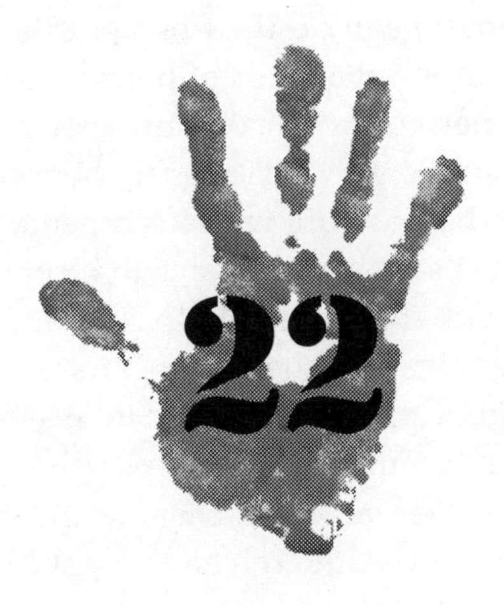

22

He watched Marty nervously eat the ham steak, mashed potatoes, and broccoli that he cooked for their supper. It was apparent to him that she was afraid the food was laced with some sort of poison or drug and, it was only after he took a bite of each item on her plate, that she devoured her supper and drank two glasses of soda. Setting up T.V. trays in her room, they ate without saying much of anything, with the exception of his telling her to slow down a little or she would choke on the food. Her eyes told him to shut up. She did not have to speak in order for him to know exactly what she was thinking. He understood her anger and would allow some level of disrespect at this point in their relationship. After supper ended, he cleared away the dishes and took everything upstairs to the kitchen, making sure Marty was securely bound once again before locking the door to her room. Once the dishes were washed, dried and everything put back in its proper place he returned to Marty's room for their discussion.

"The basis for any good relationship is communication,." he told her. "From this communication comes trust and from this trust springs the desire to listen and to understand other people's opinions and feelings. Understanding does not mean that you agree with everything someone else says or does, believes or does not believe, but rather that you have taken the time to listen and respond accordingly. You always hope this to be a reciprocal situation and, that the other person or people will afford you the same courtesy."

It was essential to him that each of his adopted children listen to his philosophies pertaining to communication and listening. It was the foundation of the very relationship he was trying to build with Marty and that he had built with his other adopted children.

Marty asked when she would be able to meet her brothers and sisters. He told her that she would get to meet them soon enough, but first it was imperative that she understand what he was saying to her about communication and trust. She needed to know just what he meant about listening before responding. Once he felt she fully understood this, then, and only then, would she be allowed to meet the rest of his family. Although he knew she was anxious and suspicious, he sensed that she comprehended what he was saying to her. She would only nod her head to affirm her understanding. Her asking about brothers and sisters did not go unnoticed and, in fact, caught his interest. None of the other adopted children had ever bothered to ask about the other siblings. After their discussion, he walked her back to the bathroom where she washed her face and hands, went to the bathroom and upon returning to her room, he secured her hands and ankles once again before she rolled onto her side for the night.

Sitting in his chair slowly sipping his morning coffee, replaying the events of the night before with Marty, he leaned forward and turned on the television. Sandy Beckman, the weather forecast person for Channel 8 News was pointing to the South Shore area near Plymouth where he could see the rain icon hovering over the coastline.

"More rain today, tapering off this evening for South Shore residents," she said as the screen changed to show the five day forecast for the region.

"Ah." He thought. "The weekend is looking good. No rain in sight and the temperatures will be in the mid-thirties: Perfect weather for Marty and me to have our family outing."

He was always amazed at how sexy the weather women dressed for these news casts. Tight fitting dresses or short skirts and low-neckline blouses accentuating their feminine attributes! Most male viewers probably never hear what the weather is going to be for the day. They are too busy drooling on their television screen. Ratings: It's all about ratings, and the producers do not mind selling their air time using beautiful women.

While he was thinking about weather women, a blue-banded ticker moved from right to left on the bottom of the television screen with the latest news of the morning. There was a volcanic eruption off the coast of Newfoundland; North Korea was rattling swords again to keep the Korean peninsula destabilized; the New England Patriots were hesitant to sign one of their running backs to a long term contract because of his age. Then he saw a box flash on the screen that said, "BREAKING NEWS!" The screen went blank for a split second before the news caster reappeared, looking truly shaken.

"There is breaking news coming out of Sutton this morning," he said. "We have just learned moments ago that police in Sutton have unearthed the bodies of five dead women found buried in the Meadow Pond area."

Although continuing to stare at the television screen, he no longer heard a word the newscaster was saying. His mind was already racing, trying to absorb the news report. His eyes were looking at footage of Meadow Pond, the Sky copter that was circling the pond zooming in every few seconds on the opened, earthen graves in and near the embankment.

"How… the… Christ? Who could have found them? No one EVER goes there! Son-of-a-bitch! MY CHILDREN! TAKEN AWAY! STOP IT! LISTEN! For Christ's sake, compose yourself and listen! CONTROL. CONTROL!"

He moved forward a few inches listening to every word the news caster said, watching the live aerial footage from the chopper. He could see local and state police still at the scene. The news-caster reported that five bodies, maybe more, were transported to Milford hospital during the previous day and throughout the night. Unconfirmed sources had said that the women were all college age, and that the bodies had been mutilated. The news commentator was not specific regarding the type of mutilation, but he knew, sitting forward in his chair, exactly what each looked like after their adoption was completed. In fact, part of each was next to him right now, preserved in remembrance.

"This breaking story was just received moments before our broadcast. Our news team is on their way to Sutton right now, and we should have live coverage from the scene by our 8AM broadcast. All we know at this time is that there are said to be five bodies of young, college-aged women, who were discovered yesterday buried around the shoreline of Meadow Pond in Sutton. You can see from our Sky copter that there is activity on the west side of the pond, putting the crime scene close to Route 146 which runs south from Worcester to Providence. The initial report states that each of the young women suffered some type of physical mutilation. We do not know how extensive the mutilation was, nor do we have any information on the actual cause of death for these victims. Attempts to discuss this developing story with the Sutton Police Department have been unsuccessful. A police spokesperson told us a few moments ago that Chief of Police Ron Kosciak will have a statement sometime this morning along with a representative from the Massachusetts State Police. We will keep you up to date as this story unfolds. We will be interrupting our regularly scheduled programs throughout the day to keep you updated on this story."

Sitting back in the chair he was still recovering from the initial shock of the news-cast. The report did not give much information regarding "who found the bodies", or the "how the bodies were found". He knew these questions would be answered later in the day when Kosciak held his news conference. But right now, he was stunned that his kids had been found and were now in a cold morgue at the hospital. His anger mixed with a sense of mournful loss as the first waves of surprise subsided. Then his calculating, controlled, thought process began to take over once again. There was no thought of getting caught. He was too perfect in his execution. They wouldn't find any clues that would to point in his direction. He was too methodical. His confidence and arrogance overrode any thoughts of caution as retaliation became his second most important goal. Marty was still uppermost, and he would proceed with her adoption immediately. He could handle Kosciak and anyone else responsible for taking away his children in due time, and handle them he intended to do.

Ken Garber sat at his desk reviewing information about the girls that investigators were able to gather during the eighteen hours since the last victim was found buried out at the pond. This information included everything from the height and weight of each victim down to what each victim ate for their last meal. Parents, relatives, friends, classmates and neighbors were all questioned without any being thought of as potential suspects. Boyfriends or partners were questioned by respective police departments in the areas where each girl lived or went to college, and all alibis checked out. Campus staff at each of the colleges attended by the victims - including professors, cafeteria personnel, janitorial and maintenance personnel as well as administrative personnel all checked out without so much as a recent parking ticket.

None of the girls were known to use recreational or hard drugs or to frequent areas where these drugs might be purchased. Religion did not seem to be a connection as some of the families were not active in any church or religious group. Only two of the girls were members of sports teams. All excelled academically, though none attended the same college or were members of any collegiate club or honor society that was associated with the other colleges. Being full time students, none of the victims even held a part time job. One of the girls spent two weeks as a patient in the Worcester

Medical Center for pneumonia last year. None of the other girls had been admitted to a hospital within the last five years. Three were licensed to drive while the others were not. Cell phone records showed that none of the victims called one another nor were any of the other numbers on their respective phones connected in any way. Police departments from each town or city where each victim lived were contacted and asked to procure and send along any lap top or PC the victims owned so that each could be inspected to determine if any of the victims were communicating via Facebook or e-mail. Ken thought this was a slim possibility but, one he could not afford to overlook. He believed these girls were, in fact, all complete strangers and, at this time, it looked as though there was absolutely no connection between any of them. It seemed, by the evidence already collected to this point, that these girls were chosen completely at random by their killer.

Police departments from all over the state were faxing or e-mailing information hourly as local and state police investigators in Sutton and Auburn feverishly worked through the data looking for anything that might give them a clue. Even police departments from adjoining states were sending information that they thought might be helpful. In a very short amount of time, this investigation was becoming the single largest investigation of its kind going on in the U.S. It is said that at any given moment, there are between 20 to 50 unknown serial killers active in the United States. This brand new investigation with multiple, female victims found buried at a single site, would rocket to the front page of every newspaper and headline every internet site in the world.

Ken ordered a profile board to be set up in an adjacent staff meeting room where pictures of each girl were posted across the top. Information pertaining to each cascaded down the face of the board like an informational waterfall. Different sized and colored papers with information scribbled or written were tacked to the cork board – the lives of each displayed for all to see and review. Less than a day ago, none of these girls, except Christine Sawyer, were known to anyone in this room. Today was a different story.

Ken rocked in his chair with his head tilted back staring at the ceiling of his office. There was no apparent pattern to the killer's selection. However, there was a pattern regarding the method used to murder each of the victims. Randomly selecting each girl from an area over a one hundred mile radius of Sutton meant that their chances of finding this person were getting smaller by the minute. The killer was able to travel a long distance to abduct a victim, and then was able to transport the victim back to the burial site at Meadow Pond. The abductions taking place at different times of the day or night suggested that the killer had a flexible schedule and perhaps did not even hold a full time job, allowing him to move about freely at any time of the day or night. A killer with ample time and the ability to move about the state without leaving a trace of evidence, anywhere, would be almost impossible to track down. Ken knew their best chance was tied directly to finding out where the drugs used to kill the girls came from. If they could locate the origin of the drugs, they might be able to find out how the drugs were procured and by whom. It was a long shot, but it was a shot none the less. He would assign an investigator to begin this part of the investigation immediately.

Doc Cavanaugh's initial findings from each of the autopsies confirmed that all of the girls were disfigured by their killer. Like Christine Sawyer, each was missing either their two ears or the eyes and lips. Ken wondered about the significance these trophies held for the killer. Why remove these body parts instead of a finger, hand, or the heart? He had read many police reports where the eyes had been removed, but he could not remember any instance where ears, eyes and lips were the coveted prize. A psychiatric profiler might be able to determine the significance eluding Ken's thoughts, and, if so, might give them more insight into the motive for the killings.

Ken knew he needed to get going. The press conference with Ron was due to begin in about an hour. Ken wanted to share notes with Ron before the onslaught of questions from reporters who were sure to bombard them during the meeting. He was glad Ron would shoulder the brunt of the meeting and did not envy the police chief one bit. Having been in that spotlight too many times himself, he knew what it felt like being a burger cooking on the back yard grill!

24

Marty did not know what time of day or night it was when she opened her eyes. Although emotionally and mentally terrified, her body finally reached the point of physical exhaustion after finishing her meal the night before. She slept without waking, although dreams filled with dark terror kept her body twitching and moving as her eyes rolled behind closed lids. Once again she looked around her room partly amazed at the detail with which it was recreated and frightened when remembering how he had obtained the information in the first place. How close did he stand next to her bed while she slept unaware of his entry or exit? He must have come into the house from the downstairs because; her room was on the second story without any trees or trellis for him to climb. A chill feeling ran through her body as she thought about being totally exposed and vulnerable while he stood in the darkness of her bedroom taking notes, watching her breathe beneath the blankets. Much of her uncertainty pertained to the fact that she did not know where she was or what time of day it was. She felt disconnected and at his mercy. This was exactly what he wanted – to keep her off balance and uninformed. She was his plaything and he required…no…demanded complete and total control. So far he had not physically hurt her in any way. In fact, he seemed gentle to some degree and thoughtful about her needs and comforts. She wondered just how long that would last. He did not seem interested in her in an intimate, sexual way. Somehow, he seemed very genuine about wanting to have her become part of his adopted family. Marty hoped she was right!

Without a clock in the room, it was difficult to determine the passage of time. She may have slept two hours or ten hours. There was no way for her to know. Marty could only assume how long she had been a prisoner and she knew what the assuming anything is never a good idea. Her next thought catapulted her mind out of the grogginess of just having woken up to a clarity and awareness that initially startled her.

"NEVER assume anything," she thought. A mentally, crystal-clear directive, blossoming from a word in a phrase to a glimmer of hope in her mind. "Never assume; always know. Knowing is planning. Planning is the key to winning. I need to think. I need to remember everything he has said and done since I woke up in this room – every action, every word. Learn more about him. Get him to talk more about himself, more about his other kids. Play along with him and make him think I am willing and wanting to be a part of his family." All of these thoughts were rolling through her mind one after the other like a line of cars stuck on the freeway. One thought after the other, after the other, after the other - a never ending line of thoughts.

The already familiar sound of the door being unlocked signaled his return. Marty realized she was almost glad to hear the sound of the lock because the urge to pee after a lengthy sleep was again becoming the foremost thought in her mind. The two sodas she drank with her last meal were looking to escape, and the high limit alarm in her bladder was howling with reckless urgency.

"Hello, Marty," he said closing the door. Marty noted that this time he did not lock the door. As the door closed, he turned and walked over to the side of the bed never taking his eyes off of hers. She knew instinctively he would never let her leave this prison. He let her see his face right at the outset knowing she could recognize him and identify him if the opportunity ever presented itself in the future. No, her future was here, in this building, in this room and, at some point he would tire of her and have to kill her.

She waited until he stood next to the bed before she spoke. "I have to go to the bathroom," she spoke softly as a request, and after a brief hesitation, added, "Please."

He noted the submissive request feeling that Marty was coming around quicker than the other children before her. None of the other children ever responded with a please or a thank-you.

"Sit up on the side of the bed," he said as he gently gripped her upper arm to help her balance and swing her feet and legs onto the floor. "Because you are being very polite, I am going to take the ties off of your ankles and leave them off. I am going to keep your hands bound until I think I can trust you enough to remove them too. Do you understand what I am saying to you Marty?"

"Yes, sir, I understand," she said looking directly into his eyes to show she knew exactly what he meant. "I have given a lot of thought to what you said about my parents abandoning me at some point in time and, how they really do not love me. I know I am a burden on them, and they wish I was not their daughter. They yell at me constantly for things that are very trivial. I felt like I couldn't do anything right in their eyes. I don't know how you knew about my predicament, but I am thankful you cared enough to adopt me." She was instantly afraid she was not convincing enough and, that he would see right through her attempt to win his confidence. Waiting ten to fifteen seconds and seeing that he was thinking about what she said, she continued, "Would it be possible to go to the bathroom now? I really have to go bad."

His train of thought broken for an instant by Marty's request, he responded; "Yes, Marty, I'll walk with you down the hallway. When you have finished in the bathroom, I'll bring you your breakfast." He was puzzled by Marty's response. Was she really glad to have this opportunity? She had looked right into his eyes without flinching and showed no signs of hesitancy with her words. She seemed very genuine and sincere. He would bide his time and observe her over the next few days. He would listen and try to determine her sincerity. If… and at this point it was a very BIG if…if she was sincere, then she might be the best child a parent could ever hope to adopt. His other children took longer to realize how fortunate they were to have him as their father. In fact, each one of them needed to be shown just how lucky they were to be chosen for adoption by him. If Marty already realized her good fortune, perhaps she could be spared the lessons the other children experienced during their adoption process. If not, then he would have to teach her just as he taught them.

He felt a sense of relief waiting in the hallway for Marty. Knowing the police took his other children away, he was feeling pressured to accelerate Marty's adoption in order to complete the process and perhaps move to another home in another part of the country. It was not the fear of being caught that prompted his thoughts of relocation, but rather, that it would be much easier to adopt other children in an area where the local authorities were not already searching for him. If Marty was as sincere about her acceptance as she seemed, they would be able to move almost immediately which would please him very much. As he was processing these thoughts, the door to the bathroom opened and Marty stood next to him in the hallway.

"Would it be possible to have a radio in my room to listen to and help pass the time? I know it is a lot to ask, but when you are not there with me the time passes very slowly." Again, as she spoke, she kept her eyes directly on his eyes.

"Yes Marty. I have a CD player upstairs I can set up for you when I bring you your breakfast. However, I do not want you to play it too loudly. I'll give you a headset to wear so that I do not hear it. I am a person who appreciates peace and quiet. I love spending time thinking and contemplating."

"Thank you very much," she replied walking back to her room.

As they entered Marty's room he said, "I will leave the door to your room unlocked for now. You will be able to use the bathroom whenever you feel the need. I will, however, keep the door at the end of the hallway locked. If you try to open that door, I will be forced to bind your ankles again and lock the door to your room. I am trusting you fully understand what I am saying to you and, what the ramifications will be if you try to escape."

"Yes sir," she said. "I am totally aware of what you are saying. I will do exactly what you tell me to do and will not try to escape." Taking a slow, deep breath, she added, "And, thank you."

Looking deeply into her eyes - trying to detect any uncertainty, and not seeing any - he turned and began to walk out of the room.

When he reached the doorway, he stopped, looked back at Marty, studied her for a few more seconds, turned and walked into the hallway. As he walked he thought, "Control, control, control. Too good to be true, so it probably isn't. One step leads to the next. Be vigilant in your preparation my friend. Very, very vigilant. Control, control, control!"

Marty listened to the sound of his footsteps fade until she heard the door at the end of the hallway close and lock. Silence filled the room immediately.

"Does he believe me?" she thought sitting on the edge of her bed. "Was I convincing enough? I must have been. He left the door unlocked and at least now I can walk around down here. I'm not tied up like a steer at a rodeo!"

Being able to walk was the first freedom Marty had regained since her abduction. She felt that if she maintained her attitude of acceptance with him, she might be able to maneuver herself into a position for escape when, if, an opportunity presented itself. She would need to be aware and ready at all times if that opportunity did become available.

She walked over to the window and pulled the curtains open. Behind the curtains: a gray, concrete wall. There was no window to look out of. No hopes of seeing something familiar to indicate where this building might be located. Not knowing how long she was unconscious after being shot in the leg with the drug, she didn't even know if she was in Massachusetts. For all she knew, she could be in Idaho or even California! However, somewhere deep within her, she instinctively knew that she was close to home. She also knew that by now her parents were going crazy not knowing where she was or what could have happened to her. She knew they would do whatever they had to do to locate her and bring her home safely. Marty stood quietly in the center of the room, closed her eyes, let her head tip backward thinking about her mom and dad trying to keep the hysteria from breaking back into her mind.

I was surprised at the size of the crowd gathered outside of the police department building for the news conference. It was a cold wintery morning, and I hoped the cold would keep some people away. I was wrong!

The news about so many young, female murder victims being found at Meadow Pond guaranteed a circus-like atmosphere by the reporters sent here to ask the questions, and I knew the responses I gave would be the headlines later today on every news station throughout the country. As I stood looking out of my office window at the reporters and townspeople exhaling their wintery breath into the morning air, I felt not only the cold of winter outside on the street, but also a chill of uncertainty growing in my stomach as I prepared to start the news conference.

Ken Garber arrived a few minutes before and we agreed I would take the lead and he would interject when he felt the need to do so, or when he was asked a question directly. Ken made no bones about it – he did not want to take point on this one.

Opening the front door to the station, I walked out ahead of Ken and stood behind a microphone on a concrete landing about four feet above the sidewalk in front of the station. The microphone was purposely set up above the level of the crowd so I could see everyone as they spoke or moved and, to create an invisible barrier between the police and the reporters. Any reporter or civilian who started to walk up the steps toward the microphone would be asked not to do so. I hoped this maneuver would help to keep the crowd a little more under control and would diminish any overzealous, rowdy behavior from the media as they pushed and shoved for position and acknowledgement trying to get their questions asked and answered first.

"Have you found any new victims out at the pond and, if not, is there any information indicating that there ARE more victims out at Meadow Pond?"

The first question was shouted out by a young reporter from the Civic Ledger, a local paper from an adjacent town. Turning my head I smiled at Ken who also saw the humor. The veteran reporters with access to statewide and national broadcast coverage were beaten out by a small town newspaper reporter with a circulation of about three thousand. I took ten seconds to let the moment hang in the air as the veteran reporters all turned to look at the youngster who had just upstaged them.

"Good morning." I said, without answering the first question right away. I wanted to start by controlling the pace of the meeting. If I answered the question right away, the control would go to the reporters. It was imperative to let everyone know that this was our news conference and not theirs.

"Let me start by saying this is an extremely sad day in the town of Sutton. As all of you know, we have transported five victims from the Meadow Pond area to Milford Hospital where forensic evaluations are being performed on each of the young women we found. We do not have any information to share with you regarding the cause of death for any of these victims, nor at this time will we be able to release the names of any of the victims to you. We can tell you that each of the victims is a college age female, we have determined that they all live within a one hundred mile radius of Sutton. To answer the first question: no, we have not found any more victims as of this morning."

"Chief, Kosciak - Chief." A female reporter I recognized but did not know her name, shouted out over the three rows of people standing in front of her. Turning toward her voice, our eyes met as she asked, "Do you or the State Police believe there is a serial killer living in this area and, do you have any indication as to how long the killer may have been active?"

"The evidence we have gathered to this point would indicate that this could be the work of a serial killer. However, the investigation is just getting under way and we can't positively state that as a fact at this time."

"Chief, do you have any motive or motives for these killings? Were any of these young women sexually assaulted?" another reporter shouted from the back of the crowd.

"As I have just said, the investigation is just beginning and we can't give out any information that might hinder or prevent us from finding the person or people responsible for these killings."

"You think there may be more than one person responsible for these murders?" yet another reporter shouted out.

"We cannot overlook any possibility at this time. We will make determinations as we go along during our investigation." My response was calculated. I was hoping the killer would believe the police were looking for more than one person instead of a solitary serial killer, although everyone on the investigative team pretty much knew this was the work of a single killer and not a team or group of individuals going around abducting young women, torturing them and killing them.

"Chief Kosciak. Is it true the first victim found was Christine Sawyer, the young woman who disappeared about eight weeks ago on her way home from a party, and is it true, that some sort of drugs or chemicals were used to kill her?"

This question rocked me down to the soles of my size 11 police boots as I wondered, "How the hell the drug information got leaked to the press? Who in their right mind, would want to give out that information?" I stood non-responsive and almost catatonic at the microphone. Ken, sensing my momentary lapse of concentration brought on by the surprise question, stepped up to the microphone and said, "As Chief Kosciak has stated, we cannot give out any names of the victims at this time, nor any information regarding the cause or causes of death. The investigation is ongoing and we will not compromise the investigation by giving out details that would harm the investigation or our chances of catching whoever is responsible for these killings. We can only, at this time, verify that we do have five young, female victims all about the same age, who were found at the pond and, who all lived within one hundred miles of Sutton."

Ken turned to me asking if there was any additional information I'd like to add. Turning back to the microphone, I responded, "Ladies and gentlemen, we do not have any further information to give to you at this time. We will contact you for an update in the very near future. Please do not print anything that is speculative in your reports. We ask that you state only the facts as we have given them to you. Thank you for your cooperation."

Turning to go back into the building, the usual post-meeting questions flew at the backs of our heads from those reporters not willing to accept the fact that the news conference was over. A few of the reporters, still needing to feel as though they were doing their jobs, ran frantically up to the doors of the police station bumping into the glass and one another. As the door closed, it separated the pile of flattened journalist faces pressed against the glass from us as we stood on the inside entry way to a waiting room just off the main corridor to the front desk. I brought my middle finger up to my mouth and inserted it backward against the inside of my cheek, pulling it out quickly causing my finger to make a popping sound as it exited my mouth.

"That, my friend, is sound of my head falling out of my ass! What a freakin' schmuck! I let that question about the drugs completely shut me down out there! I could not believe someone actually gave that information out to the media. Who would do that knowing the families of these girls would find out? It just does not make any sense to me!"

"You reacted just like anyone else would have at that instant," Ken said. "Let it go. For Christ's sake Ron, don't get down on yourself so early in the game. Shit, this nightmare is just getting started and we don't have a fucking clue yet who this monster is."

He turned and walked back out the front door, looking back briefly as if to ask if I was going to be o.k. I nodded without saying anything, turned, and started toward my office and a hot cup of coffee.

"You. Get over here right now! I thought I told you to clean up this kitchen! Look! See this? You did not put the mop away right. It belongs in the left corner of the pantry not the right corner. What are you, some kind of damned idiot?"

"I'm sorry mother. It won't happen again. I promise. I forgot that it goes in the left corner. Next time I WILL put it in the left corner."

"Shut up. I don't want to listen to your bullshit! Get your ass upstairs and get undressed. I'll be up in a few minutes. Get the tub ready. I'm giving you a bath to clean YOU up!"

"But, mother...I..."

"Don't say another god-damned word! I don't want to hear you say anything. Just do what I tell you to do. Now! Get up there and get ready for a bath. I'm going to teach you not to forget the things I tell you!"

He walked up the stairs to his bedroom wondering if all twelve year old boys lived like this. It was like this every day and had been since he could remember. The only time he actually felt out of danger was when he was in the cellar closet. At least down there she would leave him alone for days at a time. He would be hungry and thirsty, but he would not be hurt.

Within a couple of minutes he was undressed feeling completely humiliated in his nakedness. He wasn't stupid. He knew she made him undress to humiliate and embarrass him. This was how she "controlled" him. This was how she "taught" him.

The sound of the water filling the tub told her he was standing alone, naked, in the bathroom. A distorted smirk crossed her lips as she looked up the stairway. She took the first step up the stairway and stopped. No. She would wait a little longer before going up the stairs to give HIM his bath. She enjoyed these games she played with him every day. She relished the total power and control she had over him. Especially right now, knowing he was naked and stripped psychologically of everything he was.

The water level reached the right height in the cast-iron and porcelain, claw-foot tub. As the sound of the water pouring into the tub stopped, he sensed her standing behind him. He did not turn around to look at her, but, instead stepped into the tub and closed his eyes as he felt the warm water encompass his legs and torso. He kept his eyes closed tightly not wanting to see her step over to the side of the tub and kneel down on the small, pink, throw rug on the floor. She reached over to a towel rack on the wall taking the terry-cloth, wash cloth in her hand. Soaking it in the tub water, she took the cloth out of the water and snapped it across his face with every ounce of her strength. His head twisted backward in reaction to the pain on the side of his face. His entire right cheek, ear and temple burned with fire from the impact. He tried not to cry out, but, he could not hold it back. His cry filled the bathroom. She reacted with immediate and total retaliation. Reaching into the water, she quickly put her hand between his legs grabbing his scrotum in her fingers. Before he could cry out again, she squeezed tightly, watching his eyes open for a split second before rolling back in his head.

Losing consciousness, his body slid down into the tub: his head slipping under the surface of the water. She held him under the water watching the bubbles rise to the surface as air escaped from his lungs. Just before the bubbles stopped and she thought he would inhale, she pulled his head out of the water exposing his face. She listened as the air rushed back into his chest knowing she pulled him up just in time. Then, as he began to regain consciousness, she would push his head back under the water and repeat the cycle over again. After she tired of this part of the game, she would make him stand while she dried him, being extra rough drying his genitals.

She watched with enjoyment as his knees buckled from the pain in his groin.

The last humiliation came before she took him back down to the cellar closet. Instead of dressing him in his clothes, she dressed him in young girl's clothing: making him wear panties, training bra, nylons, a skirt and blouse or a dress. He was too big for her to drag down the stairs like she did when he was six or seven years old. Now, she used an old, antique, metal, rug beater to hit him with as he made his way down the cellar stairs to his wooden prison.

He stood in the middle of his kitchen wondering why these memories were coming back with more intensity and frequency. Usually, right after an adoption process began it was the other way around - the memories faded, were less intense and less frequent. Now, it seemed, he was having flashbacks every day. The part about the flashbacks bothering him the most was his inability to control when they occurred, or to remember what he did while he was experiencing them. Standing in the kitchen, he realized that during a flashback he was totally immobilized. He was vulnerable. Exposed!

The buzzer at the front door had brought him back to reality. He was in the kitchen and was about to look at his appointment book when the latest memory re-played in his mind. This was the beauty of his work. He made his appointments to suit his schedule not his client's schedules. He could see one client per day or four or five clients depending on his needs and his wants, not anyone else's. He could begin an adoption in the morning, service a couple of clients in the afternoon, and be back to his place later in the day before his new adoptee was awake. It was even better when his clients came to him at his massage parlor. It worked so perfectly. If he wanted to take a day or two off, he could do so by simply saying no when a client called to schedule a massage. It was the perfect business to own. He could even work nights and do whatever he wanted during the day. No one noticed him because he was so low key. Go to your appointment; set up the portable massage table; light the scented candle; play the "landscape earthen songs" and open the jar of warmed massage cream - rub-a-dub-dub. One or two hours later, he would be back at his place, doing whatever he wanted to do. He was a known un-known. He chuckled at the simplicity of the ruse and how people just naturally accepted him as trustworthy and an all-around nice guy. His business had grown so large over a short period of time; he was now turning down new clients. He was so good at what he did, people would not even think about calling someone else to relieve those aches and pains in their muscles and joints. Control, control, control.

Mike and Karen McMaster were unsettled as they ate breakfast. Neither one of them could put a finger on the cause of their uneasiness, but, each spoke about having upset stomachs as they pushed bacon slices around on their plate with their forks. Karen, not having heard from Marty since yesterday when she left for school, was curious as to why Marty did not call to check in with her. Marty wasn't expected home the night before because she was going over to Kelsey Hebert's house to finish a school project they were working on for their biology course.

Karen, proud for not smothering Marty or attempting to know all of Marty's business by asking the bazillion questions every mother wanted to ask, felt that her daughter was in college, always showed respect, continued to make honor grades, and was never in any type of trouble that a normal young person wouldn't experience, and therefore she had earned the right to be treated as an adult. Sitting at the table with her husband, she wondered if it was time to call Kelsey's house and ask how the girls were making out with their project. Her motherly instincts began to override her normal parental allowances. She could feel intuitively that something was wrong, and it was time to find out what that something was.

I was sitting behind my desk savoring the hot cup of coffee I had poured right after the press conference. I purposely sat with my eyes closed, as if tasting the coffee with closed eyes made a difference, when line three on my telephone began to ring.

"Yeah, Derek." I said, opening my eyes watching the steam rise from the coffee cup. "What do you have for me?"

"Chief, I just received a call from Mike McMaster over on Bourdon Road. He says his daughter Marty is missing. Says she was supposed to go over to a girlfriend's house to sleep over last night, but she never arrived. In fact, the girlfriend said Marty never showed up for school yesterday morning."

Sitting up quickly, my swivel chair lurched forward as I awkwardly placed the coffee cup down on my desk, spilling my coffee and splattering most of it onto my paperwork. Reaching for a paper towel and cursing silently, I said to Derek, "Get Kim in here on the double. I want her to go out to the McMaster's house with me!" After a few more expletives, I hung up, continuing to wipe up the spilled coffee while feeling a new wave of apprehension filling my thoughts. Although, the McMaster girl's disappearance could be as innocent as sneaking off with a boyfriend for a night, I knew in the pit of my stomach that she was the latest victim.

It only took Kim two minutes to make it to my office. Derek filled her in on the missing McMaster girl and she knew why I wanted her along. She stood in the doorway to my office allowing me to stand sullenly staring out of my office window, looking across the street at the white gazebo in the center of the town common. I did not move in recognition of her presence. She did not have to ask what was going through my mind. She understood the pressure that was mounting with each new surprise and revelation. But, because Kim knew me so well, she knew that my personal commitment to finding the killer of these young women was more important to me than what my professional responsibilities were demanding. I was a police officer because destiny had scheduled this journey for me. The ticket was purchased and stamped by a higher power and there was nothing I could have done to change the itinerary.

After three or four minutes, I turned away from the window, saw Kim standing patiently waiting and said: "Sorry, Kim. I was just thinking…"

Kim cut me off in mid-sentence saying, "Chief, I know what you must be going through right now. What do you say we get over to the McMaster's house and catch us a bad guy? We can talk in the car if you need to do a little venting outside of these office walls."

I appreciated Kim's direct nature. It was one of the things that made her one of my best officers. She had a clarity and ability that helped her to cut through a lot of the "gray" in a given situation and make decisions quickly when it counted the most.

On the drive over to the McMaster's, I let Kim do most of the talking. My thoughts were constantly changing and crowding my brain while we drove through the quite, country-like streets. I was not paying attention to anyone or anything, even though I was looking right out the windshield of the cruiser. As Kim pulled into the McMaster's driveway and shut off the engine to the cruiser I continued to stare out of the windshield.

"Chief, we're here." Kim said quietly afraid to jolt me out of my trance like state. "We're at the McMaster's house. Chief." She said hesitatingly while gently touching my left arm. My entire body reacted with a jerking motion at her touch.

"Holy shit," I said shaking my head, beginning to focus. "Sorry. I was thinking about the time frame we are working with. Marty was probably taken on her way to class yesterday. I'm thinking that our killer has taken her. The fact that she is the same age as the other girls and is a college student leads me to think this is not a situation where there has been a miscommunication between parents and daughter, which means she has been in his control for over twenty-four hours. With no concrete leads to follow, we are going to have to beat the bushes to find someone who might have seen something odd, or someone acting suspicious whose behavior was out of the norm. As soon as we talk with Mr. and Mrs. McMaster, we'll know what route Marty takes to school and we can have our people retrace her steps to try to find someone who might have seen something."

Standing beside the cruiser, I looked over at Kim and said, "Twenty-four hours already Kim. Twenty-four hours and I don't have a freaking clue how I am going to help this girl."

Peggy stood outside on the front steps of the old Baker Building waiting for Christopher to come and open the faded, double, oak doors. The Baker Building was a town landmark on the outskirts of the town. Hidden away from the main streets by large Catalpa trees running alongside the grey building on both sides, it is barely visible until you drive right up to the front steps. Although a dozen or so small, privately-owned businesses - from a printing company to a health spa - occupied the building at some time over the past 10 years, today, "Soft Touch Massage" is the only business keeping the pulse of the antique structure beating. Originally, the Baker Building was a department store that sold everything from women's clothing to specialty Christmas decorations imported from Europe. Today, most of the offices and open floor space sit vacant, collecting dust and dirt that magically materializes and covers everything from ceiling to floor over years of non-use and neglect.

Christopher Bradford wanted the building just the way it was – unoccupied, with the exception of his massage parlor and tanning salon. He purchased the building from the Baker family three years before for about fifty cents on the dollar. He was fortunate the real estate market was in a tail spin just when he was looking for a new home to share with his adopted children. During the purchase process, he spoke with the town planning board about his plans to initially open the massage parlor and tanning spa, with expectations of renting or leasing out the remaining square footage to local entrepreneurs. The town fathers were immediately relieved that someone was going to maintain the old building and try to bring new business into the town. The town fathers actually facilitated the purchase of the building by writing a letter to the bank's loan officer supporting Christopher's request for financing. However, other than remodeling for the massage parlor, tanning salon and his six room apartment, no renovations had taken place as far as anyone in the outside world could see. Though some renovations took place quietly on an as needed basis - Marty's bedroom being the latest project just completed.

After a little over three years, no one in town seemed to mind that additional space was not rented or leased. Everyone loved the way Christopher's fingers glided over their bodies releasing all of their pent up tension and anxiety as he meticulously massaged every spot where the tightness might be hidden away. Peggy Kosciak was no exception. As Peggy stood waiting for Christopher to come to the door, in her mind, she was already relaxing on his massage table feeling the wonderful effects of his magic hands rubbing away the pain left from years of dealing with fibro-myalgia. She knew the immediate relief she would feel in her aching muscles and pained joints as soon as he applied the warmed massage cream to her arms, legs and especially the back of her neck. She was getting a little impatient feeling the urge to knock on the door instead of ringing the bell when she saw Chris's familiar face approaching from down the hallway to let her in for her monthly appointment.

"Peggy. Good morning. It's nice to see you again. Has it been a month already?" hesaid, opening the door, and stepping aside to let her enter the foyer.

"Yes, it has Christopher, and I could not wait to get here. My fibro has been acting up the last few days. It seems like a bazillion years since the last time I was here."

"Well, you just come right down the hallway and we'll get to work giving you some relief. I wouldn't want you going around town telling people I have lost my touch." he said, with a quiet chuckle Peggy could barely hear. "After all, you are one of my best clients and I brag about you to everyone who comes in and complains about minor aches and pains. They have no idea what kind of pain you live with every day of your life. And, I don't mean your husband the Chief!" A laugh rolled out of his throat. Peggy rolled her eyes and laughed out loud acknowledging his play on words.

"Yeah, he can be a real pain some days!" she replied, removing her coat as they walked side by side down the hallway to the massage parlor. "It would take a lot more than a massage to get rid of that pain! That pain is almost always in my butt!" They both laughed as Christopher gave Peggy a gracious bow inviting her into the massage room.

Peggy liked the way Christopher decorated the room. The massage table was set up in the center of the room, which measured about twenty feet by twenty feet. On one wall there was a sound system already playing soothing, seasonal music - CD's for every mood stacked perfectly in piles next to the player. A large tapestry with a woven, life sized, garden scene of fountains, blue hydrangeas, azaleas, yellow and orange tiger lilies, red bee balm, purple butterfly bushes and a variety of other flowers and shrubs, hung ceiling to floor on an adjacent wall giving the room a feeling of both depth and openness. As you walk into the room you feel as though you could keep walking right into the tapestry and touch the crocuses along the walkway. A long table fit against the third wall, and on the table were Christopher's oils, creams, lotions, hot stones and towel heater used for the massage. The fourth wall, the wall Peggy loved the most, was full of different sized and colored candles placed on off-set, small shelves giving off the only light in the room. Approximately fifty candles, with their flickering flames dancing on the ceiling, walls and floor created a relaxing movement. There were no windows to violate the serenity and peace of this anatomical sanctuary. This was the perfect place to indulge one' self and hide from the hectic life cycle of the outside world.

As usual, Christopher left the room for a few minutes allowing Peggy to undress and position herself on the table. Although she felt very safe with Christopher, she always wore a pair of cotton bikini briefs and a sports bra during her massage sessions. It wasn't that she was modest but rather that there should be no uneasiness for either she or Christopher during the session. She realized some clients preferred being naked during their massages, but for Peggy, this was a time to relax and heal – to clear her mind.

Christopher stood in the hallway outside the massage room thinking about Chief Kosciak's wife lying on the table a few feet away on the other side of the wall. This was one of those situations where he would have to exercise self-control rather than give in to his inner impulses. How easy it would be to begin his retribution against Ron Kosciak right here, right now, by not letting Peggy get off of the table alive. How easy it would be to snap her feminine neck and give her muscles a permanent rest from her daily pain. "Just reach under her shoulders as she lies on her back with her eyes closed waiting for your fingers to work their magic." he thought. "Push your hands back under her shoulders a few times and repeat this movement to relax her. Then, quickly, quietly, effortlessly, move your fingers upward and begin to lightly massage the back of her neck with your thumbs positioned right over her windpipe. Roll your left hand up and over to the forehead leaving your right hand behind her head gently holding and supporting the nape of her neck. Place your left hand over her forehead and quietly, reassuringly, tell her to relax. Relax. Relax. Now, snap her fucking head and listen to the last gasp of life as her body goes limp on the table."

Standing in the hallway with these thoughts running through his head, his hands and arms moved in unison to his inner impulses playing out his desires as a mime moves without words on a city street.

"Christopher, are you out there?" Peggy's words broke through bringing his thoughts back to reality.

"Yes, Peggy. I'll be right in. Just relax for a moment and enjoy the music."

Peggy would live for another day. Today was her VERY lucky day. She would not be as fortunate the next time they met. Instead of giving into his vengeful feelings, he concentrated on being in control and having the patience to think things through - planning is always the route to success – Control. Control. Control. If he killed her today, it would only be a matter of time before her husband traced her to "Soft Touch Massage". He knew exactly where she was right now and the time frame would be difficult to explain away. He would be a suspect – a prime suspect. Actually, Peggy's being here today would take him out of the spotlight. She would talk about her massage with her hubby in every soothing detail. Ron, being the macho chief of police, would listen and put it out of his mind within minutes, and therefore would put Christopher out of his mind as well. After all, he was just Christopher Bradford the masseur: the man with the magic fingers. These thoughts repeated in his mind as he turned and entered the room to relieve Peggy of her discomforts, along with some of her money.

29

It felt good to walk around her prison room. It was unsettling to know this room was not her real bedroom, but at the same time, because it was a twin to her bedroom at home, she felt somewhat relaxed because of the familiarity. Looking into the mirror on the wall behind the dresser, Marty stared into her own eyes wondering why she was chosen for the adoption. What was it that made her stand out in the crowd? When did he begin to stalk her and how long had he studied her daily life before the day of the kidnapping?

"I'm glad my brain is finally clearing." She thought. "I don't know what he used to drug me, but it sure as hell has a nasty kick. You look like hell, Marty. You haven't looked this bad since your last kidney stone! Christ. How the heck am I going to get out of here? No windows. Doors are locked. But, I do have the comforts of home. Yeah. Real comfortable…locked in a cellar in the middle of God only knows where, hands still tied up, with a freakin' psycho-asshole waiting to live out his distorted fantasies with me as his new play toy! Jesus, help me out here. I need some divine intervention."

Marty guessed that a couple of hours had passed since he left her alone with her newly granted mobility. Because he had cut off the plastic ties around her ankles, Marty knew she was gaining at least a little bit of trust with her feigned interest and subjugation to his demands. Moving over to the night stand beside the bed, she bent over and pulled open the single large drawer. Empty. She then went back to the dresser and began to open each of those drawers, finding various articles of clothing: socks, nylons, panties, bras and, oddly, she came across her diary in the back of the bottom left drawer. Opening the diary, she realized that this was, in fact, her real diary. She heard herself take a quick, deep breath of surprise. Why would he take her diary? What significance did it play in his game of cat and mouse? Not wanting him to know she found the diary, Marty put it back into the drawer, positioning it exactly the way she had found it. To successfully outwit him, she would have to seem totally unthinking and, continue talking to him about understanding his motives and thanking him for rescuing her from unloving and cruel parents.

"Keep earning a little more trust every time he comes into the room." She thought. "Be cooperative without seeming overanxious. If he suspects that you are baiting him and leading him on, he will probably kill you right then and there."

While Marty talked to herself, she continued to look around her room for any item that might help her escape. It wasn't until the third or fourth time she looked at it that the lacrosse stick caught her attention. In fact, she was beginning to look away from it leaning up against the wall in the corner of the room before its image ignited a spark of curiosity making her turn her head back and look at it once again. "Why would he leave my lacrosse stick in the room?" she asked herself with an unsettled feeling. "He must know I am an excellent player. He must also know I could use the stick to put his lights out when he enters the room. One good whack on the side of the head and he would topple over like a china closet in an earthquake. No. He's not stupid. Don't underestimate him. It's too easy. There has to be a catch somewhere. I just have to figure out what it is. Don't jump at the obvious. Think, Marty, think!"

Marty walked over to the lacrosse stick to inspect it and make sure it was the real McCoy. It was an exact duplicate of her stick without the nicks and chips from playing many games at the school. "So, why would he leave a weapon like this in the room?" she thought again. Knowing the importance of having this stick, something with which she could defend herself, gave Marty a small feeling of confidence if things should go badly in the near future. However, for some reason, unknown to her, she did not touch the stick, but left it standing in the corner of the room. A feeling, a hunch.

Marty wondered why it was taking him so long to bring breakfast. She knew by the growling of her stomach that she was long past being hungry. She was ravenous. What she wanted most of all was a hot cup of coffee from the coffee shop. "The coffee shop - of course!" she said out loud. That was where she remembered seeing him. Almost every morning he would watch her as she sat by the window. He always stood over against the far wall away from everyone else, but always scanning the room with those dark, intent eyes. That was why she noticed him in the first place. In trying to be inconspicuous, he actually made himself stand out more. Marty wondered if anyone else in the coffee shop noticed him staring at her. Perhaps someone would listen to the news reports about her disappearance and put two and two together realizing that his behavior in the coffee shop was out of the ordinary. Maybe they would call the police and report him. By giving the police his description, police artists would be able to generate a composite sketch which they could show on the television news casts. There was still a chance that, by some miracle, the authorities were already on their way to rescuing her. She walked over to her bed once again and sat down waiting for him to return. She had hope. Not much hope, but at least it was better than no hope.

Marty closed her eyes and took in a deep breath. As she exhaled, she thought about her parents going out of their minds with worry. They would know by now that she was in danger and most likely fighting for her life. In fact, they would have discussed the possibility that she was already dead - the fear every parent has in the back of their minds as their children grow and mature to an age where they start to go off by themselves without parental protection.

The door at the end of the hall made the familiar clicking sound as he entered from upstairs. The closing of the door meant that he was in the hallway walking toward her room. Marty was beyond being scared at this point. Her fear was beginning to turn into something quite different. As he walked into her room holding a breakfast tray with scrambled eggs, toast, bacon and a large cup of hot coffee, she sat on the edge of her bed not as his prey but as an adversary getting ready to do battle.

Marty began to stand beside the bed to thank him for bringing breakfast for her when he said, "I see you found your diary."

Without thinking, she took a step backward losing balance, almost falling onto the bed while staring at him. The surprise on her face was very evident as he began to speak.

"Oh. Don't worry. I just thought you might like to write some additional entries while you are staying here with me. A diary is a very personal and valuable book. Most young women who have them cherish them and protect their written secrets. I knew your diary would help you make the transition to your new home and family easier. Think of it as a welcoming present."

Marty was still stunned knowing that he was aware of what she was doing while he was out of the room. She felt exposed again. Violated again. But, most of all, she reacted the way he expected her to react. She was playing into his hands. If she were going to get out of this "family," she would have to step up her game. However, the realization that he was watching her had taken the air out of her lungs. Right at this moment, she was like a sail boat in a wind storm with torn sails. As she sat gathering her thoughts, he began to speak.

"By the way, I know where you are and what you are doing every second I am away from this room. That is why I felt comfortable leaving the Lacrosse stick in the corner over there. Don't get any ideas about hitting me over the head when I come into the room. I'll see you waiting for me no matter where you are. I have an oblique angle lens which captures every square foot of this room on my screen upstairs. I can see everything that goes on in here."

Whatever confidence Marty was feeling a few moments earlier vanished immediately. She thumped down onto the side of the bed waiting as he pulled the tray table in front of her.

"Thank you. That was very thoughtful of you to think I might want to write in my diary. You're right as usual. I do value my diary. It is a very important and personal part of my life. Thanks for helping me to protect it and keep it safe. I certainly have a lot to write about now with my adoption and all. Is it all right if I write about my new life here with you and the other kids?"

She spoke without really being aware of what she was saying. A part of her mind was working independently of her present situation trying to maintain control and gain any speck of trust that would help lead to her escape. While the independent part of Marty kept a vigilant watch, the other part was still reeling from the reality of her situation and the knowledge that he was in complete control of her life at this point in the game. Although temporarily stunned, she was beginning to evolve from kidnapping victim to mental chess player. "With each setback comes more knowledge about your opponent," she thought. "With more knowledge gained about your opponent, the weaker your opponent becomes. Take a deep, mental breath of air, close your eyes, exhale slowly and make the next move - "WINNER TAKE ALL."

30

Doc Cavanaugh could not remember the last time he was this exhausted. Taking only two or three hour naps during the course of five post mortems was taking its toll as he woke up once again to the sound of the alarm clock next to the cot in his office at the hospital. As his swollen and sore bare feet touched the cold, tile floor, he actually smiled as the coolness spread over the bottom of each foot sending a soothing feeling through them and up each leg. Doc exhaled into the stillness of the office, letting the moment linger as long as he could.

Jerry Bickford was still sound asleep in a second cot brought in after post number three was completed about six hours ago. Doc appreciated Jerry's offer to assist on all five of the exams. He certainly did not have to stay, but Doc would owe him big time for his help and would gladly pay the tab on this debt as soon as the opportunity arose.

He and Jerry had not found any new revelations during the latestpost mortems performed on each of the victims. All were branded on the left side of the neck. Three puncture sites for the injected chemicals were found inside the design of each brand. None of the girls were sexually molested and all were facially mutilated with the removal of their eyes and lips or their ears. However, since these were all classified as Medical Legal cases due to their being homicides, filling out the mounds of paperwork would take almost as long as the exams themselves. Doc did not look forward to the next twenty-four hours he would spend behind his desk with pen in hand filling in the non-ending lines and blocks of information required by medical law in these types of cases.

The attention to detail the killer of these young women exhibited, actually impressed Doc. Both he and Jerry scoured each body for any minute portion of a fingerprint that might have been left behind. They even checked the back side of the eyelids for print patterns as well as the surfaces of every tooth in each girl's mouth. A hundred or more swabs were used to take samples from every cavity on each body looking for foreign materials. There were none to be found. They combed out each girl's hair - both scalp and pubic - looking for hair particles that did not match the victim. There were none to be found. Finger nails and toe nails were scraped for any tissue residue that might have been scratched from the killer during their struggle. It was a long shot that also did not pay any return on their investment. Each of the young women was as clean as Christine's car was when the police found it after her disappearance eight weeks ago. Other than gravel, insects and other flora found in and around the embankment of a pond, there was nothing else to give them a clue about this killer.

Jerry Bickford heard Doc's release of satisfaction when the cool flooring began to soothe his aching feet. Opening his eyes just enough to watch Cavanaugh relish these few minutes of ecstasy without Doc realizing he was being watched, made Jerry chuckle to himself as Doc's facial expressions changed comically with his rising level of enjoyment and relief. When Doc finally stood up next to his cot, Jerry pretended to wake up and shake out the cobwebs.

"Hey, Jerry." Doc said, looking down at his assistant. "How about you and I walk over to the greasy spoon diner to get something to eat? I think the special is beef and bean burritos. It might even be two for one day. I'm hungry enough to eat a half dozen. I'll buy since you're working on my nickel."

"Actually, Doc. That sounds like a great idea. I'm starving too, although I think I'll pass on eating six.

Joe's Diner was not really a greasy spoon. The restaurant served very good food. The menu offered a wide variety of appetizers as well as some good old-fashioned, home cooked meals. Specials ranged from meat loaf, mashed potatoes and green beans smothered in beef gravy, to fried steak with all of the "fixins". One of the house favorites was the "Belly-Bustin", two pounder, Swiss, bacon burger with Joe's secret sauce. This culinary beauty was served with both fries and onion rings. The burger was served on one plate with the fries and rings being served on a second plate. Anyone who could down one of these monster burgers plus the rings and fries, ate for free. Only one person in the six years this burger had been on the menu, earned a place on "The Wall of Fame" for finishing the entire meal. One would think that this person would be a three hundred pound lumber jack, but the gourmet busting champion was a twenty-three year old college girl, weighing in at about one hundred-thirty pounds, standing all of five foot four inches tall. The story goes, that her friends did have to physically carry her out of the diner back to her room at the college dorm, and that she did not eat for a week after her Olympian efforts. She did however, spend many hours in the bathroom groaning and moaning the night of the event.

Doc and Jerry shimmied into a window booth with a heavily padded vinyl seat. They ordered and then sat discussing the examinations while they ate. Jerry happened to glance over at the customers sitting on stools eating and drinking at the counter. He thought he recognized the man standing near the last one next to the cash register. It had been at least five or six years since he and the guy at the counter took the same firearms course at the police station in Worcester, but Jerry remembered Christopher because he had addressed him as Chris when they first met and was promptly told his name was Christopher. So, for the remainder of the course, Jerry addressed him only as Christopher. They got along well enough during the three days of instructions and testing, and each earned their respective firearms license. Then they said their good-byes and life went on. After all these years there stood Christopher not more than twenty feet away. Jerry told Doc he saw an old friend, excusing himself for a few minutes.

Christopher saw Jeffery approaching the register and recognized him immediately. Although tensing up on the inside, Christopher looked very relaxed as Jerry reached out to shake his hand, saying, "Christopher. I thought it was you standing over here. How have you been? It's been a hell of long time since we took that firearms course."

"Jerry. Yeah, right. It's Jerry?" he said, seeming to search for positive identification.

"Sure. Remember we took the firearms course in Worcester?"

"Oh. Yeah. Yeah. Now I remember. I'm so sorry for not remembering right away. How the Sam Hill are you? Do you still keep your license active?

"Yeah, I almost forgot to renew it a year ago. Got it renewed just before it expired. I wouldn't want to spend another three days at the police station sitting through those classes."

"That's for sure. What brings you to Joe's diner? I didn't think you lived in Milford."

"Well, I'm working with Doc Cavanaugh on the examinations being done on theyoung girls they found out at Meadow Pond. You probably heard about them on the newsover the last couple of days."

"Yes. I did hear something about that, but I'm so busy, I have not spent much time in front of the T.V. lately. Any ideas as to what actually happened to these poor girls?"

"I really can't speak too much about it right now. Most of the information is hush, hush and filtered through the police department first. Just the way these cases run. I will say these young women did not deserve to die this way. I'd like to beat the life out of the monster who did this."

"It's a shame Jerry. I feel for their families. One can only imagine what kind of torment they must be feeling."

As Jerry was about to respond to Christopher's remark, the waitress came over to the register with Christopher's order. "Here you go Mr. Bradford." she said, handing him the bill at the same time. "Two orders of fish and chips with extra tartar sauce." Christopher took out his wallet and, at the same time looked over at Jerry. "It was nice to run into you, Jerry. Thanks for taking the time to come over and say hello. Perhaps we will run into one another again." Christopher reached out and shook Jerry's hand once more, picking up the orders of fish and chips before turning towards the door.

"Christopher." Jerry said. "How about we make a plan to go the range for some practice one of these days?" We could spend an afternoon comparing notes and firing off a couple hundred rounds or so. What do you think?"

Christopher froze in his tracks just for an instant. But, it was an instant that went unnoticed by Jerry who stood waiting for a reply.

"You know; Jerry, that's a great idea. I haven't done any shooting in a long time. Listen, write down your cell phone number, and I will give you a call in a few days to set something up. We could go over to the Rod and Gun club right here in town."

Jerry reached over the counter, took a napkin out of the holder and wrote his cell phone number down for Christopher, gave him the napkin and shook his hand one more time.

"Make sure you call me, Christopher. I think we would have a great time. It was nice to run into you."

Christopher nodded his head in agreement, folded the napkin with Jerry's phone number, but instead of putting it into his pocket, he threw it in the trash barrel just outside the diner as he walked down the steps to the parking lot. There was no way in hell he was going shooting with Jerry Bickford! He had only tolerated him for the three days of the firearms course. What shit luck to run into him while stopping to pick up some food on the way back to Marty after giving a massage in Milford near the hospital. At least he knew that he was safe at this point. If they had found any evidence at all implicating him in these murders, he would not be getting into his van to go home and, Jerry Bickford would not have come over to talk with him.

Jerry watched Christopher's van pull away from the diner onto route 16 and head west toward Sutton then took his seat across from Doc Cavanaugh again. "A chance meeting?" he thought. No. There was something else happening. An odd feeling began to invade Jerry's mind. He really was not quite sure what it was, but, it did make him feel odd. Jerry took another fork full of the baked haddock, listening as Doc picked up their conversation without skipping a beat. Giving the departing van one quick glance, Jerry put the encounter out of his thoughts and enjoyed the rest of his meal.

"Get your ass in here right now! Bring the skin cream with you. It's under the bathroom cabinet. Don't take all god-damned day either. My back is killing me!"

He listened to the high pitched screaming from her bedroom. She sounded like she had dirt in her larynx giving her a gravely, raspy voice with a soprano pitch. It was a voice that pierced every nerve in his body as it raced through his ear drums and pounded the inside of his skull. Stooping over to open the bottom cabinet door, he knew what bringing the skin cream into her room would lead to. He knew just what she wanted. Every breath he exhaled was louder and deeper than the one before as the tension mounted within his body. Each step toward that bedroom made him feel more disgusted and nauseated. Out of all the different games she played with him, this one was absolutely the most demeaning and humiliating of them all.

Entering her bedroom he saw her propped up by six pillows, naked, lying on the bottom sheet with the blankets and bedspread pulled down by the footboard. Although in her mid-fifties, her body was amazingly beautiful. Two perfectly rounded breasts above a slim waist that most women would kill to have. Slender dancing legs added to the woman who, by most standards, would be any man's dream. Although not the most facially beautiful woman in the world, she was far from being unattractive. Any other sixteen year old male would have given anything to be in his shoes right now: looking at a naked woman, wanting his hands all over her, rubbing body cream into places most boys don't see until they are men.

"The towel is on the chair over by the window. Pick it up and bring it over here with you." As she barked out orders, she rolled onto her stomach and instructed him to massage the cream into her back muscles. Not too hard, yet not too soft. She wanted it just right. Wanted it PERFECT EVERY TIME!

"You're rubbing too hard. Rub softer and use more cream. Move those hands down to the small of my back and back up to the top of my shoulders. Jesus! You have done this a hundred times. You shouldn't need me to tell you what to do. You take all the pleasure out of it. What the fuck, are you some kind of idiot? You're sixteen for Christ's sake. Most boys your age would have a hard on, but not you - Mr. Limp Dick himself!"

He began rubbing a little softer and she began to quiet down and enjoy her massage. After fifteen minutes, she turned her face and looked up at him standing beside the bed. She opened up her legs exposing herself, looking at him intently, not saying a word. She stared letting her eyes bore into his eyes. He put his fingers into the jar of cream and then placed his hand between her legs. When he was done massaging her legs, she rolled over onto her back putting both arms down by her sides on the sheet. He hesitated for a few seconds frozen in place, looking down. Knowing what was expected of him next.

Sensing his discomfort and enjoying the fact that she was in total control, she asked: "Well?"

"Oh! That is so relaxing," she said as he continued rubbing and massaging the cream into her skin. The massage continued until every muscle in her body and every joint in her arms and legs felt relaxed and tension free.

"You know what I want now, don't you?" she asked. He looked away from her toward the floor trying to hide the revulsion surging up in his throat. "Yes. You know exactly what I want and just how I want you to do it. Come on! Up you go now. Be careful. Don't get clumsy and ruin it. This is the best part. Come to mama."

He positioned himself between her legs, lying on his stomach - the only sound, her slow, guttural moans.

This would be one of the last times his adoptive mother would abuse him. Over the last two years, he had been secretly hiding money he stole from her pocketbook while she slept. He did odd jobs for their neighbors, who paid him for cutting the grass, weeding the flower gardens, and other small projects. He had over five hundred dollars hidden in his bedroom waiting for the day he would leave this house and this bitch forever. That day was fast approaching, and when it came time, he would pay her back for all the years of degradation and humiliation suffered. Standing in the bathroom washing his face for the fifth time, the last thing in the world he ever wanted to do was be sexually intimate with another woman.

Christopher found himself standing beside his van in the garage at the rear of the Baker Building. The garage door was open and he hurried to close it concerned someone might have seen him standing in a trance, staring away into space unaware of his ramblings.

"What the hell is going on?" he thought out loud – hearing his words fill the garage as he continued regaining his composure. "Jesus Christ! This is starting to happen way too often! I can't go a full day without reliving what that son-of-a-bitch did to me all those years. I don't even remember parking or getting out of the fucking van to open the garage door! She's been dead for years and, she's still controlling my life!"

Standing in the garage, Christopher recalled the day he finally reached his breaking point:

Six months after the last massage and "sexual favors" event, Christopher came home from school one afternoon to find his adoptive mother waiting for him at the kitchen table. She said she just wanted to talk with him, but he sensed from years of abuses suffered at her hands that there was more to her request than met the eye. She asked him politely - something she never did - if he would please bring a cold drink up to her bedroom and, that she would talk with him there. The nausea was immediate and intense. Panicking, he paced back and forth in the kitchen listening to her footsteps reach the top of the stairs, then the closing of the bedroom door. Back and forth, back and forth, he paced again and again not knowing what to do. He knew he would not let her do those things to him again. Not today. Not any day. She had to stop! He had to stop her!

Suddenly, the shaking stopped. There were no tremors in his arms or legs. The nausea in his stomach disappeared and the cold sweat escaping from his pores was gone. It was as if someone injected him with a gallon of self-confidence. The calmness and control he felt was surreal. Without any cogitation, Christopher moved over to the pantry, found the plastic bottle of liquid drain cleaner and, filling a tall glass, thought: "This will really clean her pipes!" Adding a few ice cubes, he looked at the glass thinking how much it looked like a tall, cool glass of water. It was crystal clear and he hoped, as he climbed the stairs that the ice would not melt too quickly.

She actually looked pleased to see him as he opened the door and entered her bedroom. Seeing the glass of "ice water," she reached out and took it from him without taking her eyes off of his face. Christopher watched with absolute joy as she brought the glass to her lips and took two giant swallows. Christopher did not notice that he was instinctively backing away from her bed as the corrosive chemicals burned their way down her esophagus into her stomach. The caustic mixture tore away at the flesh in her mouth; burning her throat with corrosive fire. Her abdomen was dissolving from the inside out before the first attempt at a scream tried to make its way out of her dissolving voice box. Only a horrific, fear-filled gurgling sound managed to exit her distorted mouth as she ran from the bedroom, down the hallway, toward the stairs – her voice box a melted piece of flesh.

Christopher followed behind her. As she approached the stair railing at the top of the staircase, Christopher lunged, pushing his adoptive mother over the railing and watched spellbound as she fell onto the hardwood flooring below. The gurgling sound stopped on impact: her face and chest slamming onto the polished, oak slats. Standing at the top of the stairs, Christopher knew he was free –at last. He knew that the rest of his life belonged only to him.

Disposing of the body was even easier than Christopher thought it would be. First, he dismantled her body into segments, appendage by appendage, joint by joint. It amazed him just how small the human body could be once taken apart and put into plastic freezer bags. He then ran each part through an old meat grinder stored in the pantry. After the grinding was completed, each piece of the grinder was cleaned and soaked in scalding hot water for two hours, removing any traces of its last use. Her flesh and bone, now the consistency of ground beef, was then boiled, packaged and put into the refrigerator until nightfall.

Christopher left the house that night around 10PM. Riding his bike with the plastic bags inside his back pack. He rode to the outskirts of the town, entered the woods, and hiding his bike, walked far into the woods spreading the remains of his dead tormentor on the ground for the animals to eat. Even if someone were to come upon uneaten remains, they would never know who it was in this condition! He was rid of the bitch who tortured him. He would tell the authorities she just didn't come home, simply walked away. With that thought, a wide smile sprouted on his lips. He was, after all, quite a planner and thinker.

Smiling once again because the memory of revenge was so sweet, Christopher shut the lights off in the garage and walked up the stairs to his apartment. He would bring Marty her fish and chips. Jerry Bickford was already a distant memory – for the moment!

32

I stood on the front step of the McMasters' home, looking across their yard at the surrounding neighborhood. Upper middle class homes lined each side of the street with two-car garages and variously colored SUVs parked in driveways waiting for their next trip to the corner store. This was not the type of affluent neighborhood from which a kidnapper would choose to abduct a young girl and ask for a large ransom. These were not the homes of doctors or lawyers, of business owners or financial wizards. These were the homes of blue collar, work long hours, middle class Americans who struggled to keep their heads above the flood waters of a weakened economy.

Kim stood directly behind me on the walkway as we waited for the door to open. "Do you think they heard the bell?" she asked, just as the door made the sound of wood rubbing against wood while opening into the house. The wood was obviously swollen from winter snow melting on the threshold causing the door to swell and jam.

"You must be Chief Kosciak," the man said as the door opened wide enough for us to enter.

"Yes, Mr. McMaster, my name is Ron Kosciak and this is Kim LaFleur, one of my investigative officers."

"Please, call me Mike, Chief." He replied, motioning us to follow him down a hallway to a room in the back of the house - pushing hard to close the front door all the way. No one spoke until we entered a sitting room with a crackling fireplace, where a small-framed, middle-aged woman sat with her legs tucked up on a sofa, watching the flames as though she were hypnotized by their rhythmic motion.

"Hon, this is Chief Kosciak and his assistant, Kim LaFleur."

"Chief Kosciak, Officer, thank you for coming so quickly." She said softly continuing before I could reply. "We are extremely concerned about our daughter, Marty. You probably already know she never arrived at school yesterday, nor did she go to her girlfriend's house last night as planned. We have talked with Kelsey Hebert and her parents, but Kelsey has no idea what might have happened to her. Kelsey tried calling her on her cell phone a number of times, but the phone went directly to voice mail. Kelsey thought Marty was probably sick and just took the day to stay in bed. She is beside herself for not calling us to ask why Marty had not gone to school."

"Mrs. McMaster," Kim began. In situations like this, we always try to review any situation that might contribute to, or lead to a person's disappearance. We need to ask you both a few questions to help us get going in the right direction. We do have the information you have shared with us from your phone call to the station. Please do not take any offense to the questions we are about to ask you. They are very standard questions asked in order to eliminate some possibilities and help us to focus on others."

Mike McMaster already knew what type of questions we needed to ask and sat next to his wife while signaling with his hand for us to sit in two adjacent chairs.

"Does Marty have any history of drug or alcohol abuse?" Kim asked looking at the McMasters watching their response and listening for their reply.

"No. Not that we are aware of." Mike responded. "She is an honor student, and we never even smelled cigarette smoke on her breath. She may have tried smoking pot, but we don't believe she is smoking it right now. Marty has a few beers or a drink or two when she goes to college parties. But, she has never come home drunk or even tipsy. To us, she's a parent's dream."

"Does Marty have a boyfriend?" was Kim's next question.

"No. She does date occasionally, but does not have a steady boyfriend." Mrs. McMasters said. "I know my daughter very well Officer. My maternal instincts would know, or at least, I hope they would know if Marty was in a deep relationship with anyone or sneaking around with someone she knew we wouldn't like. She has been very focused on what she wants to do with her life and very focused on her education. We have been fortunate she thinks the way she does and prioritizes her life by setting healthy goals."

"By the sound of what you are saying and listening to your sincerity, you both have been very blessed. But, I think Marty has also been blessed by having you both as her parents." Kim followed.

I sat in the chair listening to the conversation and thanking God that Kim was so sensitive and caring. She did know how to conduct an interview, but also knew how to keep the interview very human and respectful.

"This question is sort of sensitive, and, again, please do not take this question out of context. Have either or you, or both of you, had any disagreements, verbal arguments or physical confrontations with Marty within the last month or so that might have caused her to run away?" Kim asked, again watching both of the McMasters very closely as Mike answered her question.

He did not look at Kim as he responded; he looked straight into my eyes without any hesitation and said, "Chief, we are a good family. Yes, we have our disagreements. Yes, we have our arguments. But, we do not have knockdown, drag out, confrontations with physical violence, breaking of furniture or injury to anyone. You can question our neighbors. They will tell you we are a good family and live peaceful lives."

Kim shifted in her chair and asked, "Has Marty been acting differently in any way over the last few weeks? Has she had any uncharacteristic mood changes?"

"No." Karen answered. "She has been her normal, joyful self, who, right now, I miss with all of my heart."

The rest of the interview lasted about a half hour. Kim continued to ask questions about strangers who might have been seen in the neighborhood, workmen who may have been hired to do yard work or projects around the house, neighbors who were having any remodeling done to their homes, sales people who might have stopped by the house within the last few months, new neighbors who might have moved into the neighborhood within the last year, any male relatives who had been stopping to visit more frequently than before, anyone calling Marty who never called her before, or any off-color or obscene phone calls being received?

Before we stood up to leave, I leaned forward in my chair, looking at Mike and Karen, knowing I had to tell them my suspicions regarding Marty's abduction and the probable connection her disappearance had to the five girls who were discovered at Meadow Pond a few days earlier. As I shared information regarding the case and the victims, without using names or physical conditions, Mike and Karen were both visibly shaken. Karen, who had been sitting without moving during the interview, lowered her head and began to sob openly. She did not raise her hands to hide her tears which fell freely onto the legs of her slacks. Mike put his arm around her and gave her a hug as he, Kim and I stood to leave. I assured him that we would do everything we could to locate Marty. Before leaving the back room, I asked the McMasters to tell us which route Marty took when she walked to class each morning. As we left the room, Karen was sitting in the same position on the couch by the fire once again captured by the flame's movement.

"Chief, thank you for coming over. We appreciate anything you can do to help us – to help Marty. But what can I do to help? I feel totally disabled by this. I want to run out and start searching for her, but I don't know where to loo.! I have driven over every road in this town two or three times hoping to catch a glimpse of her walking or riding in someone's car. All I know is that Marty left this house on her way to school and never got there. How can that happen? How the hell can a young girl just vanish without a trace or without anyone seeing anything?

"Mike," I said standing on the front steps of his home, "We will do everything we can as quickly as possible to find out what has happened to your daughter. I already have officers canvassing the town door to door asking if anyone has seen anything or anyone out of the ordinary over the last few days. I will be speaking to Captain Garber over in Auburn at the State Police to share all of the information you and Karen have given us so that he and his people can use it within their investigation. Mike, we will do everything humanly possible to find Marty and bring her home safely to you and Karen. You have my word on that."

Mike put his hand on my shoulder, squeezing as he said, "Ron, father to father, I believe you."

Mike was still standing in the open doorway as Kim and I drove away. He looked out at the same neighborhood I had looked at an hour before - a neighborhood he would never look at the same way again for the rest of his life.

Derek Larson stopped at "Arts and Things" on his way home from the police station to pick up craft supplies for his wife, Cheryl. Molly called to let Cheryl know that her order was delivered so that she would have it in time for her class the next evening. Cheryl taught classes in a large room attached to the garage, and like Molly, sold many of her craft items at local town fairs and on the Internet. Derek, driving by the store on his way home, volunteered to stop for Cheryl so that she would not have to drive into town herself.

As Derek reached out to grab the front door knob to the store, the door suddenly opened as Molly was leaving for a short break. Both jumped back in surprise, startling one another.

"Oh! My God." Molly said putting her hand over her mouth, reacting to almost running into Derek on the sidewalk.

"Hey, Molly, nice running into you - literally." He responded. Both laughed together, then stepped into the store.

"You must be here to pick up Cheryl's order." Molly said.

"Yeah, I told her I'd stop by so she wouldn't have to come into town. Just let me know what she owes you."

"Don't worry about that Derek. Cheryl always pays me at the end of the month. All you have to do is load it up and take it away."

"Will it fit into the bed of the pick-up, or do I need to rent a tractor-trailer to get it all home in one load?" Derek asked with a smart tone to his voice.

"Funny man. Funny man." Molly replied. Changing the subject, she asked, "I've been hearing about those girls they found out at Meadow Pond. Is it true that one of them is Christine Sawyer?"

"Unfortunately, it is true. We're still verifying the identities of the others. That process could take a few more days. But since you have brought the subject up, have you seen or heard anything unusual over the past week or so that might be worth our looking into? Any instance, no matter how trivial it might seem?"

Molly, standing by Cheryl's order at the end of the counter replied, "To tell you the truth Derek, yesterday a man came into the store looking to buy a replica of the three monkeys sitting together, you know the, ah, hear no evil, speak no evil, see no evil? I know I have those mixed up," she said chuckling.

Derek nodded his head yes.

"Well, he was really creepy and stared at me with coal, black eyes. They were the blackest eyes I have ever seen in my life! I told him I did not sell them but that I would do a quick search on the 'Net for him to see if I could locate a seller in the area. He continued to stare at me while I was on the computer and never moved a muscle…just stared. Then, when I handed him the paper with the address on it, he made sure to purposely brush my fingers a smirk. I felt a chill run up my spine and I swear he left a bad aura in here for an hour after he was gone."

"I'd say that qualifies as very unusual to say the least." Derek responded. "Have you ever seen this guy before yesterday?"

"No. Not that I can remember. He's never been in the store while I was here. If he had, I would have recognized him."

"Molly, I'm going to have a State Police sketch artist come over to the store later today so that we can get a composite of this guy. It may be he's just an odd ball who enjoys making people feel uneasy, but I don't want to overlook the possibility that he is more than that. What would be a good time for you?"

"Any time, Derek. Just have someone give me a call so that I can have one of my part-timers in here to run the store."

"Not a problem. Thanks for your help with Cheryl's order. Oh, and with this information. If this guy should come back to the store just wait until he leaves and give us a call right away. We'd like to know if he's still in the area. Also, try to get a description of his vehicle and the license plate without putting yourself in jeopardy."

After loading Cheryl's order, Derek drove the six miles home thinking about the man Molly had described. Something in his gut told him he needed to follow up on this information right away. He called Kim from the truck and filled her in on his conversation with Molly. She said she would let the chief know and call the state police to set up the sketch artist right away. Pulling into his driveway, Derek could not get the three monkeys out of his head. Something, something about those monkeys bothered him and would continue to bother him the rest of the day.

34

Jerry Bickford and Doc Cavanaugh completed the last autopsy late in the evening. The greasy spoon lunch was still swimming around in Jerry's stomach causing some discomfort as he left the hospital parking lot and headed home for a well-deserved shower. He was thinking about the last forty-eight hours and was not paying a great deal of attention to the drive with the exception of the road ahead. He did not notice the white van following him at a discrete distance a few car lengths behind. Turn for turn, stop light for stop light, the van kept the appropriate distance and followed Jerry until he arrived at his condo.

Christopher was thinking about his and Jerry's surprise meeting at the restaurant earlier in the day. At first he dismissed it. But as the afternoon progressed, Christopher realized Jerry was one of the only people involved with the case who knew anything about him. More importantly, Jerry knew Christopher carried a concealed weapon. If the police ever caught up with him, he wanted that fact to be a surprise. If Jerry had even the tiniest question in his mind about Christopher, it could be the beginning of the end. Jerry had to die. It was a plain and simple fact. It was that easy a decision to make. Jerry Bickford had to die today. Despite planning to leave town in a couple of days, he did not want to leave anything to chance. "Control,

control, control," he thought to himself as he parked his van a couple of blocks away and began the walk back to Jerry's condo.

Upon arriving at home, Jerry went straight to the refrigerator and took out a cold beer, kicking off his shoes as he walked into the bathroom to start the water for his shower. Walking into the bedroom, he left a trail of socks, shirt and jeans and under-shorts on the floor along the way. "Oh! Christ! Does this ever taste good," he thought taking another swallow of his favorite brew. Walking back into the bathroom he saw the steam rising out of the shower and could not wait to feel the hot, jetted water rolling down his body, relaxing his muscles and wash away forty-eight hours of morgue. Stepping into the shower, he took the soap and began lathering up while letting out a loud and long "Ahhhhhh." "I want to shake the person's hand who invented the shower." Jerry thought continuing to lather his face rubbing the soap into his pores. After the last couple of days, this was one of the best showers he had ever taken. He lingered in the shower longer than usual allowing himself to enjoy these cleansing moments of self-indulgence. He put both hands against the shower wall, leaning his face directly into the water to feel its full impact.

When Jerry turned the water off, he opened the shower door and reached for his terry-cloth towel hanging on the rack. Grabbing the towel, something did not feel right. It seemed much closer than it should have been. Wiping the water out of his eyes, Jerry stepped out of the shower and turned to his right. There, sitting on the toilet seat, was Christopher Bradford… pointing a gun at Jerry's face.

"What the fuck! Christopher! What the fuck are you doing here? Why the gun: for Christ's sake?" Jerry yelled, dropping the towel onto the bathroom floor while backing up against the wall.

"Hi. Jerry." Christopher replied, very quietly, continuing to sit on the toilet seat pointing a Glock at Jerry's head. "Let me just say I don't have any other choice but to kill you. Our meeting earlier today has put me in an awkward position. But, look at it this way, when they find your body at least you'll be clean."

A smirk opened to a wide smile as Christopher squeezed the trigger. Shot point blank in the forehead, the impact of the bullet pushed Jerry upward against the wall, splattering blood and tissue onto the tile around his head as his body slid down to a sitting position on the tiled floor.

"Dead mans' halo." Christopher said, pleased with himself, blood beginning to pool on the bathroom floor.

Kim called me right after talking with Derek regarding Molly's encounter with the stranger at her store. I told her to have Todd Mercer take a cruiser up to Worcester to check out the store that actually sold the statue of the three monkeys. I also instructed Kim to make sure Todd asked the owner of the store how the statue was paid for by our person of interest. If he used a credit card, we would have his name and address and could follow up on it right away. If he paid in cash, we would not be able to do anything, but would send the state police artist to the store to produce and a second composite of our stranger.

"At least something is finally starting to happen," I thought, sitting at my kitchen counter finishing off a large, grilled chicken salad with extra cheese. This would be my only real meal of the day, and I stopped at home to thoroughly enjoy every bite along with one of my usual diet sodas.

Cleaning up the kitchen after dripping salad dressing on the counter-top, kitchen stools and floor, I left the house and drove back to Milford Hospital 30 minutes away. Drive time is good thinking time, and I reviewed everything we knew from the investigation thus far to be sure I wasn't missing something.

Four officers were knocking on doors asking questions regarding peculiar people or odd occurrences with people in town over the last week or two. Todd was on his way to Worcester by now. The State Police artist would have arrived at "Arts and Things" for the composite sketch. Kim was walking the same route Marty probably took the morning of her abduction and we should receive the psychological profile of our killer from Ken Garber's people this afternoon. My next stop was a visit with Doc Cavanaugh to follow up on the autopsies of our five victims. I would get copies of the reports over to Ken Garber as soon as possible as well as to my staff at the station in Sutton. Everything seemed to be in place.

One of the perks of being a police officer is you usually have special areas to park your vehicle in hospital, town or state facilities. We don't have to ride in circles for fifteen minutes like everyone else looking for back up lights signaling a soon-to-be empty parking space. When I arrived at the hospital, I headed toward the cellar door of the hospital for the second time in two days. Walking down the corridor, I expected to see someone moving from one room to another or waiting at an elevator door, but the hall was empty. Even though I was the Chief of Police, I still looked into each darkened doorway or hideaway for the "Boogie Man". "What a wimp," I said to myself.

As I reached the doors to the morgue, I realized that I will never get used to how unsettling and quiet morgues always seem to be. Opening the door, I walked into the examination room and found it empty. The autopsies having been completed, the bodies of the five girls were now hidden behind the doors of the stainless steel refrigeration units at the far end of the morgue. Other than the low humming sound of the fridge's compressors, there was no sound what-so-ever. Turning to Doc's office, I thought maybe I had missed him. Perhaps he was already at home getting some real sleep after putting in over forty-eight hours performing the post mortems.

Poking my head around the corner of Doc's office door, I spotted his feet sticking out from behind his desk - his body hidden, lying on the floor. I ran over, pushing his chair out of my way and it was then that I could see pooling on the floor. Doc had been shot in the chest. Bending over him, I did not see any signs of life and could feel no pulse in his neck. I immediately pulled his phone over to the edge of the desk and dialed "O". Being in the hospital already, the quickest response for emergency assistance would be thru the operator at the front desk.

"This is Chief Kosciak from Sutton. I am down in the morgue with Doctor Cavanaugh. He has been shot in the chest! Get a doctor and crash team down here ASAP!"

"Okay, Chief. I'm calling the ER right now. We'll have someone down there right away."

I began CPR not knowing how long ago Doc had been shot. My own heart was pounding wildly as I compressed his chest over and over again. Occasionally, I stopped the chest compressions to breathe new air into his lungs. Compression, compression, compression. "Come on Doc!" I heard myself saying. "Come on man, BREATHE, damn you! Come on! Breathe!"

I heard frantic footsteps pounding down the hallway long before the doors to the morgue burst open and a gurney accompanied by a doctor and two nurses rushed into the morgue.

"Over here! In the office!" I yelled at the top of my lungs. "We're in here, Hurry!"

The ER doctor physically pushed me out of the way as he knelt down next to Doc assessing the damage and Doc's condition. "Help me put him up on the gurney! Quickly God-dammit! Come on! Move. Move, people! Let's go!" he shouted, not worrying about hurting anyone's feelings.

I helped lift Doc up onto the gurney – not an easy task considering his size and weight. Once on the gurney, the ER doctor cut away Doc's blood stained shirt and pulled the two electrode paddles off of the defibrillator. Within seconds the defibrillator snapped out its electrical current and Doc's entire body stiffened, arched and raised off of the gurney.

I stood behind the crash team wanting to reach over and start pounding on Doc's chest myself, as if I could do better than the team urgently and efficiently working on him trying to save his life. Again the snapping sound. Again Doc's body arched and stiffened as the electricity tried to restart his heart. Doc's heart still refused to respond. Finally, on the fourth snap the doctor said, "We have a heart beat! We have a friggin' heart beat folks! Yeah! Doc, you old son-of a-bitch, you might just make it!"

The medical team rolled Doc out of the morgue as Janey Blair, the hospital's chief of security, entered the room with two of his officers.

"Chief, what the hell is going on?"

"Doc's been shot." I responded, out of breath and still incredulous at the whole occurrence. "I came in to meet with him about some autopsy reports and found him on the floor bleeding out behind his desk."

"Who the hell would want to shoot Doc?" she asked. We were all wondering the same.

"I want you to call the Milford PD and get them over here right away. Then, I want every video tape taken within the last three hours ready to replay by the time they arrive. Chances are our attacker was picked up on one of those cameras entering and/or leaving the hospital. I am going to stay here and wander around just in case this person likes to hang around and revel in his or her work. Who knows, I might just get lucky."

"Okay, Chief. I'll have one of my officers go with you. Let me know if there is anything else you need from us," Janey said as she turned and left the morgue.

"Let's go up to the ER first." I said to the security officer. "I want to check on Doc."

Running up the hallway toward the elevator my stomach felt nausous. I knew Doc's life hung by a very fine thread and that thread was as taut as a thread could get without breaking. The only thing that seemed to make sense was that someone wanted us to know he or she is not afraid to come after us in order to prevent being exposed. Coming after Doc, right here in the hospital, is as bold a move as I've ever seen in all of my years as a police officer. Hastening my pace to get to Doc, I honestly worried where this event would take us, and who might be next on the hit list.

Entering the hospital was easy. Just walk right in! A baseball cap, sunglasses and a shoulder sling purchased at a local pharmacy in Milford solved the security camera problem. Being the beginning of winter, the scarf around his neck hid the rest of his facial features.

Doc Cavanaugh was as surprised as Jerry Bickford had been when the bullets tore into his chest sending him sprawling onto the floor. Cavanaugh's fall was a little more dramatic when his large torso bounced off of the desk moving it about a foot as he crashed to the floor. Christopher, watching Doc collapse, thought to himself, "He was, after all, a very large man. The law of physics would dictate that the bigger you are, the harder you fall."

After killing Jerry Bickford, Christopher knew that Cavanaugh also had to die. Jerry would have talked to the good doctor about him over lunch after their surprise meeting at the diner and may have even mentioned Christopher's weapon's permit. There was the possibility the doctor might play criminal-psychologist at some point in the investigation and therefore he was a liability. Christopher needed to avoid being discovered at any cost. The costs, in this instance, were the deaths of Jerry Bickford and Doc Cavanaugh. He laughed and gloated driving back to the Baker Building satisfied that his tracks were covered and he was safe from detection. The only person Christopher felt needed pay back now for having taken away his children was Chief Ronald Kosciak.

Once the van was parked in the garage and the doors were locked, Christopher went up to his apartment to watch Marty on the monitor. She was not in her room, and he immediately went over to the door leading down the stairs to the cellar. Opening the door at the top of the stairs, he looked to see if the door at the bottom of the stairs was closed. Seeing that it was, he thought, "She must be in the bathroom." He walked back to the monitor waiting for her return to her room.

Christopher could see the CD player he set up for Marty sitting on the table next to her bed. He chose the CD player instead of a radio so Marty would have no information from the outside world, especially news about his adopted children. She would meet her sisters soon enough.

Marty appeared on the screen and Christopher breathed a sigh of relief. There was a small part of him that was beginning to worry Marty might have found a way to escape. If she did escape, he would have to leave town immediately and not have time to properly prepare his departure over the next few days. When he did leave, it wouldn't take long for people to notice that Christopher Bradford was missing and perhaps connect him to the murdered girls found at the pond and the abduction of Marty McMaster. So, when he did leave, he wanted to go out with a big bang and leave on his own terms. He did not want to run away with his tail between his legs.

Christopher watched Marty for the next hour, enjoying her every move and gesture on the monitor. Earlier in the day, Marty ate the fish and chips Christopher brought back from Joe's Diner. She seemed very content and at ease in her new home. Christopher wanted to believe that Marty really was thankful for her adoption, but the sly, untrusting, cunning part of him still doubted and therefore was always prepared for alternative situations. As he watched the screen, Marty walked over to the camera, looked up, smiled, and waved at Christopher.

"How the hell does she know I am here? What kind of game is she playing?" he thought standing to walk out of the room toward the cellar door. After unlocking and opening the door at the bottom of the stairs, Christopher walked down the hall toward Marty's room. Half way down the hall Marty came out of her room and stood looking at Christopher.

"Hi." She said smiling at him.

"I saw you look up into the camera and wave at me." I knew it was only a matter of time before you located the lens, but how did you know I was upstairs?" He asked not trying to hide his curiosity.

"Oh. That's not a secret, Every time you drive in or out of the garage, I can hear the motor faintly through the wall. I just wanted to say hi and welcome you home. After all, you have been treating me very well since my adoption. I have my own private room and a private bath. You give me plenty to eat and I have my own music. You haven't harmed me since you rescued me. Who knows what my father and mother would have done to me!"

Marty turned and walked back into her room. Christopher stood alone in the hall assessing what Marty just said to him. Again, there was part of him that wanted to believe she was sincere and grateful. However, he would not allow himself to trust her. He must maintain control. Control, control, control!

Marty sat quietly in her room waiting for Christopher to enter wondering if she overplayed her move in the game. Sitting for what seemed an eternity, she finally heard the hall door close and lock as Christopher went upstairs.

"Maybe I over did it," she thought, sitting alone once again.

I was running down the corridor to the emergency room the split second the elevator door opened on the first floor. The security guard with me was barely able to keep up. I expected to lose him at any moment as his breathing became very labored and loud. Rounding the last corner into the ER, I looked back to see the guard stop and sit in a chair by the nurse's station in Pediatrics. Not missing a step, I sprinted until I reached the triage desk in the middle of the ER. I began looking from cubicle to cubicle hoping to find Doc and his team. When I could not find Doc, I nearly lost it. Thinking Doc was dead from his wounds and that he was somewhere on a gurney with a sheet pulled over his face, I closed my eyes and bowed my head about to pound my fist on the counter top of the nurse's station, when I felt a tapping on my shoulder.

Emily, one of the ER nurses, looked into my eyes and said, "Chief, try to relax. They took Doc Cavanaugh directly to surgery on the third floor. It's his best chance of survival. We have the best ER teams in the state and he is in the very best of hands right now. You need to hold it together for Doc's sake. He would want your strength working for him right now along with your prayers."

I knew Emily was right and was relieved to know that Doc was still alive. While Emily was talking me down from my emotional episode, Andy Stephens, the police chief from Milford walked into the ER with a few of his officers. Andy and I had worked a few felony cases together over the years, but neither thought we would ever be working a case with Doc upstairs fighting for his life.

"Ron. What the heck happened here?" Andy asked as we walked out of the ER to the parking lot.

"All I know right now, Andy, is that someone shot Doc downstairs in his office -- got him right in the center of his chest. I don't know how many rounds he took, but when I arrived he didn't have a pulse and he was not breathing. I called for help, gave him CPR and the rest was up to the guy upstairs. I asked Janey to get the surveillance tapes ready for us to review. Maybe we'll be able to pick out our perp entering or leaving the hospital."

"Well, I'll have two of my officer's talk to everyone at the main entrance and the ER entrance. We'll talk to everyone in the whole damned hospital if we have to! I think our shooter is long gone though." Andy said, as we walked to the video surveillance room to review the tapes.

Janey was waiting for us when we got there. I asked her if there was a surveillance camera at the entrance to the morgue. She said there was, and I asked her to pull that tape up for us to watch first. I told her I wanted to start playing the tape about one half hour before I arrived. An officer sitting at the console had already reversed the tape to one hour before the shooting. Fast-forwarding the tape to a time about five minutes before my arrival, we saw a single figure walk down the hallway and stop in front of the morgue doors. I had the officer slow the tape down to normal speed. The person in the video turned, looked up into the camera, and nodded. Wearing a baseball cap, sunglasses, and a winter scarf to cover the face and neck, there was no way we were going to be able to identify our shooter. We were able to estimate the height, and weight of the individual, but could not determine the person's race or gender due to the disguise being worn.

Everyone in the room watched the video again as it played a second time. The results were the same. It took three minutes for the shooter to enter and exit the morgue, vanishing only minutes before my arrival. One minute and forty-four seconds elapsed from the time the shooter left until I stood in front of the camera entering the morgue: meaning Doc was probably dead for no more than two minutes before I started CPR. Using this time frame, we immediately called to the surgical team on the third floor thinking this might be vital information in determining Doc's condition and probable recovery problems. Even if it did not help Doc, it made us feel like we were contributing something to the "Ole War Horse's" situation.

"I was THAT FREAKIN CLOSE to being there! SON-of-a-bitch! That pisses me off. Just a minute and a half earlier and I could have nailed the bastard!" I said leaning against a file cabinet next to the console.

"Ron. If you had surprised the shooter in the morgue, you might have been our next victim." Andy remarked. "At least, right now, Doc is still alive and I fear we will be hearing a lot more of his sarcasms over the years to come. He's a tough old bird. We all know that."

"You're right, Andy. It's just that Doc and I go back a lot of years. I feel like my dad is up there lying on that table."

While Andy and I were talking, Janey switched the video to the camera covering the main entrance to the hospital. Once again, as our shooter entered and exited the hospital, he took the time to stop and nod at the camera. This person was one ballsy bastard.

We were leaving the video room when the telephone rang. The officer at the console picked up the receiver and listened intently. "Yes." he said, still listening. "Yes." He replied a second time. While he was still listening, I motioned to him asking if the call pertained to Doc Cavanaugh. Shaking his head yes, I immediately reached over grabbing the phone out of his hand and started speaking.

"This is Chief Kosciak. What's Doc's status up there?"

"Chief," The surgical nurse responded, "Doc is still in surgery, but he is holding his own. His vitals are good and getting stronger as the surgery progresses. He took two bullets to the chest. It is a miracle of miracles that he survived these wounds. If you hadn't come along when you did Doc would by lying in his own morgue right now instead of on this surgical table. Everyone up here says thanks for saving his life. He's a friend of ours too."

Turning to the people in the room, I said, "The ER nurse says Doc is doing better. He is far from being stable, but they think his chances of surviving are getting better by the minute. They'll keep us updated as they learn more."

I felt a deep, deep relief knowing Doc was okay for now. His being alive was the first step. His surviving the night would be his second and more questionable challenge.

There was not much Andy or I could do at this point and we decided to head back to our respective police stations. We briefly spoke about the Meadow Pond crime scene and the murdered girls. As we separated in the parking lot and began walking to our cruisers, my cell phone rang.

"Chief, Kim here, we have another homicide."

"What? Did they find another body at the pond?" I asked turning to catch Andy Stephen's attention.

"No, Chief. It's Jerry Bickford. His partner found him dead in their bathroom a few minutes ago."

"What!" I yelled, feeling my body shudder from the news. "What's the address? I'm going over there right now." As I spoke to Kim, I stopped and shouted over to Andy who was just getting into his cruiser. I motioned for him to come back over as I watched him reaching for his cell phone. When Andy was a few feet away, he asked, "Jerry Bickford?"

"Yeah, I just got the call too. Found him in his bathroom. This has to be connected to Doc's shooting. They were working together on these autopsies. Why don't the two of us go over to Jerry's condo since both of our jurisdictions will be involved in the investigations?"

Andy agreed and I told him I would follow him over. As we drove out of the hospital parking lot I could not help but think two of the world's most generous people had been shot within the last couple of hours. One of them was already dead; the other fighting for his life and, could, at any minute, be the second one to die.

Following Andy over to Jerry Bickford's condominium, I could not help but think about the events of the last three days propelling me faster and faster down this winding, tragic road of disaster. I felt our investigation was getting out of control as I reached into to my shirt pocket for a cigarette.

"What: A freakin cigarette? I haven't smoked in twenty-three years!" I thought. "This case is really starting to rattle my nerves."

The last time I had reached into my shirt pocket for a cigarette was ten years ago on Interstate 95 heading up to Massachusetts from Florida driving a "vintage" rental truck that didn't go over fifty miles per hour. I used to smoke one package of cigarettes a day and did so for over twenty years. Finally, deciding it was time to quit, I attended a smoking cessation class for eight weeks, taught the class for two years and thought I had overcome my addiction to tar and nicotine. Honestly, I have done extremely well over the years, but, when I am under massive amounts of pressure, I get the urge to light up without even knowing where the urge is coming from.

I was picturing the bodies of five, beautiful, young women filling the refrigeration compartments at the hospital. A sixth young woman was missing and a state medical examiner was dead on his bathroom floor from a gunshot wound to the head, while Doc Cavanaugh fought for his life with two bullet holes in his chest. In my mind I knew the same person was responsible for all of these events. I also theorized at this point that the killer was retaliating for the discovery of the bodies at Meadow Pond. But, why would the killer want to take the lives of Jerry Bickford and Doc Cavanaugh? What possible reason could the killer have? They were just performing their normal medical duties. They were not responsible for finding the girls. There had to be some other connection to this case, but right now, I did not have a clue what that connection could be. The real problem I was facing: if Doc Cavanaugh died from his wounds, I might never find out the answer to my question.

My cell phone began to ring again, and I took a very deep breath anticipating additional fecal matter was about to hit the fan.

"Chief, it's Kim, again. We have a run down on the guy who purchased the statue of the three monkeys up in Worcester."

"Go ahead, Kim. I'm all ears." I responded.

"The guy did'nt use a credit card to pay for the monkeys. He paid cash. But the store owner's description of the man matches the one given to us earlier by Molly Harrington. The store owner said something else to Todd that mirrors what Molly said to Derek after this guy left her store. The owner said the man's presence left an evil behind aura that lingered in the air after he had left the store. He watched the guy walk out of the store, across the street to a white van and drive away. Before you ask, no, he did'nt think to get the license plate number. We couldn't be that lucky."

"Make sure you get the State Police sketch artist up there for that composite. We need to compare the one from Molly Harrington when we get it. I think we need to follow up on this guy. He may not have anything to do with this case, but I'm not willing to let any leads go unchecked. At the least, he is on our radar and worth some looking into. It's not a crime to be creepy, but you sure do get people's attention when you leave the black plague behind you wherever you go." I said, already thinking about the white van.

"O.k. Chief. I'll make the call to the Staties."

I do not believe events happen randomly or by chance. There must be some sort of logical pattern of evolution and connection between people and their daily environments. Here I was, driving behind Andy on my way to a brutal crime scene, that was somehow connected to a serial killer running around our county abducting, torturing and killing young women, when I receive a phone call about a weird guy purchasing a statue of three monkeys. The phone call stirred my questioning mind, making me wonder just how all of these events tied together.

"If the man with the white van is our killer, why would he purchase a freakin monkey statue?" "How would that...Holy Shit!" I yelled out loud. "Holy, friggin shit! That has to be it" I yelled out even louder, turning on my police lights to get Andy's attention. I stepped on the gas to get closer to his cruiser signaling him to pull over.

As both of our vehicles pulled off to the side of the road, I took out my cell phone to call Kim back. Andy walked up to the passenger's side and climbed into the Explorer as Kim answered my call.

"Kim, I think I have figured out the connection." I blurted out like a school kid who thinks he has the correct answer to the teacher's question.

"Chief, Is that you? What connection are you talking about?" she asked.

"The monkeys, Kim! The friggin' monkeys! The guy who bought the monkeys, he's our killer. See no evil; hear no evil; speak no evil. The monkeys represent the missing eyes, lips and ears taken from the dead girls. Do you see the correlation? It has to be him! He bought a keepsake to remind himself of who he is and why he does what he does. We need to get those composites ASAP. Call Ken Garber and tell him to get a second artist. We need to expedite those sketches so that we can get a look at this guy NOW!" I said with the first sense of hope I had felt since this nightmare began three days ago.

"You got it, Chief. How long before you'll be back?"

"I'm not sure right at the moment. I'll give you a shout on the radio when I finish up with Chief Stephens at Jerry Bickford's condo."

Looking at me from the passenger's seat, Andy said, "Well, it looks like you may have found the lead we need to get this investigation off of the ground. If the artist's sketches portray a real likeness of this guy, we may be able to start looking through our records and the National Crime Information Center for a look alike with a previous criminal record."

"Ya know, Andy, something in my gut tells me we won't find a record on this guy. I bet he doesn't even have a parking ticket. Just a hunch. I'm not even sure why I'm so sure. But, even with this new information, I'm still at a loss as to why he would kill Jerry and try to kill Doc. It just doesn't fit. There would have to be a specific reason for this guy to try killing two people in one afternoon, in broad daylight, one of his victims in a hospital morgue, for Christ's sake!"

Andy shook head in agreement. "Your right, there is no way anyone would come out into the open to commit two murders in one afternoon at a place like a hospital unless that person feared being exposed. There is somethng about our killer he thought Jerry and Doc knew. If this guy killed them just because he's pissed off, then he's crazier than we think he is! No, this guy had something to lose if he allowed Jerry and Doc to live. Exactly what that something is, is the real question we need to answer right now."

Doing Doc was easier than Christopher thought it would be. The disguise worked perfectly and he was able to enter and exit the hospital without anyone giving him a second glance. He fit in like a car in a giant parking garage - just another car in another spot. His theatrics with the security cameras gave him a lot of satisfaction made him feel invincible, untouchable.

Doc didn't even have time to say a prayer. Christopher calmly walked into the morgue, into Doc's office, removed his sunglasses, winked at Doc and then shot him twice without ever saying a word. Christopher relished the drama. Doc never knew what hit him, who shot him, or why he was going to die alone on the floor of his office.

"They see me, but they don't see me," he thought as he drove back to the Baker Building without any worry of being caught. "I'm right out there in plain view, even touching some of them every day, and they STILL do not see me." A smirk formed on his lips as it had so many, many times before. The "smirk of the smart" he liked to call it. The smirk that came from being confident and in control.

Christopher thought about Ron Kosciak, as the trees, fields, farms and stone walls of the Massachusetts countryside whipped by the window on each side of the street. Although most of the farm owners could no longer afford to raise cows or run dairy farms, families kept the farm houses and barns in their possession, selling off tracts of land from their acreage to raise money for expenses. It was one way to keep the land barons from gobbling up all of the historical structures, raising them to the ground and building new condominiums where farmhouses once stood. Christopher wondered how long it would be before all of these historical sites ceased to exist and the countryside was transformed forever. A feeling of sadness came and went quickly as his thoughts turned back to Chief Kosciak.

"Right now, Kosciak is running around in circles. He has so much on his plate he doesn't even know where to start eating. He has corpses stacked up like cord wood, a missing girl, two homicides committed within hours of each other and not a friggin' clue to go on," he thought. "I know he won't stop looking for clues. He seems to be a very tenacious sort of cop, and I do owe him payback for taking away my kids. Maybe, I ought to pay him a nocturnal visit and shoot him up on some of my special juices. Maybe, I should shoot his whole family up. What about Marty, though?" She seems so sincere about having been rescued from the bondage of her parents. She has made no attempts to escape. Yes, she did search her room, found the hidden camera and looked around, but, who wouldn't do those things. Her words sound convincing. I want to believe her. She is so emotionally strong. The other kids all fell apart and whimpered, crying for their mommies and daddies. Marty hasn't fallen apart since our first meeting. If she is really speaking the truth, we could start a family all over again together. Marty would be like my first born child helping the new adoptees make their transition into our family."

Christopher was brought back to reality by a car suddenly pulling out of a side road and almost hitting the van as it sped away in the opposite direction. "Stupid son-of-a-bitch!" he yelled into the closed door window leaving a foggy patch on the glass from the heat of his breath. "Jesus, some people just don't think."

"Christopher. Christopher. What to do with Marty?" The thought of Marty being with him of her own accord was almost too tantalizing. "Although I enjoyed adopting the other kids, having Marty adopt ME would be the most incredibly wonderful thing in the world! That is, if she is sincere about her feelings. How can I be sure? Why do I have this nagging, mental, caution flag? Come on man. You are far from stupid. Do you take the chance or not?"

Pulling the van into the garage he remembered Marty telling him that she was able to faintly hear the motor of the van whenever he left or returned. He hit the horn quickly three times before turning off the ignition letting Marty know he was back. Stepping down out of the van, he walked over and closed the garage door making sure it was locked securely. "Never know what sort of low life might be out there waiting to break in and steal something," he thought walking over to the stairs leading to his apartment. "Christopher. Christopher. What to do about Marty?" his last thought switching off the garage light.

40

Marty heard the three toots of the van's horn as she stood in front of the dresser mirror brushing her hair, one of the few comforts of home she held onto for dear life - almost a literal statement. She wondered how long it would be before he came downstairs, hoping he would walk through the door with some food and something better tasting to drink than the highly chlorinated bathroom tap water. She fantasized about french vanilla coffee.

Even though Marty listened to music while he was away, thoughts of escape never stopped churning through her brain. The songs were like quiet back ground music playing at a restaurant during dinner as she considered her next move in the game. While he was out doing whatever it was that he did, Marty spent the time thinking about her situation. She knew her life was in jeopardy every second she was around him. He was unpredictable. He was unreadable. He did not respond in any way to her verbal attempts at winning him over, so she had no idea if she should continue to "butter" him up or take a step back to see what he would do. If she pushed even a little too far, and he believed she was lying and bullshitting him, he would bind her ankles again and lock the door to her room. If, however, he did believe her, he would keep things status quo and she would take that as her license to continue feigning her allegiance to his family. At this moment, in this cat and mouse game, he was the cat and she was the mouse.

The key rolled the lock's mechanism as Christopher opened the door to the cellar hallway. This time Marty did not come out to greet him and he wondered if she might be sleeping. Perhaps she had the ear plugs in from the headset for the CD player and did not hear the three toots from the van's horn. Turning into the doorway of Marty's room he saw that he was correct. She lay on the bed with the headphones tucked into each ear listening to her CD's. In that instant, an indescribable relief came over him. He knew there was a part of him desperately wanting to believe in Marty and her desire to stay with him as part of his family. Could he, trust her after all? This intriguing thought gave him hope - something foreign to Christopher.

Marty turned her head on the pillow, and looked over at Christopher as he held out a bag with hamburgers and onion rings along with an iced coffee.

"I took a chance on the coffee and asked for milk and three sugars." He said as she accepted the meal and drink.

"Actually, that is exactly how I like my iced coffee," she replied. "You know me pretty well don't you?" she asked watching his face for any negative expressions or intonations.

"I did spend a lot of time studying you before the day I began your adoption, so I you might say I learned a few things here or there along the way. Are you comfortable enough down here? Is there anything you need? I have tried to think of everything to assure your stay will be comfortable."

Marty, having watched him very intently since he walked into the room, saw no signs indicating she had overstepped and decided right at that instant to go for the gold.

"I have been thinking since the last time we spoke that there is one question I would honestly like to ask you, but I do not want to make you angry, so I am hesitant to ask it."

"Well, Marty, there is only one way to find out now, isn't there? You just need to ask the question and wait for my response. I cannot guarantee if I will get angry or not because, I don't know your question." There was no change in his facial expression while he responded to her statement.

Once again Marty was at a loss and did not know if she should ask. Should she take the risk?

"If I am going to be part of your family, and you are going to be my dad (this word she chose purposely), then, I would like to know your name. It's very difficult talking with someone when you don't know their name; especially if that man is going to be your father." She stated as she sat up on the side of the bed looking directly into his eyes.

Christopher stood for a few minutes studying Marty. Once again, he could find no signs of dishonesty in her eyes. She really did seem to be telling the truth. She was just speaking her mind, or was she? The nagging doubt once again pushed its way to the front of his brain. Without saying a word, he reached into his pants pocket and pulled out a switchblade knife, pressing the button allowing the blade to move and lock into its extended position. Marty, reacting instinctively to his swift, unannounced movement and, seeing the blade, began to raise her hands and arms instinctively in order to cover and protect her face from the ascending knife. As she closed her eyes waiting for the searing pain that was sure to follow, the plastic, electrical tie binding her wrists fell to the floor at her feet.

Picking up the electrical tie, Christopher walked to the doorway of the room, turned, looked at Marty and said, "My name is Christopher." before walking down the hallway, leaving Marty sitting on the side of the bed in shock not believing that she was still alive.

41

We found nothing at Jerry Bickford's condominium in the way of evidence to help us answer any questions. The shot was expertly fired into the center of Jerry's forehead. The back of Jerry's skull was splattered on the wall looking like a modern style acrylic painting of reds and grays against the bathroom beige. There were no bloody footprints smeared on the floor. No words or riddles written in blood on any walls or on the bathroom mirror to indicate motive. This crime scene looked like an execution style murder with only one goal - the total elimination of the victim. In Jerry's case, this goal had been achieved to the fullest measure.

Looking down at Jerry's lifeless body sitting in a pool of blood, one leg stretched out straight, the other bent up under his buttocks propping him against the wall, reminded me of a Raggedy Anne doll my sister used to play with when she was a young girl. Connected, but very disconnected at the same time. Jerry's head was bent down with very little blood at the bullet's point of entry. The majority of the blood flowed down his back onto the floor. Death came immediately upon the arrival of the projectile, with little or no suffering involved during his final process of living - the process of dying.

Jerry's partner, Michael, found the body when he came home early from work. Michael was a restaurant manager, working split shifts and odd days each week. Today, Michael came home early to surprise Jerry with baked, stuffed lobster, corn on the cob and rhubarb pie for supper. The bag with the live lobsters still moved in the kitchen sink where Michael had placed it when he first came in. There would be no boiling pot of water for these exoskeletons tonight. Michael would not remember the lobsters tonight, and by morning the bag would no longer be moving in the sink.

Michael knew immediately when he walked into his home that something was not right. The bathroom door was wide open and the shower's water was running. Jerry would never shower with the bathroom door open – a quirk that Jerry was saddled with from a very early age. He required all of the doors and windows in a bathroom to be closed. Michael, thinking Jerry may have fallen in the shower, ran into the bathroom to help his partner. Standing in the doorway, Michael saw Jerry's colorless, blood-drained body on the floor under the towel rack. A pool of dark, burgundy-colored blood spread out on the floor around Jerry's body following the grout lines of the square black and white tile. A bath towel covered only a portion of Jerry's groin. Without thinking, Michael bent down and covered Jerry, wanting to protect Jerry's dignity even after death. Michael told the first officer responding to the scene about moving the towel. He knew he would automatically be considered a suspect because he and Michael had been a couple for many years. Michael wanted to be up front with everything right from the start of the investigation. His and Jerry's relationship would be investigated as the police looked at every detail to determine if this was a domestic crime instead of an execution style killing. At this moment, Michael really did not give a shit about any of that crap. His life's partner and his love lay dead, murdered. Michael was going into shock as the realization of what had happened to Jerry began to shatter every part of his world.

"My God, Jerry, what did you get yourself into this time?" Michael thought as more police patrolmen and detectives entered and left his home without so much as a "How are you doing?" offered to the surviving gay man sitting on the couch.

I spotted Michael as Andy and I entered the living room. He was sitting alone staring out the sliding glass doors to the deck unaware of our arrival. Having met Michael a few times over the years at various medical events Jerry attended, I walked over to him and shook his hand as he stood to greet us.

"Michael, I'm very, very sorry," I said. "Jerry was assisting Doc Cavanaugh over in Milford with the autopsies of the girls we found buried at Meadow Pond. In fact, someone also tried to shoot and kill Doc this afternoon in his office at the hospital."

"Someone tried to kill doc too?" Michael said, looking very surprised and confused at the same time. "I moved the towel. To cover him. I told the officer. I know I shouldn't have, but Jerry was just laying there...exposed. I...I..."

"Michael. It's okay. It's okay. We understand. Most partners would have done the same thing. What you did is a natural and loving response."

Michael shifted his position on the couch, posturing himself like someone regaining dignity and confidence. "You said someone tried to kill Doc. What do you mean, tried?"

"Right now, Doc is fighting for his life in surgery. However, they did tell us just before we left to come here, that his chances of surviving were improving by the minute. Being completely honest, Michael, I believe Jerry's and Doc's shootings were done by the same person. One or both of them must have known something about the killer. There would be no other reason for someone to attempt killing both of them in such a short span of time. They paid the price for whatever it is one or both of them knew."

"What the fuck, Chief? What in heaven's name could Jerry have known about anyone that would cost him his life? Jerry was the easiest going man I have ever known. He was honest and straight up. He wouldn't hurt anyone or anything for Christ's sake!"

"I can't say I know what you are feeling, Michael, but I do want you to know how sorry I am about your loss. If there is anything that I can do, professionally or personally for you, do not hesitate to give me a call." I, handed him one of my cards. "I mean that, Michael. Do not hesitate to call me. Is there anywhere you can stay until all this is sorted out? Unfortunately, this process may take some time. I'm sure Chief Stephen here will allow you to get some personal belongings to take with you."

"Yeah, Chief. I can move in with my sister up in Gloucester for a few months until I sell this place and find somewhere else to live. I can't live here after losing Jerry like this. I don't really give two shits about much else right now. Jerry was the reason I was able to wear a smile every day.

"Okay, as long as you will be alright."

Michael thanked us as I turned to walk away. Andy spoke with Michael about his personal belongings and Michael was gone in just a few minute, bag in hand.

"What a way to remember someone you love: bleeding out, naked, and contorted on the bathroom floor, a hole in the front and back of his head and nothing in the world you can do to help." I thought as I walked into the kitchen, the paper bag in the sink catching my attention as it moved about, a claw breaking free of its paper prison.

Not having spent much time with Peggy over the last three days, we decided to meet at Calabria's, a local Italian restaurant serving the best Chicken Marsala in central Massachusetts. Chicken Marsala is one of Peggy's favorite meals. She orders it nine times out of ten along with her traditional glass of Chardonnay. I am a Chicken Parmesan connoisseur and was looking forward to sitting with Peggy, eating a hot meal, and talking about the last few days.

When we go to Calabria's for dinner, we go to visit our friend Giuseppe, (Joey), the owner of the restaurant. Joey usually works the bar when we are there and tonight was no exception. We began talking with him as he mixed Peggy's Southern Comfort Manhattan - not quite a glass of Chardonnay, but none-the-less refreshing - and my Captain and coke, catching up on his latest news and adventures. Joey was born with a natural ability to make people feel at home and relaxed. Peggy and I felt like family the first night we met him when the restaurant first opened. Calabria's became our home away from home.

Driving to Calabria's I called Milford Hospital to check on Doc's condition. One of the ER physicians who worked on Doc told me he was now resting in the intensive care unit. They had talked about life-flighting Doc to Mass General in Boston, but one of the bullets grazed the aorta next to the heart and they wanted to minimize his movement to prevent a rupture. The doctor said Doc's chances of survival at this stage were thirty to seventy percent. I did not like hearing those odds, but Doc was alive and still fighting. The doctor continued telling me that either bullet could have punctured and destroyed Doc's heart. Both bullets were that close. One quarter of an inch and we would not be having this conversation about Doc's survival. We would be discussing his funeral.

Peggy was already sitting at the bar when I walked into the restaurant. Joey was just setting my first Captain and Coke on the napkin as I pulled the stool into position.

"Joey, tonight I appreciate this drink more than you know," I said settling into a comfortable position. "Honey, how was YOUR day?" I asked raising my glass to take my first sip.

"Hi, baby." Peggy said, reading the specials on the menu.

I already knew she would order the Chicken Marsala and chuckled to myself as I asked the question. "What are you going to order?"

"I don't know yet. I was thinking about the sixteen ounce Rib-Eye with the blue cheese sprinkles. You know me though I'll look for twenty minutes and end up ordering the Chicken Marsala!"

We said Chicken Marsala simultaneously as I mimicked her. After her initial "you're an ass" response, she smiled and blew me a kiss. This verbal exchange hardly ever varied. I would ask; Peggy would reply that I was an ass and then we would eat. I was no longer surprised at how predictable we had become.

"What about you?" Peggy asked. "What are you going to have?"

"I'm going for the Chicken Parm," I said, thinking again of my predictability.

Joey looked over at us to see if we were ready to order. I shook my head left to right signaling we needed a few more minutes. He shook his head up and down in return acknowledging my message. Some people know how to communicate without talking. Joey knew us and we had an unspoken code used to talk with one another while waiting for Peggy to make up her mind.

"What's happening with the Meadow Pond case," Peggy asked.

Not having seen Peggy at all today, she was not aware of Jerry Bickford's murder or the attempted murder of Doc Cavanaugh.

"Doc Cavanaugh was shot in the chest this afternoon and..."

"What!" Peggy responded in a high, surprised tone, everyone in the restaurant and bar turning their heads in our direction. "What do you mean? What the hell happened?" she asked completely taken off guard.

"Someone went into his office this afternoon and put two bullets into his chest. We don't know who it was, but Doc is in the ICU over in Milford fighting for his life. The surgeon gives him a thirty percent chance of survival."

"Oh, my freakin word!" She said, "Poor Doc."

"That's not the end of it. Jerry Bickford was shot and killed this afternoon in his condo around the same time that Doc was attacked. Michael found him in their bathroom when he got home early from work."

"What the…why would anyone want to hurt either one of them? Poor, Jerry." Peggy said.

Joey, overhearing my conversation with Peggy interjected. "Chief, I know Jerry and Michael very well. They come into the restaurant often. I can't believe it. Jerry was a great guy. Do you have any idea who is behind the attacks? How is Michael doing? I know he and Jerry were extremely close."

"We don't have any concrete evidence linking the two shootings yet. We have to wait until the ballistic tests come back to see if the bullets match up. If they do, then we know both Jerry and Doc were shot with the same gun. Until then, all we can do is assume, and I don't like assumptions. Michael is going up to Gloucester to stay with his sister for a while. He's doing as well as anyone could, having just lost his partner in such a violent way."

There was a silent pause between the three of us. Finally, I said, "Joey, I'd like the Chicken Parm and a mixed salad with ranch dressing."

Peggy, taking my cue, ordered her Chicken Marsala. Joey reached over the bar as a waitress was passing holding her tray up in the air, and grabbed a basket with hot bread, placing it in front of us, as we mixed our own dish of olive oil, grated cheese and spices.

"So, what's new in your neck of the woods?" I asked Peggy, trying to change the mood.

"Not too much. School is the same. The kids are a riot, and that little Jeremy makes me pee my pants laughing all day long. He is just so damned cute. I could hug him to death. I'm going over to Libby's after we're done eating. She has some new clothes for the baby she wants me to see. I thought maybe I would take her and the baby out for some ice cream while Eugy is at work."

"Great idea," I replied. "It's Lib's birthday pretty soon isn't it?" I asked, as my plate of Chicken Parm and salad were placed in front of my hungry eyes and grateful nose.

"It's next week. We're going over to "Soft Touch" so she can get an hour-long massage. It only costs sixty-five dollars and it's a nice gift for her birthday."

"Sounds great, tell her to move over 'cause I'll need one of those rub-a-dub-dubs by this time next week."

"Rub-a-dub-dubs? You're such a twit!" Peggy said smiling, taking her first bite of Chicken Marsala, accompanied by her usual, musically-toned, hum of contentment.

Christopher stood at the top of the cellar stairway after leaving Marty sitting on her bed completely freed of her restraints. He slowly walked over to the monitor in the computer room watching her for a few minutes before taking a shower. After all, he had been very busy today and earned a much needed rest. Removing the two human roadblocks this afternoon had left him feeling a bit tired and achy.

The nagging question repeating itself in his mind as he watched Marty standing in front of the dresser raising her newly freed arms to study them in the mirror: "Is she for real?" Followed by, "Do not lose control my friend!"

The hot, soapy lather felt soothing as he stood in the water's stream enjoying the peace and quiet. The spraying water, being the only sound in the bathroom, helped him focus his thoughts as he planned his retribution against Chief Kosciak. Deciding the chief and his wife Peggy, as well as their daughter Libby would all be punished, he knew whatever plan he developed would not be received well by the Kosciak family. Although his plan was only in its infancy, he relished the idea of killing all three, one at a time, while Kosciak watched. Libby wold be first. Peggy second. Then, the chief, his heart ripped to pieces, helplessly looking at his dead family lying on the floor, the recipient of final justice.

Finishing his shower, Christopher changed into casual slacks and a pullover T-shirt. Grabbing a diet coke out of the fridge, he sat down studying the eyes, lips and ears collected from each of his adopted children. Remembering each one of the girls, their individualities, the time spent with each here at home, and the closeness he felt for every one of them, helped him to relax and reminisce. Collectively, the girls reacted much the same during their adoption processes, and that was why they were taught that: in this home there was no evil to see, no evil to hear, no evil to speak. Their screams and resistance showed how tenaciously and deeply rooted the evil was that clung to their souls as he proceeded with their ritual of adoption. He taught each of them that here, with him, they would be safe from being cast away by loved ones, or even worse, from being humiliated and abused like he was. At least here, with him, they would be taken care of and remembered. His love for them was unquestioning and unconditional. Once the adoption process was completed by each of the children, they were enshrined and appreciated daily by their adoptive father.

Christopher held family meetings with the children on a regular basis. Most often he discussed the next child he was considering for adoption and asked their opinions and thoughts. Today though, Christopher wanted to talk to them about something quite different.

"Time for a family meeting kids." he said addressing the glass jars sitting on the table top. "As you all know, I have begun the adoption of another daughter whom I want to become part of our family. But, I'm having some difficulty and reservations about her sincerity and honesty. I think she really does want to be my daughter. She seems very open and receptive to everything I've told her. She knows about each of you, and I'm sure she will be glad to finally meet all of you when I decide it's time to bring her upstairs. But, she seems too good to be true. What do you think? Should I trust her, or should I consummate her adoption the same way I consummated each of yours?"

Standing next to the table, looking into the jars, Christopher began to move his head and hands like he was listening to someone respond to what he had just said.

"Yes. You are correct. Hmmm…I could do that I suppose. Do you really think that? I don't know if she would agree, but I could ask her. So, you are all in agreement? Marty could be the "big sister" we have all been waiting for? Angie, I can always count on you to be the odd person out in these conversations. Yes, I know - control, control and control. You have an iron-clad memory, my dear. Children, I will have to give this some more thought. Thanks for listening to me ramble on. I will give this conversation more time to mature before making up my mind. Do you children want to meet Marty?" He smiled at their answer, turned away, took a few steps, and turning back toward his children, said "I love you all very, very much."

After finishing our dinner, I left Peggy at the bar talking with Joey about his latest weekend spent in the town of Harwich, located on Cape Cod. Driving over to Auburn to meet with Ken Garber, I thought about Doc lying in his hospital bed with IV's, drainage tubes, monitor leads and electrodes hooked up to and running out of every part his body. Doc's wife passed away a few years ago, and his only child, a daughter living in California, was on her way home to be with him at the hospital. Maybe subconsciously the sound of her voice would help Doc rally from the semi-comatose state that the attack had left him in. So far, Doc survived the initial attack and subsequent surgery, and I prayed upon arriving at the State Police facility, that he would be strong enough to survive the night...and beyond.

Ken was waiting for me in the control room where pictures and information about each of the murdered girls hung tacked to the portable cork-boards set up against two of the room's walls. The posted information gave the boards a crossword puzzle like appearance, with information written or drawn on multi-colored squares of paper, all being worked on simultaneously. Photos and information about family and friends, boyfriends, athletic coaches, college professors, employers, social history, likes and dislikes and police records covered most of the space on both boards. The

Staties were doing a great job re-creating the lives of each of these victims. Standing in front of the boards reviewing the information, I noticed Ken's people circled in red any information considered to be a priority worth investigating. Even though I knew Ken's staff was sure to be thorough, I still took the time to review the information that was not marked in red as well.

"Ken. There doesn't seem to be any area in these girl's lives indicating they might have known one another or even crossed paths. A couple of the schools the girls attended do have athletic programs which overlap and their teams do compete, but the girls did not play on any of the teams that actually competed against one another. Right now, the information is telling me our killer picked all of these girls at random. There are no connections between any of them. All this information and not one lead to follow," I said out loud turning to look at him.

"Yeah, Ron. I know what you mean. This is like looking for the proverbial "needle in the haystack." Only problem is we have six haystacks to look through at the same time. That's a lot of hay, my friend. By the way. How's doc doing? I heard about what happened to him this afternoon."

"He's in the ICU. He's one tough son-of-a-bitch, I'll give him that much. Have you been able to determine how many white vans are registered in this area? I know we sent the request out to the DMV only a few hours ago, but I was hoping you might have some feedback by now. I'd like to start running down each owner - no pun intended - and see if we can find one registered to our guy."

"Not too much on that yet. Not enough time at the end of the day for the registry to process the request. But, we do have the first composite sketch that Molly Harrington, from Arts and Things, gave us this afternoon. The artist is still up in Worcester working with the store owner on the second sketch."

"Super. Can I take a look at the first one?"

Ken walked over to the table set up next to one of the cork boards, picking up a piece of paper containing my first glimpse of our potential killer. My blood was pumping fast as I anticipated what this guy was going to look like. As Ken handed me the sketch, I focused on the facial features hoping there would be some sort of immediate recognition. There wasn't any. Although there was a familiarity, I did not recognize this man's face. The familiarity bothered me, but I couldn't put my finger on why.

The man looked to be in his mid to late thirties, Caucasian with no distinguishing marks or scars on his face. His hair was neatly cut, and he didn't wear any beard or mustache. Although his eyes were dark and piercing, in a crowd he would disappear without much notice. Sort of a regular guy. I was disappointed as I continued to evaluate the sketch with no recognition bulb going off in my head. And yet, there WAS something familiar about him.

"I don't know, Ken," I said handing the sketch back to him. "There is something, but there isn't anything I can run with."

"I know" said Ken. "I felt the same thing. In fact, a couple of my officers felt the same when they first looked at the sketch. This guy has one of those familiar faces. It drives me nuts, but it is what it is. I'll fax the second sketch over to you as soon as it's completed."

"Thanks, Ken," I said, turning back to the boards, to continue reviewing the information.

"You heard about Jerry Bickford, right?" I asked.

"Yeah, we received that call soon after it happened. We heard about Doc right after that. Are you thinking the two shootings are related?"

"We are definitely on the same page here, Ken."

I told Ken my revelation about the three monkeys: see no evil, hear no evil and speak no evil. My theory struck him the same way. Could something so simple be the key to opening up this investigation? Could a killer who was so meticulous in every move he made up to this point, make such a simple mistake?

I spent the next hour studying the information on the two boards. My eyes were about ready to fall out of my head from concentrating so hard. At this point we would have to wait until the second sketch arrived and we received the information on the white van from the DMV. Three monkeys and one sketch was all the information we had right now. I still felt stuck in the mud as I stood looking at the pictures of five, beautiful, young girls whose lives ended way too prematurely, and a sixth, I was still hoping we could save before it was too late.

After talking with his children, Christopher sat quietly at his desk watching Marty on the monitor. Wearing the earphones for the CD player, she listened to the music and seemed content lying on the bed tapping her foot to the rhythm of the CD's current song. She did not look up at the monitor, but instead, seemed to relax and accept her present situation. Everything she said and did substantiated her apparent desire to be accepted as part of his family. Even the children, with the exception of Angie, told him they wanted to meet Marty and see for themselves just what kind of big sister she would make. They would be able to tell in an instant if Marty were faking and playing all of them. After all, each had been in her shoes and knew what the adoption process was all about. Christopher sat pondering his next move. Should he bring her up and introduce her to the family, or should he continue to proceed with the adoption process the way he normally had proceeded in the past?

"What to do?" he said out loud. "What to do?" he repeated.

"You KNOW what you have to do." A voice said responding to his question. "You know exactly what you have to do. There is no question here to be answered. You do not vary or change your course one bit when it comes to the adoption process. This is something you already know, and yet, here you sit wasting god-damned time blubbering all over yourself, trying to convince yourself that someone would actually want to be part of your family. YOUR fucking family!"

Christopher turned in his chair to face the doorway looking for the source of the voice.

"Why do you have to come now?" he asked, looking into the shadows of the hallway just outside of the room's entrance. "Why now?" he repeated.

"You know why, Christopher." was the response from the hall. "Why do you question me? You are the one sitting here in your fantasy land wishing for things that cannot be. You are the one changing the rules mid-stream. Changes which will get your ass caught and sent off to be executed in some state, fucking prison. It's a good thing I did come along otherwise you would be suckling up to this girl like a newborn to its mother's tits! Think man! Think! What the hell are you doing?"

"But, Marty is sincere. She really does want to be part of the family. She has said…"

"She has said! SHE HAS SAID! Who gives a rat's ass what she has said! She just wants out of here any friggin' way she can! She is not an idiot. You abducted her, drugged her, tied her up and brought her here. What the fuck! Do you REALLY think she wants to be part of your family? For someone who is supposedly brilliant, you sure are pretty god-damned stupid at times. You do not have a choice, Christopher. She gets adopted just like the rest of the children, and if you don't do it accordingly, I will! There is no discussion here! You know I mean business."

"I know, but I was hoping…."

"Jesus Christ man! What do I have to do or say to make you see the light? This firl is playing you for a sucker! She is playing with your mind and will kill you in a split second if you trust her and give her a millisecond of an opportunity to do so. She is good, I'll give her that much. Only captive for a few days and she is already inside of your head playing mind-games with your thoughts. I'm surprised you even had enough self-control to kill that Bickford guy and the doc this afternoon: Which, by the way, you did a nice job with."

"All right! All right! I'll get ready for the adoption. I just wish for once I could do what I want to do. Just once! You're always sticking your nose in and ruining it for me. I do not understand why it always has to be YOUR way!"

This time there was no response from the hallway. Only shadows and darkness remained along with the silence. Christopher stood up from his chair and walked into the hall looking both ways, but no one was there. He knew as he stood alone in the gray shadows, that he had no choice. He would prepare to complete Marty's adoption immediately. Tonight, Marty would become one of his children. She would remain with him forever just like the children before her. Christopher still did not want Marty to be just one of his children. He knew she was special and wanted her to be the big sister for the family. He wanted her to sit next to him and share the immense pleasure of the family. However, his opinion had been overruled and he could not refuse to obey the voice in the shadows.

46

I stayed to have a cup of coffee with Ken in his office. We talked more about the probability that the same killer was responsible for Jerry and Doc's attacks as well as the deaths of the five young women from Meadow Pond. The oddity was the purchase of the three monkeys. For some reason it just did not fit. Why would a killer who was so meticulous with every detail of each crime try to purchase the monkeys in the area where he had buried his victims? Did he really believe that he was that invincible? Was he that confident that he would not be caught and exposed? After beating our heads against the wall for a while, I excused myself and headed home for a shower and a few hours of sleep. It was night time again, and I wanted to spend an hour or so with Peggy before she went to sleep. My drive home was filled with thoughts of Doc and Jerry. I heard myself sighing deeply, recalling the last few days and the time I spent time with both of them at the hospital. Both were good men: One of them, a very good friend and confidant.

"I want a piece of this bastard," I thought as the headlights of my Explorer reflected off the street sign to my house. Within a few minutes I was closing the front door to my house, and immediately felt the warmth of the pellet stove as I started to take off my jacket.

Peggy, hearing the door open and close shouted down from upstairs, "Is that you?"

"Who the heck is you?" I replied.

"I see the day has not ruined your sense of humor, sweetheart," she said, starting to laugh as she came down the stairway. "I'm glad you decided to come home for a while. You need to unplug and get some rest. Besides, your wife misses you and needs to snuggle on the couch with her hubby."

Peggy, wrapping her arms around me and burying her head into my chest, suddenly pulled away and said, "Snuggling will come after you take a shower, my love. You have a lot of mileage on that shirt you're wearing." Laughing and holding her nose, she turned and said, "I'll get you a towel while you jump in the shower. If you'd like, I could get two towels?"

"A two towel shower it is," I responded. I've always lived by the old saying, "Never look-a-gift-horse in the mouth." Tonight was no exception.

After a long shower, Peggy and I each ate a dish of ice cream sitting on the couch next to the pellet stove, enjoying the small fire and its warmth. It was already about ten-thirty when my cell phone rang. Peggy rolled her eyes at the interruption.

"Chief, Kosciak." I said shrugging my shoulders apologetically at Peggy.

"Ron, Ken Garber."

"Hey, Ken. Didn't get enough of me today?" I said, as Peggy raised her right hand shooting me the bird with a big smile on her face.

"Well, actually, I was just looking at the second composite of our perp. It definitely matches the first sketch, but, I think this one has much more facial detail around the eyes and mouth. I wanted to let you know that I'm faxing it over to your office so you'd have it first thing in the morning."

"I tell ya what, Ken. Why don't you fax it over to my house? I'm sitting here with Peggy. I'll give you the number."

I rattled off the number, and within a couple of minutes. I heard the electronic bleeping sound all fax machines make when they are transmitting. I stood fidgeting over the fax machine watching the pencil-lined face materialized on the plastic tray. Patience is not one of my strong points, and I found myself tapping my foot on the hardwood floor as if it would help to speed up the process.

Picking up the sheet, I looked at the man's face staring back at me, and experienced the same feeling of semi-recognition that I had experienced after looking at the first drawing earlier in the evening. The man's features were strangely familiar, but I could not place him. Yes, there was more detail from the second composite, but still not enough for me to recognize him. "Shit!" I blurted out.

"What is it hon." Peggy asked, walking over to rub my arm.

"I keep looking at these drawings but I can't place where I've seen this guy before. It's probably because he looks similar to a hundred guys I've seen over the years. Maybe it's just me being impatient and wanting to recognize him. Ken said the same thing. It's like we are supposed to know who this guy is. Frustrating as hell!"

Peggy looking over my shoulder at the drawing was shocked at the composite of the man's face on the fax paper. I felt her hand drop off of my arm down to her side. I heard her inhale sharply, filling her lungs without exhaling right away. Turning to look at her, I saw an expression of realization and disbelief on her face.

"What is it Peg?" I asked very slowly. "Do you know this guy? Seriously, do you know him?"

Peggy did not say a word nor did she utter a syllable. She slowly nodded her head up and down indicating recognition of the man in the drawing. She put her hand up to her mouth, as if to prevent the words of recognition from coming out. I knew she did not want to believe she knew this person looking back at her from the fax.

"Honey, you've got to tell me who this is," I said, putting my hand on her shoulder giving her a squeeze of assurance. "Come on, baby, who is it?"

Finally Peggy gasped, "That's Christopher Bradford, my masseur. You remember him. He just gave me a massage yesterday."

"Are you sure? I mean, are you absolutely positive that it's him?

"Honey, I'm telling you without a shadow of a doubt that that is a sketch of Christopher Bradford. You met him once about a year and a half ago at the mall. Don't you remember? You said he had dark, penetrating eyes."

"A year and a half is a long time." I replied. "I don't remember meeting him, but, that's probably why I thought I should have recognized him when I first saw the sketch. Holy shit, hon, you may have just solved this case. I've got to get dressed and get over to the station. This can't wait until morning. I've got to call Ken Garber right now and get him moving too. We have to try and nail this son-of-a-bitch tonight. Marty McMaster may still be alive. Every minute I sit on my butt is one minute less she may have to live, and besides, this monster had his slimy hands all over you. This gets more personal every minute. Real personal.

Peggy looked up into my face, held it in both of her hands and said, "You be careful. This guy doesn't care who he hurts. He's killed five women that you know of, abducted another girl, taken out Doc Cavanaugh and murdered Jerry Bickford. He will not hesitate to kill you the instant he lays eyes on you. Promise me you will be extra careful tonight. Don't be a freakin hero and go barging in there by yourself. You go by the book and follow the proper procedures. Promise me!"

Looking into her eyes, I reassured her, "Yes." After going upstairs to get dressed, I came back down to find Peggy waiting by the door with a hot cup of coffee to go.

"Thought you might need a -pick me up- coffee. I'll take a rain-check on the snuggling."

"I love you too, baby," I said kissing her as the door closed, not knowing what the rest of the night would bring.

47

"Kosciak to Larson, come in Derek." The radio at the police station echoed into the quiet of the night filling every room on the first floor with its reverberating clang. Derek was in the back room making a cup of coffee to help him cope with the long, lonely night-time shift when he heard me calling. Picking up the mike in the break room, he answered: "Larson here, Chief. Go ahead."

"Derek, I need you to call the Assistant District Attorney and have her call me right away. I'm on my way to the station, but, I need to talk with her ASAP and right now every second counts. I will fill you in when I get there. Just make sure she calls me now. It is extremely important. Make sure she understands the urgency of her response when you speak with her."

"Understood Chief, I'm on it right now."

I closed my cell phone and opened it immediately to dial Ken Garber's number. Listening to the ring of his phone, I felt an excitement in my stomach I had not felt since I was a sergeant in the army stationed in Viet-Nam. I used to get this high-energy feeling each, time we took off to fly a mission and every time I was involved in prisoner interrogations. Almost every day of my tour was dangerous, bu, there were certain days when the stakes were raised to a higher level and could cost you everything - everything being your life. It had been over forty years since the adrenalin pumped this fiercely through my veins. I felt the electricity of anticipation preparing me for what might happen tonight if Christopher Bradford did turn out to be our killer. Remembering what Peggy said to me before leaving home, I thought. "By the book Kosciak, by the book."

"Hello, Ken. Ron Kosciak. Sorry to bother you, but I need you to meet me at the station in Sutton right away."

"Not a problem, Ron. Give me twenty minutes. What's going on?"

"I was at home and Peggy saw the fax you sent with the composite of our killer. As soon as she looked at it she said she knew the guy. I almost fell on the friggin' floor. She says his name is Christopher Bradford, a masseur over here in Sutton. She just went to him for a massage yesterday. My skin's crawling just thinking about that bastard touching her. I'm on my way to the station right now. One of my officers is calling the assistant District Attorney. We'll need a search warrant mucho, pronto. She should be calling me any second. I'll see you at the station in a few."

"Okay, Ron. I'm puttin' my ass in high gear. Be right there."

As Ken hung up, my phone was already ringing.

"Chief Kosciak," I said steering to the left, barely missing a raccoon sauntering across the street dragging a piece of garbage rummaged from a nearby dumpster. It never gave me a second glance, tripping over its nocturnal meal with its front feet, as my Explorer cut one way and then back onto the right side of the street. "Furry little shit," I thought hearing the district attorney's voice on the other end of the line.

"Ron, Cindy Littleton. Officer Larson said there is some sort of emergency you need to talk to me about?"

"Sorry to bother you this late at night, Cindy, but we have a significant lead on the murders of the five girls who were found at Meadow pond the other day. We have a suspect whom we have identified from two composite sketches drawn by the State Police artist with the help of two different witnesses. I need a search warrant immediately, so we can go over to the Baker Building where this individual lives to interrogate him and search his property at the same time. He owns the building and his personal residence is also located on the premises. I just want to make sure the search warrant covers the entire building to include business and personal. How long would it take you to secure a search warrant for me?

Captain Garber from the Auburn State Police is going to meet me at my station here in Sutton within the half hour. I figure it will take about one hour to get the necessary people together and be ready to search that building. We believe another young woman is also being held captive in the building, so every minute is crucial to her survival."

"Okay, Chief. I understand what you're saying. I need the individual's name and the address of this Baker Building you just mentioned."

As I gave Cindy the information, my mind was racing at a hundred miles per hour. I thought about Marty McMaster and getting to her before this idiot could abuse her any more than he already had. Remembering those young girls with their disfigured and torn faces, I was almost sick thinking about what might be happening to Marty. I could only hope that if Christopher was our killer, and was the same person who killed Jerry and attacked Doc, that he had been too busy to spend much time torturing Marty. I needed Christopher Bradford to be the serial killer, and I needed Marty McMaster to be alive and not tortured to the point where she would never recover from the emotional and physical damages sure to be her legacy as a result of this ordeal.

"Chief," Cindy continued. "It will take me time to wake up the judge and get him to write up the warrant. It may take more than an hour, but I will explain to him the critical circumstances and try to move him along as quickly as I can. I will call you when I have the warrant. You go ahead with your people to the building. I will meet you there with the paper, and then you can go ahead with the search. Stay back a block or so away from the Baker Building, on Rivulet Street. I am driving a black, BMW convertible. I'll park and wait for you or vice-versa. Do not jump the gun here, Chief. If this is our guy, we want it done by the book. Understood?"

"How many people are going to tell me that tonight?" I thought answering Cindy in a most respectful way. "You bet your ass I'll go by the book. I don't want this monster to get away on some technicality. I wasn't born yesterday, Cindy."

Having to wait for the warrant was driving me crazy. Every part of me wanted to storm into that building immediately. But, with only two sketches, and no physical evidence to implicate Bradford, we were forced to follow the letter of the law. I knew instantly my emotions had overtaken my common sense. Before she could reply I said, "Cindy, I'm sorry. This case has me on edge and I don't want this bastard to get away."

"Ron, don't worry about it. I understand completely and I didn't take offense to anything you just said. Besides, I know Peggy, and if she can put up with you, so can I," she replied laughing as she hung up the phone.

"Oh. Great," I thought. "Another freakin' comedienne!"

All I could do now was assemble the team and get them ready for the unknown. Being night time, this mission would be much more difficult to run because of the darkened and shadowed areas within and around the building. The team would need to study the schematic of the building that Derek had spread out on a desk top in our center office before entering and beginning our search. These old buildings were like a rat maze in a laboratory – one wrong turn and you would be lost for valuable minutes trying to find your way out again. Those few minutes could very well cost someone their life. It would be imperative that the teams be made up of at least two officers. Two members per team would reduce the chance of getting disoriented and would help the officers cover each other's backs during the search. It is never good procedure to send only one officer into any situation of this type. Too many police officers and first responders are buried in cemeteries because their hearts overrode their heads. It is difficult for a police officer or EMT to stand back during an emergency situation waiting for back-up when the situation mandates the need for a partner.

I walked impatiently into my office to get my Kevlar vest and helmet. There was no choice but to wait for Ken Garber and the remainder of our group before driving over to the Baker Building to meet Cindy with our search warrant. I hoped Christopher was not there when we arrived so we could initiate our search for Marty before dealing with him. However, if we had to deal with him first, then so be it. He would be handled with any and all force required. There was a voice inside my head repeating over and over: "I hope he resists arrest."

48

Marty did not hear the cellar door unlock or open. The CD player's earphones were solidly inserted into her ears keeping all outside sounds at bay. Christopher walked sullenly down the hallway toward Marty's room. He did not enjoy being chastised so harshly. Why wasn't his opinion ever good enough? It was never good enough when his "mother" was still alive either. Just once he wished his opinion would carry some weight, or at least be considered. But no, once again he was the dummy, the dunce. In his heart he did not want to consummate Marty's adoption in the usual manner. Instead, he wanted to open up his home to her and introduce her to his children. He believed Marty not only genuinely wanted to become one of his children, but actually wanted to take on the role of the big sister, caretaking for the other children.

He stood in the doorway to Marty's room watching her for a few minutes. Her foot still tapped out the beat to the music while lying on her bed unaware of his presence. Upstairs, in another part of the Baker Building the adoption room was prepped and ready for the consummation procedure.

"I don't want to do this!" Christopher thought to himself clenching both hands into fists by his side to maintain control. Knowing that he did not have a choice, he took a deep breath and walked up to the side of Marty's bed. She was startled at first to see him standing there, but regained her composure very quickly.

"Hi. Christopher," she said lightly, following with a smile.

"She always looks right into my eyes." he thought before responding, "Hello Marty. I have given you a lot of thought in the last hour or so. I've decided I am going to take a chance and bring you upstairs to meet the rest of my family. Although I will not bind your feet, I will have to bind your wrists. I am the one taking the chance and do not want you trying to escape. Do you understand?"

"Yes, Christopher. I understand completely. It's okay, really. I won't try to escape, but, can I ask you one little favor before we go upstairs?"

"Of course, Marty, go ahead and ask." he said feeling defeated and powerless to prevent the adoption.

"Would you mind if I take my diary upstairs with us? If I'm going upstairs to meet the other kids, I'm assuming I will be staying upstairs with them in another room."

"You are absolutely right, Marty. You will be staying in another area upstairs. In fact, you will be right alongside the other kids watching over them for me. Yes, go ahead, get your diary and then I will tie up your wrists."

Marty stood up, walked over to the bureau and opened the drawer that held her diary. Holding the diary in one hand, she held her wrists together allowing Christopher to slip the plastic electrical tie in place, securing her wrists.

"I'm sorry, Marty, but I just can't take the chance right now. Perhaps, after a little time, you will have earned the privilege and I will remove the tie again. Walk ahead of me down the hallway to the door leading to the upstairs."

Marty did as she was asked, stepping out of her prison into the hallway for the last time. She was relieved to be going upstairs to meet the other kids. At least she would have someone to talk with for a change. Her room in the cellar was starting to drive her crazy. You can only listen to so many CD's and go to the bathroom so many times in a day.

Marty stood at the door leading to the upstairs waiting for Christopher to unlock it so they could proceed up the stairs. She was getting very curious to see what the upstairs looked like and hoped to get a glimpse of the outside. She might recognize something out of a window giving her clues as to where Christopher was holding her prisoner. Marty was not overconfident, but her level of hope was rising with every step she took closer to the top of the cellar stairway. She knew she would have to be quick if the opportunity for escape arose, and she was prepared in her mind to act swiftly if it did. Family or no family, she would seize whatever opportunity presented itself over the next few minutes. Escape was still at the top of her agenda.

Christopher reached around her right side and inserted the key into the door lock. He turned the doorknob and the door swung open. Marty looked up the stairs and was disheartened when she realized the upstairs was very dark. "He must have all of the window shades pulled," she thought, walking up the stairs to the first floor of the building. However, as soon as Marty reached the top step she spotted the hallway to the front door. Positioning the diary in her left hand, the binding of the diary was exposed to her right hand. On the dimly lit stairway, Christopher, two steps behind Marty, did not see her maneuvering the diary into position. He also could not have anticipated what followed as Marty reached the top of the stairs.

Because Christopher was a couple of steps behind Marty, he was a foot lower than she was standing on the top step. Although Christopher was used to the darkness of the upstairs, he too was coming up the stairs from the bright room where Marty was held captive. His eyes were adjusting to the darker upstairs as he stood for just a second waiting for Marty to continue walking into the hallway. When he saw Marty's body swiftly turning toward him, he instinctively knew he had misjudged her intensions. Marty's hateful, fiery look seemed to burn through his eyes into his head and, in that same instant, Christopher knew it was too late for him to react as the ball point pen hidden in the binding of Marty's diary entered his left eye socket piercing his brain.

Marty watched Christopher's body go limp, crumpling and falling backward down the cellar stairs, blood gushing from the eye where the pen was firmly impaled. Christopher, not making a sound, was dead before his body hit the bottom of the stairs with a dull thud. His arms and legs, twisted and broken, jutted out in unnatural directions. His head, twisted and contorted, was almost facing backward like a ventriloquists dummy lying on a table at a side show waiting to be picked up and brought to life. Marty stood watching for a few moments, hoping Christopher was dead, but half expecting to see him come back to life and charge up the stairs.

"Could he be playing dead?" she thought, watching for the slightest movement of his motionless form. No, he seemed to be dead. She could not believe her luck, hitting her mark on the first attempt. She knew the risk she took, but also knew her fate if she did not take it. Looking one final time at Christopher's lifeless body, Marty turned and started walking toward the front door of the building. Having taken only a few steps, she thought about the other children. They were hidden in this building somewhere, and, with Christopher being dead, they would need her help to escape. Stopping in the middle of the hallway, Marty began looking for doors to rooms where the kids might be kept. Seeing two doors on opposite sides of the hallway, Marty moved the closest and tried turning the knob. The door opened easily into a medium-sized room where she saw the monitor Christopher mentioned during their earlier conversation.

"This is where he sat watching me," she thought. "No wonder he knew everything I was doing when I was doing it."

Turning to inspect the rest of the room, Marty noticed the glass jars placed next to each other on a table against the wall. In the dim light, she could not tell what the jars contained and took a few steps closer to her newest surprise.

"What the...?" Marty started to say out loud, but before she could get the entire thought translated into words, an ether-soaked cloth was pressed onto her mouth and nose from behind sending the room spinning and then fading away into darkness.

Police work is sometimes more about waiting than it is about doing. Within forty-five minutes after speaking with Cindy Littleton, our task force of 14 officers, Ken Garber and myself, were parked a few blocks from the Baker Building waiting for the search warrant to arrive. One of our officers dressed in street clothes used his private vehicle to drive by the building to determine if any lights were on and in what areas of the building. He would also see if any vehicles were parked in the vicinity of the building, radioing the information to the team. It was a very low risk maneuver in order to ascertain the probability of running into someone when we finally entered the building. The drive-by was negative in that there seemed to be no lights on in the structure what-so-ever. No lights usually meant no people. This was a good sign for us once we gained entry. There were no vehicles parked in front of the building, either, which meant no quick getaway for our suspect if he was in the building. So far, everything seemed to be in our favor. In this type of operation you needed all the favors you can get!

We waited half an hour before I began getting nervous about our search warrant. What if the judge decided we didn't have enough information or legal grounds to issue one? My frustration was beginning to show when I finally saw headlights pulling up behind our convoy parked along the sidewalk on Rivulet Street. I watched

Cindy Littleton get out of her BMW and approach my Explorer. She had a disgruntled look on her face as she reached my driver's side window.

"Chief Kosciak, you will never know what I had to go through to get this search warrant. The first judge was away for a few days of fishing in Maine; the second judge did not answer his telephone, and the third judge was watching a reality T.. shows and didn't see that I had called until about thirty minutes ago! Jesus H. Christ almighty! Sometimes I wish I was a real estate lawyer. The most they have to worry about are a few percentage points on the interest rate and whether or not the toilet flushes properly."

"Cindy thanks for hand-delivering this. Makes the job much easier for us. You're going to stay around while we do this, right?" I asked, mostly out of professional courtesy, but also knowing that having the assistant district attorney present while we executed the warrant would solidify our case if it came to trial in the months ahead if Christopher Bradford was our killer. Cindy would be our judicial eyes and ears to help us keep this operation "by the book."

Having the warrant in hand, I gave the signal to Ken and the others to move out. We would approach the building from four directions to cover all sides of the building. This would minimize the opportunity for anyone to escape unseen as we approached and entered the building. Just because we saw no lights on in any of the building's rooms did not mean the building was empty. In fact, the one person I wanted to find in the building was Marty McMaster. My hopes were flying high as our vehicles stopped at their predetermined areas. The teams dispersed, each team approaching the structure from their designated route. Ken Garber would take team number two in thru the back entrance to the building. Teams three and four each took a side entry position but remained outside of the building. I would take team number one in through the front entrance.

Kim would be first to enter the building with me close behind. Derek Larson and another officer would follow up the rear. Each officer carried a .40-caliber, Glock22 handgun. Each team was also armed with one Remington, 870-shotgun, and either a Heckler & Koch, MP5 assault weapon or a Ruger, Mini-14 tactical carbine. Night vision eyewear was being used by everyone on all four teams. Body armor and helmets would protect each of us from most ammunition fired our way. Most, not all.

Holding her Glock with outstretched arms poised to fire, Kim entered the doorway first. The door gave little resistance to the battering ram, breaking away from the door-jam immediately after the first hit. Kim slanted off to the side wall of the hallway crouching down onto one knee while visually surveying the darkened environment for any movement or possible booby-traps. Seeing none, she signaled the rest of us to enter. Once we were inside, I signaled Ken Garber on my tow-way that our team was inside the building and for his team to enter from the rear.

We quickly searched the outer office and massage parlor finding nothing out of the ordinary. Moving to the back of the office through a locked door, which we persuaded to open in the same fashion as the front doors, we found ourselves back in the darkened hallway with two doors on alternating sides and a third door at the end of the hall. Looking back over my shoulder, I could see the front doors where the moonlight reflected off of the flooring dimly lighting the hallway. There was a small amount of light coming from the other side of the door at the end of the hall but not enough to illuminate the length of the hallway. Kim and I took the first door to the left while Derek and his partner took the door on the opposite side. Each team entered their respective rooms simultaneously without any resistance. Entering our room, the first item I noticed was the monitor sitting on the desk top. There was obviously a camera positioned somewhere observing someone being kept in the room where the lens was located. Looking closer at the monitor, the room looked to be a girl's bedroom. I could feel the sweat beading up on my neck and forehead realizing there was no one in the room. The room was empty. Had this room been Marty's prison since her abduction? Was she already dead?

"Where the hell is this room? We have to find it quickly," I thought signaling to Kim that we needed to move right away to begin looking for the room. Making a visual sweep of the room we currently occupied, there did not seem to be anything else out of the ordinary: a sitting chair by the desk, a small sofa and a long wooden table against the far wall with nothing on it.

Derek's team was already waiting in the hallway when Kim and I came out of our room. They had not found anyhing of importance. Their search found a storage room filled with items Christopher used for his massage and tanning business placed on shelves and put away in totes stacked on the floor. They found no traces of anything illegal hidden away.

The only door left was the door at the end of the hallway. This door was ajar allowing a small amount of light to filter in from the other side. I took the lead, and the four of us quietly and cautiously approached the door with all weapons trained on the opening. I slowly pulled the door open exposing the cellar stairway.

Kim again assumed a crouching position while I trained my Glock straight down the stairs from a standing position. We both spotted Christopher's distorted body at the bottom of the stairs. My first impulse was to rush down the stairs to see if he was still alive.

"Dummy" I thought to myself looking at Kim, giving her the signal to proceed.

Kim slowly went down to the body and checked the carotid artery for any sign of a pulse. She looked up at me shaking her head left to right. There was no sign of life. Kim lifted her night vision goggles to look further into the brightly lit cellar area. She motioned the all clear sign, and the rest of us proceeded down to the cellar finding ourselves in yet another hallway. At the bottom of the stairs, I saw the pen sticking out of Christopher's eye. "A unique and unpredictable method," I thought. "Someone knows how to improvise."

Lifting out night-vision goggles to see more clearly, out team passed a small bathroom on our left. Moving a little further down the cellar hallway, we entered the doorway to the room being watched on the monitor upstairs. I noted that the bed was unmade and rumpled. There was a CD player and earphones on the bed linen, and I knew I had been in this room before. As I was thinking about my déjà vu moment, Kim looked at me and whispered, "This is Marty McMaster's room. Remember the day we met with her parents, they let us into to her bedroom to look around? Chief, she was here. Marty was here..

While the four of us were inspecting the room we heard footsteps in the hallway. Our team separated creating more distance between each of us, two taking low aiming positions and two of us aiming chest level -- all toward the doorway. Before anyone entered, we heard Ken Garber call out.

"This is Captain Ken Garber of the State Police. Whoever is in that room, I want you face down on the floor right now. I will not ask a second time. Assume the position on the floor now!"

"Ken. It's us. This is Kosciak. We've found Marty's prison cell."

Ken entered the room leaving the rest of his team in the hall to protect our backs. "Kosciak, you're a real dumb ass tonight." I thought, mentally scolding myself. "Why didn't you leave one or two of your team out there to cover your backs?"

"Ron, we didn't find anything coming in the back door. The garage is empty and there doesn't seem to be anyone anywhere in the rest of the building. I checked with the teams outside and everything is quiet. No one has even walked by the building since we entered. Except for our dead boy back there with the pen sticking out of his head, this place is empty."

"Well, I think our mystery just got bigger and more confusing." I said to everyone in the room. "We know Marty was being held here. We know this is a very close replica to her bedroom at her home. We know Christopher Bradford owns this place and therefore most likely is Marty's kidnapper. However, what we don't have is any connection between Marty's abduction and the murders of the five girls! What we also do not have is Marty McMaster! Her abductor is lying dead in a pile of broken pieces at the bottom of the cellar stairs with his head twisted one hundred and eighty degrees out of place, and there is no sign of her anywhere? It doesn't make any freakin sense! No sense at all! If she had escaped, we would have heard something from someone. Her parents would have called it in to the station or someone else would have found her. Having escaped from here she would have been free to go anywhere for help. She would only have to go a few hundred feet in any direction to find help. What the Christ am I missing here folks?"

Kim looked at me and simply said, "Bradford was not alone. There must be more than one killer, or perhaps an accomplice"

The white van drove over the back roads of Sutton and Auburn keeping within the speed limits trying not to attract any unwanted attention. The driver knew most of the Sutton police force was standing inside the Baker Building right at that instant scratching their collective heads wondering just what the hell was going on. Having missed the police teams by only a minute, the driver watched their vehicles converge on the Baker Building in the rear view mirror as the van turned the corner at the end of the street. There would be limited time to reach the cover of the safe house before they put out an APB on the van. However, the driver still felt very confident the trip would be concluded in plenty of time before police actually started cordoning off the roadways. The drive to the safe house would only take about a half to three-quarters of an hour keeping the vehicle within the speed limits, including all of the stop lights and stop signs along the way. After retracing this route a hundred times over the last three years, the driver was very familiar with every foot of blacktop and every pot hole waiting to bruise an unsuspecting tire. With his cargo securely bound and sleeping soundly, the drive was at least quiet and pleasant while the radio played R&B hits from the 60's and 70's.

"Too bad about Christopher," The driver thought. "I don't know why he wouldn't listen to what I was trying to tell him. Now look at him; a heap at the bottom of the stairs. Killed by a stick from a Bic. I told him to keep his eye on Marty, but I never thought he would take me that literally!" Amused, a smile came and disappeared quickly in the darkened cab of the van as the vehicle rose and fell, the front suspension reacting to the first few feet of a narrow, wooden bridge crossing over the Blackstone River.

"I'm actually surprised something like this didn't happen sooner." The driver continued to think. "Being dead is better than being in custody. He probably would have spilled his guts at the first sign of pressure during the interrogation, leaving me exposed and next in line for the electric chair. They'd probably use lethal injection in our case just to get even with us for the girls." A smug expression overtook the driver's face because he knew, that inside of his body there was not a shred of caring anywhere to be found. He truly did not give a shit about anyone or anything. There was no room for fear or indecision. Both were signs of weakness. This heart was composed of hatred. This nervous system, hardened due to years of systematic brutality.

"I bet even God himself would hesitate to interact with me, or try to save my soul. After all, it does say in the Good Book that He is all knowing, and He knows just how black and soulless I really am. How do you save something that doesn't exist?" Another facial change, as his expression went from being smug to being sarcastic and fatalistic.

"Even the ole Satan-bird himself better give me wide birth, because I will even rattle his cage if he pisses me off." The driver listened to Sam Cooke singing his 1963 blues song, "Mean Old World." The irony struck the driver as being funny, and an eruption of loud laughter filled the inside of the van. The cargo still sleeping quietly on the floor in the back of the van, was unaware her situation was deteriorating swiftly the closer the van got to the safe house.

"Mean ole World." the thought lingered in the driver's mind while the van continued its journey through the wintery, night-time shadows.

51

Our team spent two hours looking through the Baker Building after finding Christopher Bradford's broken, dead body at the bottom of the cellar stairs. An APB had been issued by the state police for the van, and an Amber alert for Marty. As Ken and I were inspecting the stainless steel surgical table and associated carts and cutting implements in a large, mirrored room where Christopher undoubtedly disfigured and murdered the girls from the pond, I had two additional cruisers searching for Marty within the town limits. This mirrored room, used for many years to hold weekly ballroom dances, had become Christopher's adoption chamber where he committed gruesome anatomical destruction, no more twirling dance gowns. Each implement, surgical cart and table was spotless and meticulously cleaned just like Christine Sawyer's car when it was found in the state park after her disappearance. We were beginning to form some consensus about what had transpired just before our arrival as we continued examining the room. Ken and I agreed Marty was the person who stuck the ballpoint pen through Christopher's eyeball into his brain. This type of assault would have been improvised on the spur of the moment, not like the use of a handgun where you planned to take someone out. Marty probably surprised him as she reached the top of the stairway before Christopher could make any adjustments to her assault. It was obvious to us that after the attack Marty would have been alone in the hallway and quite able to run toward the front door, open it, and gain her freedom. There would be nothing nor anyone in the hall to stop her. If she knew there was another person helping Christopher, she would not have killed him while still being in the presence of the other killer. No, she thought she was free as soon as Christopher took his fall from grace. Therefore, the only logical conclusion was that the other person must have surprised Marty, overpowered her, and abducted her a second time. We believed Marty was still alive. We reasoned the second killer would not have carried off a dead girl's body when he could leave her in this mirrored room on display for someone to find. Another disfigured girl lying on a surgical table would offer much more gratification for the killer than dragging her dead body around the countryside. At least that is what Ken and I thought. We might be way off base with our hypotheses, but sometimes hunches play out better than physical evidence. In this case, hunches were all we had to go on.

Located on one of the carts were three bottles, each containing one of the chemicals used for the lethal injection procedure. Hypodermic needles were covered on the same tray by white, surgical towels. I could only imagine the heightened ecstasy Christopher or his partner must have felt while performing their Marquis De Sade acts with the mirrored walls illuminating and magnifying their unrestrained, torturous sickness.

"More than evil," I thought. "Much, much, more than evil. There aren't any words in the English language to describe how sick these bastards truly are," I said out loud shaking my head in disgust.

One of the mirrored panels moved inward as Kim entered the room.

"Chief, the coroner is here to take Bradford away. Is it okay to let him go?" she asked, looking at the instruments and implements precisely placed next to each other on the portable carts.

"Yeah, Kim, it's okay. Doctor Faldwell from the ME's office came by and let us know his initial exam of Bradford was done," I said without looking away from the bottle of Pancuronium on the cart. "I need you to come right back after talking with the guys from the coroner's office. We need to start thinking about tracking down this second person or people who have taken Marty." Kim nodded, and left the room, the mirrored partition closed with a thud behind her leaving the walls once again reflective all the way around the room.

"Ken, I would like to have one of my officer's team up with one of your officers to research and create a historical timeline on Bradford. We don't know much about his personal life or history. Place of birth, mother and father's names, current whereabouts of each, siblings, schools he attended, military service, marriages or ex-wives, DMV information and credit report for starters. What do you think?"

"Do you have anyone you can send over to Auburn? We're better equipped for collecting that data and have better access to NCIC than you do in Sutton."

As we stood talking, Kim opened the panel. We brought her up to date on what we were doing regarding the investigative team for Bradford's history and I instructed her to get Todd involved right away.

"Kim, even if you have to physically drag Todd out of bed by his ankles yourself, I need him on this right away."

Kim, smiling at my weak attempt to be dramatic, said that she was sure Todd's wife would have something to say about that, but that she would impress upon Todd the urgency of my request.

"Have him go right over to the Auburn facility and meet up with…" I looked to Ken for a completion to my sentence.

"Oh!" Ken responded a little embarrassed having been a million miles away in thought. "What was it you were saying, Ron?"

"Who do you want our guy to meet up with at your facility so we can get going on Bradford's information?"

"Have him see the desk sergeant. I'll leave instructions with him.

We had no idea if the person, or people who took Marty, knew about our arrival or had seen our vehicles converging on the building. Assuming the worst condition, that our presence was known, would increase Marty's chances for survival. Her abductor would probably want to keep her alive for use as a hostage should we catch a whiff of his trail and locate his hiding place. I hoped, as we left the Baker Building, that this was the case. Marty needed all the help she could get. I had no way of knowing, as I walked out of the building, that my assumptions regarding Marty's captor were so far from the truth.

Marty immediately recalled waking up like this a few days before. The foggy cloud in her head was difficult to penetrate with clear thoughts. Some thoughts seemed to begin clearly only to vaporize within seconds of their inception. She kept reaching mentally for reality, but it was always a fingertip away - elusive, but there to tease her waking mind.

In her dreams, Marty could see Christopher's bloody face falling backward down the stairs -- the ballpoint pen protruding from his eyeball just where she left it after striking her blow for freedom. But what then? What had happened just after she entered the room with the jars?

"THE JARS!" she thought, remembering them placed side by side on the table just before everything went dark. "Some of the jars were looking at me!" another thought dulled and distorted by the drug used to put Marty into an unconscious stupor. "Eyes. Lips. Ears. In the jars. In the fucking jars! I must be dreaming. This must be a nightmare! In those fucking jars!" she repeated, as her eyes slowly began to open bringing her closer to her new horror.

She realized her legs and wrists were bound once again. However, this time she was also gagged. She could breathe through her nose, but her mouth was trussed with cloth and duct tape preventing any breathing or speaking.

"Where the hell am I?" she thought. What the hell is going on? What happened to me back there?"

The clearer Marty's thoughts became, the more memories of those last minutes flooded to the forefront of her mind. She knew that the jars scared her to death when she saw eyeballs looking out at her suspended in their formaldehyde solution. But just as she was about to scream, something…no…someone put a hand over her face.

After that everything went black.

"Someone else was there!" she thought with renewed panic running through her body. "Someone else has me now! Who? Why the fuck are they doing this to me? For Christ's sake, what the FUCK is happening?"

As these new realizations settled into her mind, Marty tried to focus on the room in which she was now being held captive. Unlike the room Christopher built for her, this room was nothing more than plain, drab, gray, concrete blocks and mortar. There were no windows and only one gray, metal door in or out of the room. She was lying on an old, metal, military bed with a three inch mattress. There were no blankets or pillows or anything else in the room. One very bright, bulb hung from the center of the ceiling illuminating the room. The room was about twelve feet by twelve feet with one small air vent sticking out from one of the concrete blocks about two inches from the ceiling. Marty knew that whoever was keeping her here was not concerned about her being comfortable. Remembrances of home were a thing of the past. This room represented the true meaning of the words "total isolation".

Hearing the door opening, Marty looked over to see a person walking into the room holding a plastic bucket. The person, presumably a man, wore black slacks, black shoes, a black sweatshirt, and a black mask covering his entire face. The mask looked to be plastic which was sewn to a cloth hood hiding the entire head. The person walked over to the corner of the room furthest from Marty's bed, pulled a roll of toilet paper out of the bucket, and set both on the floor. Two plastic water bottles and a few packages of peanut butter crackers were also in the bucket. These the person haphazardly tossed over to Marty, not caring if they landed on the bed or on the floor. Still maintaining complete silence, the person walked back over to the door leaving the room. The only sound Marty heard after the person left the room was that of the lock being engaged from the other side.

"I don't know what good the bottled water and crackers will do me with my mouth taped up like this." she thought to herself. "A lot of good a friggin' bucket is going to do if I can't get my slacks down to take a leak. What does this asshole want me to do, sit over the bucket, piss my pants and let it drain through? What the hell!"

As she was contemplating the situation regarding her bodily functions and the bucket, the door opened again. Raising the index finger of his right hand in front of his mouth, signaling Marty to be quiet, he closed the door re-entering the room. The man stood and stared at Marty lying on the bed. The room filled with his silence making Marty afraid for her life as she waited for this stranger's next move. After five minutes of silence, the man walked over to the bed, bent over, grabbed a corner of the duct tape covering Marty's mouth and forcefully ripped it away. The duct tape burned as its adhesive fought to hold onto her flesh before letting go, allowing the rolled up cloth to fall out of her mouth onto the mattress. Before the cloth hit the mattress Marty began to speak.

"Wha…" was all she was able to say before a black-gloved backhand smashed into the side of her face, sending her head against the cinder block wall. Remaining silent, the man walked to the door, turned one more time to look back at Marty trying to recover from the blow. He shook his head and gave a low chuckle as he closed the door.

Marty's head was reeling from the impact of the blow, saliva beginning to fill her mouth in response to the sudden jolt. She had learned a very quick and valuable lesson: do not speak unless asked to do so. Whoever this person was, he would hurt her without hesitation - he was no Christopher!

The abandoned State Hospital in Westborough was the perfect place to occupy a hidden facility for unnatural activities. Over three thousand acres of rolling inclines and crisscrossing pathways, covered mostly with trees and overgrown brush made it easy to use one of the outbuildings on the back side of the property without being detected. The hospital began closing its doors in 2009 leaving only a few mental health programs active within the main structure until its final closure in 2010. Due to state, budgetary cut-backs, grounds care was almost non-existent at this particular site, making it easy to choose an outbuilding located at the far rear of the property completely hidden from any main roads. There was only one dirt access road to the building that came in off a single lane road the town very seldom maintained. Access at almost any time of the day or night held minimal chance of being observed.

The building where Marty was being held was built into the side of a hill. It had a large, manual, spring-loaded, overhead, garage door and one man-door visible from the dirt road. Grass, weeds and nature's debris littered the area in front of the doors. If you did not already know this building existed, you could easily walk past and never notice it. Even in the winter months, the leafless scrub and brush camouflaged the building within the hill.

Splicing into a nearby power feed running through the property supplied ample electricity. The garage kept the vehicles out of sight. No one ever came to check on the building. Video monitors do not lie, and there were half a dozen cameras set up in the area surrounding the hideaway to verify that fact. If someone did happen upon this hideaway, alarms would sound and a tunnel running three quarters of a mile underground to another utility building offered the perfect escape route.

Originally this site was going to be home base for the abductees and their adoption processes. It was thought the vast size of the property would lend itself to secretive areas where remains could be buried and never found - a large cemetery without stones. But, after Christopher found the Baker Building and became obsessed with the mirrored room, plans changed. His constant whining finally drove his partner to relent and the Baker Building was purchased, becoming their prime location. Although the risk of discovery was higher at the Baker Building, one had to admit the adrenaline rush performing the procedure in front of all those mirrors, right in the middle of a town, was indescribably titillating. Until tonight, this building served as a secret place where they could hide for an unlimited amount of time if need be. Under the present conditions, it looked as though their theory was going to be proven out. With Christopher's death, Marty's kidnapping and the intense search sure to follow, it might be a very long time before the current tenants would see the light of day. Not only was there an ample supply of food, water and personal items, Marty had been brought along to supply the entertainment!

"It felt good to give that bitch a good crack in the head. I wanted to hit her again on the other side just to even things up," his thought, provoking a feeling of complete power and control. "She may have played those mind fuck games on Christopher, but, the only thing she will play in my world is a harp at the pearly gates!" His words echoed within the concrete chamber.

"Baby… you got a one way ticket to paradise…" he sang. He took a cold beer from the refrigerator, turned on the police scanner and sat to relax in his recliner. "All the comforts of home, my friend, all the comforts of home."

54

By the time we concluded the follow up meeting with the teams from the Baker Building event and I arrived home for a much needed shower, Peggy was already fast asleep. I mixed myself a Captain and coke, with only a few ice cubes, to enjoy while I sat and processed the events of the day for about the thirtieth time since leaving the police station after the meeting ended. Although we still did not have any concrete proof there was a second person involved with this whole mess, with the exception of the missing white van, my flags were standing straight up and I knew we were dealing with someone just as evil as Christopher Bradford.

After taking another long shower, I very cautiously and quietly slipped into bed next to Peggy trying not to wake her. Pulling the blankets and bedspread up ever so....o slowly, positioning my head on the pillow precisely in the right spot so I would not have to move again and, thinking I had not disturbed her sleep, Peggy's voice filtered through the darkness sarcastically saying, "So, crash, what brings you to bed this time of night? You know I won't be able to fall back to sleep. You also know that I will hold this against you forever and ever!"

"Sorry, baby, I tried to be quiet and not wake you up."

"Well, my dearly NOT so beloved, I would say on a scale of one to ten, ten being the greatest level of failure, you have earned an eleven!"

"Baby, I'm really sorry. We found Christopher Bradford dead over at the Baker Building tonight. Looks like you were right. Christopher probably was responsible for the murders and the abduction of Marty McMaster. It took us a while to process the crime scene and get Bradford's body removed."

"Holy, shit! Ugh! My skin is beginning to crawl. That freak had his dead hands all over me the other day! Holy, holy shit!" she repeated getting out of bed while pulling off her winter pajamas.

"What the hell are you doing?" I asked picking my head up off of pillow trying to focus in the dim, night light.

"I've got to take a shower!" she replied still racing to get her clothing off. "I feel dirty and disgusting, honey! He had those friggin, cold paws on me! I'm DISGUSTED!"

As Peggy ran out of the room to the shower, I thought about our rolls being reversed and what I would feel like if I were in her shoes. I kind of understood where she was coming from but, could not stay awake long enough to contemplate the psychology of the incident. Within a couple of minutes I was fast asleep. Before letting go of my last thought of the day, I wondered how many of Bradford's other clients would be running to the shower once they found out who this guy really was and what he really did. I drifted off to sleep no longer worrying about who Christopher Bradford was; his death; the abduction of Marty McMaster or Peggy's frantic shower. Sleep has a way of removing one from life's situations, and, right now I was very thankful to be removed!

The morning's sunlight shining in my eyes woke me once again to the smells and aromas floating up the stairs out of the kitchen. "Peggy: cooking omelets?" I thought. This time I was not going to wait for my cell phone to ring cancelling breakfast. I was starving! Rolling my over aged butt out of bed, attempting to slip my feet into my wool lined slippers - which always point the wrong way – I cursed when one of them disappeared under the bed. Again! Bending down, I blindly felt under the bed for the lost slipper. The slipper finally rescued, I was on my way down the stairs to find out what mystery ingredients Peggy was adding to the omelet before she folded it over on the griddle.

To my culinary surprise, Peggy was cooking her Dad's version of French toast, which, in my book, was the best French toast I had ever eaten. Her dad may be a crotchety ole bastard with a liturgy of cuss words dating back to Paleolithic times, but he was one hell of a cook. He also makes the best apple pies in the world. It may seem a bit exaggerated, but, I can assure you, it is not far from the truth. Sitting at the kitchen table, I was preparing myself for a chow down, my eyes focusing on the griddle, my stomach growling in anticipation, thankful for Peggy and thankful for my life.

"Hey, you, about time you got your butt out of bed. I figured the smell of these babies frying in the pan would get your attention. How many do you want? By the way, the coffee is ready too. Pour us both a cup."

Walking over to the coffee pot, I began pouring us both a cup of steaming hot coffee as Peggy continued. "Sorry about bolting out of bed like that last night. I was totally freaked out."

"I understand hon, not a problem with me. I'm good with it. You did what you needed to do for yourself. I'm sorry I was not able to keep my eyes open until you got back from your shower. I was dog ass tired and just could not stay awake."

Changing the subject Peggy asked, "What's the status with Marty? Do you guys have any ideas at all?"

"The only part of the investigation going right now that might shed some light on Christopher Bradford is an investigation into his personal history. We've got to turn something up somewhere or Marty's chances are slim to none! These guys just don't leave any clues behind. They ARE that good at what they do. It pisses me off to feel this helpless, but there is nothing I can do." I replied lowering my head while I stood next to the coffee percolator listening to its blurp, blurp, blurp. I knew if something did not materialize and materialize soon, Marty McMaster's chances of surviving this ordeal were minimal if not non-existent. I honestly believed in my heart Marty was still alive when she left the Baker Building, I just did not know how much longer that belief would be true.

Two serial killers working together; almost unheard of anywhere in the history of serial killings and, of course, I had to be the one smack in the middle of the exception to the rule.

There was nothing in the room Marty could use as a weapon or device to help her escape. She knew instinctively this person had covered all of the bases. The Army bed was in perfect shape. Her attempts to dislodge or remove any of the metal links that interconnected the platform were futile. The metal handle for the pee bucket was removed as well and Marty had never heard of killing anyone with a plastic water bottle or a package of peanut butter crackers. She was at a loss sitting on the bed looking at her drab, isolated surroundings.

Shaking out the remaining fog from her brain, Marty knew her present situation with this individual was much more unpredictable than when she was being held captive by Christopher. She had at least been able to start a dialogue with Christopher, something not possible in her present situation. A feeling of hopelessness began to overtake her as she sat listening to the air vent push new oxygen into her cinder block prison. Wondering if this idiot, like Christopher, was watching her right now sent a chill racing through her extremities making her shudder on the bed. Marty was correct in her assumption. There was a camera lens positioned overhead inside the air duct hidden from her view watching every move she made. What she did not know: there was an audio microphone hidden there as well, an item Christopher overlooked when installing the system in the Baker Building.

"I have used up every card I have in the deck," Marty thought to herself. "The only cards left are the two Jokers, and whoever this joker is, he knows he is holding all of the other cards." Marty was felt defeated and exhausted from days of captivity and uncertainty. Not knowing from second to second if she was going to live or die was taking its toll.

"There must have been two of them working together all along." She thought. "There is no other explanation. Whoever this person is, he or she must have been there when Christopher was bringing me upstairs. But if that is the case, what was Christopher bringing me upstairs for? Those jars on the desk full of eyes and stuff were not just decorations! They must have come from real people: people like me! You don't keep jars filled with fucking eyeballs and stuff lying around a friggin' room for the fun of it! Well, not if you are normal. Were they going to do the same thing to me? Is that what this asshole is planning to do to me? Christ! This nut case is going to have a fight on his hands. I'll go out screaming and kicking ass until my last breath!" she spoke these words defiantly, allowing them to linger in the air as renewed energy began to fill her spirit. Marty would need all of the energy she could muster if she were going to survive.

Marty's abductor watched and listened processing similar thoughts about her mortality. Sitting in his chair, the unrelenting restlessness began once again to take control of him. He would not try to fight it or prevent it from engulfing him. He relished its power and precision. There was no second guessing. There were no "maybe's" in its cunning and execution. It was black and white. You live or you die. There was not and never would be any in between. It would not happen today, but in the very near future Marty McMaster would join the rest of the children and be part of the family which now took up residence here in their new subterranean home. Soon the excitement, the rush, the power of being completely in control would be the only emotion he would feel. It would infiltrate every cell, every muscle and every bone, obliterating any simplistic thoughts of forgiveness or redemption. It had nothing to do with Heaven or Hell. It only had to do with him and the absolute power of adoption.

"Control !" he thought. The madness escaped him in the form of a twisted grin.

I spent most of the day reviewing new information sent by other police departments and state agencies regarding the murdered girls. No pertinent information was discovered concerning our killer or his victims. I was purposely holding off contacting any of the victim's families to inform them of Bradford's death and involvement in the murders of their daughters. I was hoping Todd and the Staties would find a solid piece of information leading us to killer number two. The information I was about to receive as my phone began ringing would cheer me up exponentially.

"Chief Kosciak," I said even before the receiver was in position next to my ear.

"Good morning, Chief. My name is Jenna Fitzpatrick. I'm an ICU nurse over here in Milford."

"Good morning Nurse Fitzpatrick. I hope you have some good news for me about Doc." I said with an edge of foreboding.

"Chief, I wanted to personally call you and let you know Doc is going to make it. He rallied early this morning and his vital signs are as strong as any thirty year old. We think he might be out of ICU sometime later today or early tomorrow morning if he continues to improve."

"Nurse Jenna Fitzpatrick, I want to thank you very much for your call! I've been knee deep in a swamp of sh…it! Ah! Sorry, Jenna. What I meant to say was…"

"Chief, for Christ's sake, you don't have to apologize to me! You don't think we have swamps of shit over here too? I'm so deep in shit over here sometimes, I need scuba gear to keep breathing and find my way around! Chief, you say all the shits you want. Doc is going to make it and that is all that matters right now."

"Thanks for letting me off the hook, Jenna. You're gracious as well as a hot shit. No pun intended," I said with a laugh. "You make sure you give Doc a big hug for me. I know he'll cringe when you tell him the hug is from me. Tell him I'd send along a kiss too, but I'm afraid he would relapse and kick off on us!"

"Aren't you the hugsy well-wisher," she said with a chuckle as she hung up the phone.

"I will make it one of my top priorities to meet you nurse Jenna, Fitzpatrick to deliver a personal thank you. After all, you are a hot shit," I thought, hanging up my phone, already dialing Ken Garber's number over in Auburn.

Ken did not answering his phone. As I was leaving him a message, my cell phone began to ring. It was Ken calling me.

"Hey, Ken, I was just leaving you a message on your office phone. What's up?"

"Ron. I think we may have found something out about Bradford that will give us a place to start looking. Can you get over here quick? I think it would be better if you took a look at this in person instead of me trying to explain it over the phone."

"Yeah, sure Ken. I'm out the door as we speak. See you in a few."

Driving over to Auburn, my thoughts once again turned to Marty McMaster. I was feeling personally responsible for her welfare. Everybody and their brother could tell me it wasn't my fault, but in my heart I could not let the feeling of responsibility go. If we had arrived just a few minutes earlier last night at the Baker Building, Marty might well be alive and at home with her parents, and I would be writing a police report describing the capture or death of both killers. But the reality was that the weight of this responsibility resided in my soul. No matter how hard I tried to relinquish this burden, it would be futile. The guilt was mine to keep until this all played out one way or the other.

I looked in my rear view mirror as I took a right turn on Route 20 toward the State Police facility in Auburn. A white van followed a few vehicles behind my Explorer as I continued through my turn. Watching the van, it took the same right turn maintaining the same distance from my cruiser. My blood began to rush a little faster as I turned right into a small strip mall pulling my Explorer in front of a bridal shop.

"Won't this be a tip off if the guy is actually following me?" I thought feeling a little less masculine sitting behind the steering wheel.

The van proceeded past the strip mall continuing up the street. Backing out of the parking space, I pulled the Explorer back onto the roadway watching for the white van up ahead. Half a mile up the street I spotted the van parked at a 24-hour convenience store. The driver was inside the store talking to the cashier. I pulled in to check the van and driver out. Pulling up behind the van, I parked so that my Explorer was out of the driver's line of sight, but in such a way he would not be able to move his van if he decided to run. Stepping down out of the Explorer, unclipping the clasp on my holster, I proceeded very cautiously beside the passenger' door of the van. I pulled out my Glock. There were no side windows in the van. A black partition separated the back of the van from the driver's compartment. One small peep hole allowed the driver to look from the cab into the back of the van. The van certainly fit an abductor's needs for committing a kidnapping. Every sense was telling me to be on my toes and to be prepared for anything.

There was nothing in the cab of the van to indicate that it was anything but a delivery vehicle. A few papers were on the passenger's seat and a yellow pencil protruded from the open, unused ashtray. Other than these two items, the cab was clean. But, clean, thus far, was their way of doing business.

Watching the two men through the store window, it appeared to me the two men were arguing. As I entered the store, both men stopped talking and looked in my direction. Continuing to walk past them, I walked toward the wall coolers containing bottled water and soft drinks at the back of the store. My heart was racing even faster than before as I tried listening to what they were saying to one another. Opening one of the coolers, I reached in for a bottle of apple juice, continuing to keep my other hand closed on the handle of my Glock. It was difficult to distinguish their heated words, but I thought I heard the cashier telling the driver that even though a dozen bags of his "Hot Tamale" chips were stolen off of the rack last night, it was not the stores responsibility to reimburse him for his loss. I breathed a quiet sigh of relief, calmly walking up the cash register to pay for my drink. The driver, never giving me a second look, went right back to tearing the cashier a new ass as I walked back to my Explorer and drove away.

I was only five minutes from the State Police facility, and was relieved to know my paranoia seemed to be coming from my over active imagination. Driving away from the bridal shop, I missed spotting the second white van which was pulled over watching me play policeman at the convenience store.

Jarred "Gabby" Henderson, as he was known ten years ago when he directed the "Angels of Mercy" orphanage in upper state New York, wondered why the Massachusetts State Police were attempting to get in touch with him. Today, as the CEO of a medical supply company distributing sleep disorder products all over the country, he could only guess what they needed to talk with him about. Jarred hadn't been to Massachusetts for six years and was never issued any moving violations when he did travel within the state.

As jarred reviewed the throughput spreadsheets for the last quarter, he was smiling because of the increased sales output and revenue his team had produced. Looking at the drop in operating expenses for the same period, Jarred was even more impressed as his secretary broke in over the intercom.

"Mr. Henderson, it's Captain Garber from the Massachusetts State Police again. Do you want me to put him through?" Jarred's secretary asked as if not connecting the call to Henderson would keep the police out of his office.

"Of course, Caroline, put him through. We don't have anything to be afraid of. Don't worry, they aren't going to cart me off in cuffs and put me in jail," he responded, thinking what a great experience that might actually be.

"Captain Garber. Jarred Henderson here, how may I help you this afternoon?"

"Mr. Henderson, we are currently in the middle of an investigation regarding the murder and mutilation of five young women from our area out here in Auburn, Mass. There is a sixth girl missing and we presume she is being held by one of the killers."

"One of the killers? You have more than one?"

"The first killer was found dead yesterday, and we believe there is a second killer currently holding a young girl who has been missing for the last three days. Mr. Henderson, we need to talk with you concerning the "Angels of Mercy" orphanage you directed a number of years ago. Our investigators found some information regarding one of the killers having been adopted during the time that you were there. We have not been able to find anyone who knows where the records for the orphanage are located since its closure. Your name is listed as having been the director, and that is why we are contacting you. We are looking for any information you might have regarding a man named Christopher Bradford."

The name Christopher Bradford hit Henderson right between the eyes like a line drive in a fast pitch softball game. He actually fell back in his chair at the mention of the boy's name.

"Christopher Bradford? Holy Crap!" was the only initial response Henderson could manage to get out of his mouth.

"By that reply, I assume you are familiar this man's name?"

"Christopher Bradford would be the second most likely boy to have been involved in a sick situation like this. Let me tell you…"

"Sorry to break in Mr. Henderson, but we need to send a couple of investigators out to meet with you this evening in New York so you can share any information with us you might have regarding Christopher. It will be a couple of hours before they arrive, but a girl's life in on the line and we would very much appreciate your cooperation."

"Yes, Captain. In fact, I still keep in touch with a couple of the nuns who worked at the orphanage. I'll call them to see if they know anything about the location of the records. I can't make any promises, but I will do whatever I can to help."

"I appreciate your cooperation. However, I have one question that I need to ask you."

"Go ahead, Captain, shoot." replied Henderson, already regretting his choice of words.

"You said Bradford would have been the second most likely boy to have been involved in a situation like this. Who would have been the first?"

"Keith, Willingsby. As much trouble as Christopher was, his brother Keith was three times as bad."

Ken could not believe his ears. "What do you mean brother? One is named Bradford and the other Willingsby."

"Bradford is - was - Christopher's adopted name. Christopher's adopted father flew the coop soon after Christopher's adoption leaving his wife to raise Christopher by herself. We knew of a few boyfriends she dated here or there, but there was never anyone for the boy after the step-father was gone. Keith was so exasperatingly evil and impossible to control that he was never adopted out. He remained at the orphanage until he was eighteen years old. It was unfortunate, but he spent most of his time in solitary because of the perverted things he said and did to the other children. He acted out in many different ways ...brutal, sadistic... from raping of some of the younger girls to severe beatings of some of the boys. Keith did not need to be antagonized; his need to hurt people was something that just came naturally to him. Even the older boys at the orphanage stayed away from Keith.

All a person had to do was glance in Keith's direction. Keith would flip out and be all over them punching and kicking until the staff could pull him away. It didn't matter if it was one of the kids or a staff member. It was rumored that Keith loved to torture small animals he caught in the woods behind the orphanage, letting them die slowly.

He literally had the entire population of children at the orphanage so afraid of him that no one dared to tell on him for fear he would find out. Even most of the staff stayed away from him. A few of the children he hurt required physical and psychiatric hospitalization; two are still institutionalized to this day. We reached the point where we would lock him up in solitary for even the smallest infraction of the rules just to keep him from the others. Also rumored was that some of the staff brutalized and tortured him because of what he was doing to the other kids. None of the rumors about Keith's torture of the small animals, or the supposed beatings by the staff could be substantiated. I hired outside investigators to collect evidence so that we could press charges against Keith and send him off to a juvenile prison facility, but no one would say anything against him and the system turned its back on us. I will tell you this much, Captain, if I live to be a hundred years old, I would not want to meet up with Keith Willingsby again. People talk about the coming of an anti-Christ? Well, I think Keith might have put in for the job."

With the white van registered to Christopher Bradford gone, we figured his brother Keith must have subdued Marty, put her in the van, and driven off just before we arrived at the Baker building. With the revelation about Keith Willingsby being Christopher's biological brother, and knowing just a little about the years Keith spent at the orphanage, we knew Marty's situation was looking dimmer by the hour. Torturous and deviant behavior at a young age is not a good indicator for one's future behavior as an adult. It seemed as though Keith had earned a PhD in deviance by the time he was twelve or thirteen, perhaps after graduating from perversion and sociopathic tendencies. I caught myself to correct my socially, unacceptable mistake. The term "Sociopath" is seldom used in today's world of "gentle" understanding. Now a sociopath is generally referred to as a person afflicted with "antisocial personality disorder, or ASPD.

"How could I be so unfeeling?" I thought to myself with every ounce of sarcasm I could muster. "I mean, what the hell, by changing the label attached to the mental disease, we somehow change the person afflicted with the disease? Yeah. Right." My rational thinking was making me feel frustrated, because some people's concerns afforded more compassion to those afflicted rather than proper justice being metered out for those affected. "I'm supposed to worry about calling this asshole a sociopath as opposed to a person with

ASPD?" I continued to mentally rant. "I think ASPD translates as "another sociopathic perverted dickhead. I mean, look at what these two idiots have managed to accomplish? Five dead, one missing, and that's just in the last few years."

My attention was snapped back when I realized my thoughts were actually becoming vocal statements as I stood staring at the data boards in the meeting room in Auburn. We were in the middle of a briefing with my team members and Ken Garber's team members at the State Police facility. My thoughts had wandered when one of the forensic psychologists corrected a team member who used the term sociopath.

"Hey. Hey. Ron." I heard Ken say softly just before he jabbed me in the ribs. "I don't think the word "dickhead" can be used in any of our reports, if you know what I mean."

"Sorry about that, Ken. Sorry, everybody." I said apologetically, a little more than red faced. "I didn't mean to interrupt the meeting."

Leaning over to Ken, I quietly asked how much of my thoughts I had shared unkowingly with the group.

"I think it was somewhere around sociopathic perverted dickhead," he replied with a chuckle while shaking his head.

One of the troopers sitting a couple of chairs away looked up and said, "Hey Chief, don't worry about it. There isn't one of us in this room that doesn't think these guys are a couple of dickheads! You just said what we're all thinking." Everyone in the meeting room gave an audible signal of agreement.

Now it was the forensic psychologist with the red face feeling a little uncomfortable. Not one to pass up on an opportunity to gloat, I looked at him smiling my little smile of group acceptance and unity. No, it was not a competition, but at least I knew the rest of the group also thought these guys were assholes.

Todd and one of the Staties, having returned from New York late the night before, recounted their talk with Jarred Henderson. Jarred was not able to get the records of the orphanage by the time the officers arrived, but said he would have the information within a few days. Two nuns, Sister Allison and Sister Florence were with Jarred in his office when the officers arrived. The sisters both repeated pretty much what Jarred and Ken had discussed earlier in the day with regards to Keith Willingsby and Christopher Bradford.

Although both boys were known as being extremely difficult, Keith was regarded as the most evil and dangerous child they had ever met during their careers with the order.

Sister Florence said that Keith was the leader of the two brothers. He would tell Christopher what it was he wanted him to do and Christopher would obey without question or hesitation. The sister continued to say that Christopher was subservient to Keith almost as a servant to a master. Totally dependent on Keith's every word. The two boys together terrorized the entire population for over two years, until Christopher was adopted out leaving Keith alone at the orphanage. Keith retaliated by increasing his campaign of intimidation, physical and sexual abuses, and threats of death on the children at Angels of Mercy. Even the older boys at the orphanage steered a very wide path around Keith. Although not muscularly large for his size, Keith emitted an aura of darkness and evil that chilled people to the bone.

"It was the "evil within him," Sister Allison told the officers. "That is what protected him. Standing next to him was a frightful experience. It felt as if a vile, electrical pulse was infecting your body as he pierced your soul with his black eyes. Eyes that did not look at you, but rather peeled you apart layer by layer exposing your fears, making him stronger and leaving you exhausted and feeling violated. He was beyond cold, totally unfeeling. His only joy was watching other people suffer."

For the next three years, the orphanage stood a daily vigil trying to protect the other children from Keith. Sometimes they were successful. Sometimes they were not. Solitary confinement at the orphanage was given a new name. It was called Keith's room.

Both of the sisters verified the rumors of Keith's abuses at the hands of a few of the staff members. No one ever seemed to be around when the abuses took place, but in some instances Keith was not seen or heard from for days at a time while he recovered from the beatings. Keith never attempted any sort of retaliation nor did he ever go to the sisters or to Jarred Henderson to ask for protection. Instead, he remained silent and continued to take out his rage on the children.

A resounding sigh of relief filled the orphanage the day Keith was told he was free to leave. At eighteen, he had reached legal age to go out on his own. It only took Keith half an hour to get his personal belongings together, sign the release papers, and walk off the grounds. On his way out of the administration building, Keith boldly walked over to a group of attendants standing together smirking at him. Their smirks vanished after a brief conversation with Keith, each attendant looking unsettled and fearful as the front door closed behind him..

The attendants never shared what Keith had said to them, but within a year, all three attendants were victims of some sort of fatal accident. One died in his apartment from an apparent electrocution. Police found a radio in the tub where the attendant was relaxing, having a drink after work. The second fell off of a "T" landing just as a passing train roared through. There was very little of him left to find by the time the train came to a stop five hundred feet down the track. The third was found impaled on the wrought iron fence at the perimeter of the orphanage one morning as the day shift staff came in to relieve the night shift personnel. Everyone at the orphanage always wondered if Keith was responsible for their deaths, but no one was ever able to prove his involvement. Those who remained feared they could be next!

Jarred "Gabby" Henderson was a man of his word. Two days after our officers met with him and the sisters in New York, I received a large, white envelope from Fed-Ex containing the information regarding Christopher's and Keith's history at the orphanage. I closed the door to my office and took two hours to review the enclosed pages. When I was finished reading, I was frustrated and disappointed to find no new information we could use to help find Marty or Keith. Although more detailed, the stories were pretty much what we already knew. There was no "smoking gun" to help us in our search. Every police agency in New England was looking for the white van we believed was used in Marty's abduction. A national alert was issued as well, though I really felt Keith was hiding in the area. The one item of interest I did find in the envelope was a picture of Keith taken when he was released from the orphanage. I would run the picture over to the State Police and have them age enhance the photograph so that we would have a close resemblance to what Keith looked like today. The photo would then be sent out nationwide, and all New England television stations would be asked to show the photo during news broadcasts. It was imperative that Keith's face saturate the television and newspapers in this area so that more people might recognize him if he should venture out of his hole. My hope: some person would recognize

Keith at a convenience store buying groceries, or buying gasoline for the van.

"One tip," I thought. "One friggin' tip is all we need."

It had been three days Marty's disappearance from the Baker building. I paced my office floor knowing Marty's chances of survival decreased proportionately with each passing hour. This truly was a race against time. In my opinion, whatever happened to Marty while she was Christopher's captive would not compare to her situation now that she was being held by Keith. I had grave concern for Marty as I continued reviewing the pages of information scattered across the top of my desk.

"Paper. Just meaningless pieces of paper that don't mean a thing." I thought. "Marty's out there somewhere enduring god knows what, and I'm sitting here on my ass not able to move a muscle to help her."

The door to my office opened. I looked up to see Derek walk in.

"Chief, I've been reviewing information we received over the fax machine from the State Mental Health Department in Worcester. They were responding to the inquiry we sent out a couple of days ago asking for any information on Christopher Bradford or Keith Willingsby."

"Go ahead Derek. I'm all ears." I said emphatically, knowing right away that I was curt and to the point with my response. "Sorry Derek, I..."

"That's o.k. Chief. It looks like Keith was a patient for a short time in one of the state hospitals in Westborough. The records show he was arrested for assault after beating a guy at a bar. The charges included, drunk and disorderly, assault with a deadly weapon – a broken Tequila bottle - resisting arrest, assault on a police officer, and destruction of police property – he kicked out the windows of the police cruiser. The report continues that he was able to get his arms around one of the officer's necks while being escorted into the station and almost choked the officer to death using the chain between the cuffs against the officer's wind pipe. It took two other officers to free him from his grip.

"During the ninety days Keith was at the hospital, he underwent psychiatric evaluation and was deemed fit to stand trial. During the hearing that followed, the guy Keith cut to ribbons with the broken bottle actually testified in his defense! He told the court he provoked Keith with constant heckling during the course of the night and that Keith really was acting in self-defense. The man said Keith tried to defuse the situation by remaining calm, even offering the guy a drink. At one point the guy confessed to pushing Keith off of his bar stool onto the floor. Even after being thrown to the floor, Keith maintained his composure, righted the stool, and sat down again continuing to drink his whiskey. The witness testified he was surprised by Keith's non-response to his antagonism and further stated it wasn't until he struck Keith on the back of his head that Keith grabbed the bottle of Tequila, broke it on the top of the bar, and cut him.

"Keith's lawyer maintained that the arresting officers used excessive force during the arrest. He stated that upon their arrival at the bar, they saw the guy on the floor covered in blood from the over thirty cuts inflicted by the broken bottle. Assuming Keith was the antagonist they cuffed him right away, calling the ambulance for the victim lying unconscious beside the bar. The lawyer stated that the officers, while escorting Keith to the police cruiser in the parking lot, lost their hold on his arms and he fell onto the pavement cutting his front lip and bruising the side of his face. The lawyer, at this point in the hearing, held up a video surveillance tape from the bar asking the judge to accept the video tape as evidence the officers forcefully struck Keith in the face and pushed his face into the door of the police cruiser. Needless to say the charges against Keith were dropped immediately. The judge ruled that Keith acted in self-defense and that the arresting officers used excessive force during the arrest. Keith was instructed to pay for the windows in the police cruiser. Keith's lawyer immediately filed a law suit against both the bar patron who attacked Keith and the police department for excessive force and bodily harm to his client. As far as could be determined, the city paid a substantial amount of monies in order to avoid the publicity of a trial."

"Christ. This guy has to be luckiest son-of-a-bitch in the world!" I responded as Derek took a breather and sat in the chair opposite my desk.

"Chief, I was talking with Kim about this and we have a hunch we would like to follow up on, if you don't mind."

"Yeah, I don't mind a hunch now and then. What's your hunch?"

"We know Keith was a patient at the Westborough facility. He spent three months there. He would have had plenty of time to study the buildings and the grounds.

We'd like to take a ride over there and look around. It may be nothing, but it would be a great place to hide – abandoned buildings scattered all over the property with virtually no visitors."

"It's the middle of winter." I replied. "If he's hiding out there, he would be in a building with lights and heat. I would suggest you and Kim contact the electric company. See which of the buildings on the site are currently using electricity. This will save time on your initial search. If you don't find him in any of the buildings with power, then search the remainder of the buildings."

"Good idea Chief. we'll can get on this right away. Is it alright if we work overtime this?"

"If you don't work over, I'll lock the both of you up for dereliction of duty."

Derek smiled, and walked to the doorway. Turning he said, "Chief, we'll find her. I know we will."

"I hope you're right, Derek. I pray she's still alive. I hope you're right." I said as he disappeared into the outside office.

60

Keith put on the black mask, adjusting it to fit more comfortably on his face. After watching the Boston Celtics beat the New York Knicks, polishing off some chips and onion dip, downing a cold beer and allowing the moment of peace and quiet to settle his mind, Keith figured it was time to "play" with Marty. This would not be part of the adoption process like the other girls before. No, this was something much more personal and intimate. "This is between me and you, Marty. This playtime is time for me to express my needs. You are only a means to MY end - your end, being my main goal." he thought, smiling as he walked to the room where he held Marty McMaster.

Walking down the incline to the room holding Marty prisoner, Keith picked up an old, wooden, desk chair found in many of these state buildings. He wondered why furniture in state facilities always had to be so drab and depressing. "The people who picked this crap out should be institutionalized themselves."

Unlocking and opening the door, he knew Marty would be sitting on the bed. There was no other place for her to sit in her new "digs." Stepping into the room, he saw Marty sitting on the bed turning her head to watch as he closed the door and placed the chair a few feet away from the bed.

Keith straddled the chair and sat looking at Marty without saying a word. He continued to stare at her, watching as she began to squirm under his unyielding gaze. Marty tucked her feet under herself and folded her arms across her chest in an intuitive, self-protective gesture, hiding her breasts. She refused to look away from him, staring back into his eyes defiantly. "She is a feisty little bitch," he thought without making the slightest movement. He kept his breathing easy and rhythmic, enjoying the buildup of tension, while toying with her.

Marty felt like she was going to explode as her anxiety level tried to find a release. Although she was returning his stare, every part of her being was screaming inside waiting for something to happen: for anything to happen. The silence was pounding in her head.

"How can silence be so loud?" she thought watching the muscles in his thighs tighten just before he suddenly stood up over the chair.

Without saying a word, he signaled her with his hand to stand up next to the bed. Hesitating at first, he signaled her more forcefully the second time. She knew by the sharpness of the second request, that if she resisted any longer he would strike her again as he did before. Slowly she pulled her legs out from under her and placed each foot onto the floor standing as instructed. Before she could stand erect and look at him, his hand reached out grabbing the front of her blouse pulling it downward so forcefully the buttons popped off flying across the room exposing her breasts held in place by a see-through black bra. He continued straddling the chair as the last button stopped rolling on the floor, hitting one of the walls making a little clicking sound. He moved away from the chair, kicking it out of the way. The chair slid a few feet across the floor before falling onto its side with a loud crash. Simultaneously, he grabbed the front of Marty's jeans, pulling her up against his body. The blackness of his eyes mixed with the heat of his body made Marty shudder.

Still, he did not say a word. There was no sound with the exception of his breathing which continued to be controlled even after kicking the chair away. Marty could feel the depth of the complete darkness driving this person. She knew instinctively that this person holding her against him, looking down into her eyes, was a person totally devoid of any human compassion. There was no conscience to prevent this man from violating her as no other human being had ever been violated before. She renewed her resolve to fight with every ounce of strength she could muster, but knew in her heart there was little she would be able to do when he decided it was time for her to die.

Locked together by the grip on Marty's jeans, he smelled the fear begin to permeate the air around them. Loosening his grip on her jeans he began to undo her belt. Marty stiffened as the belt was pulled out of the loops and fell to the floor. It was at this point Marty closed her eyes knowing what would follow. She heard her jean's zipper as he pulled it downward while unfastening the top button, exposing the low-cut waist band of her panties. Still, he did not speak a word. But, the breathing, the calm, rhythmic breathing continued.

Letting go of Marty, Keith stepped back and signaled Marty to pull her jeans down and take them off. By having Marty perform this task, he was making her become part of her own humiliation. He knew the disgust she was feeling right at this instant as she bent over to pull each leg of her jeans from her left and right foot. He had felt the same humiliation many times at the orphanage.

Marty moved back toward the bed leaving the jeans on the floor between her and her captor. She was praying this was as far as he would go and that she would be allowed the dignity of not being stripped naked. At this moment, her bra and panties were the only things affording her any dignity or protection. She closed her eyes so she would not have to look at him. Marty did not want to acknowledge any signal given by him which would leave her completely naked, physically and emotionally. Her eyes snapped open when she heard the clap of his hands. Her fears were well founded. He signaled her to unclasp her bra and remove her panties. The sickness in her stomach was overwhelming. Marty dry heaved numerous times while slowly removing her undergarments, letting them drop to the floor.

Keith moved over to the chair, picking it upright. Straddling the chair once again, he sat to observe Marty's total nakedness standing before him. She knew if she tried covering her breasts or pubic area he would signal her to remove her hands and arms. He might strike her again like he did before. So, Marty stood with her arms by her side unable to prevent this "viewing." She felt his eyes penetrating her body with the same intense physical violation of rape. Revulsion and nausea mixing together made her feel faint and unsteady on her feet. "This is it. I'm going to die." She thought.

"Not the most physically attractive girl I have seen," he thought. "Breasts could be a little bigger, and she needs a little more meat on her bones, but she is definitely just what I need for playtime."

Keith stood up, signaled Marty to pick up the five buttons and clothing on the floor. She stood in front of him holding all of the items while she stared at the floor. Still holding the chair in his left hand, he took the clothing and buttons from Marty, putting the buttons in his pants pocket. He held the clothing under his left arm, turned toward the door, but, as he took the first step, he delivered another backhand to Marty's face sending her backward onto the bed. He did not look back.

"I love this," he thought. "I absolutely love this."

Kim and Derek were on their way to the state hospital in Westborough after speaking with a representative from the electric company. They were surprised to learn that nine of the fifteen buildings on the property were still using electricity. Three of the buildings were currently occupied and leased by satellite programs serving mental health patients who were living in the surrounding communities. The remaining six buildings were presumed empty but required heat to maintain structural integrity.

I was driving to Milford Hospital after receiving word that Doc Cavanaugh was out of the ICU and recovering in his own room. I left a message for Peggy on her cell phone to let her know where I was going to be for the next hour or so. Her support this last week had been a key factor in helping me hold everything together. If I needed to worry about an upset wife while dealing with this case, I think I would have cashed in my chips and moved under the Blackstone river bridge to share a cigar with Harvey, our resident hobo.

Jerry Bickford's services were to be held tonight as well as the services for Christine Sawyer. I would make sure to spend time at both. Pulling into the hospital parking lot, I instinctively looked into my rear view and side mirrors for any sign of a white van. Seeing none, I entered the hospital and asked the person at the reception area which room Doc was recuperating in.

Doc looked like he was sleeping when I walked into his room. There was a maze of IV's and drainage tubes in his body, but seemed to be very restful, propped up on some hospital pillows. I stood next to his bed looking at his chest area, my curiosity getting the best of me.

"If you're here to give me a kiss to go along with that hug, I'll throw my piss bottle at you! Doc said without opening his eyes.

"I suppose you're a psychic now that you've had a near death experience, you old buzzard." I replied laughing.

"Not really. I saw you in the hallway before you came into the room. I thought if you saw me sleeping I could escape another one of those hugs you sent in with the nurse. Damned if she didn't give it to me, too!"

"Well Doc, I guess you're well on your way to a full recovery. If you're strong enough to throw a urine bottle, then you must be on the mend."

Both of us laughed a little, although laughing caused doc to go into a coughing spasm and I knew from the grimace on his face he was in lot of pain.

"So, ... what the hell happened in your office? I asked.

"Damned if I know, Ron. One minute I was alone, and then this guy comes walking into the office, winks at me and then lets me have it! Next thing I know, I'm lying in a bed in the ICU after they took two slugs out of my chest!"

"Well, I'm not sure if anyone else has brought you up to date, but we believe the guy who shot you was named Christopher Bradford."

"What do you mean, was?" Doc asked, picking up my use of the past tense.

"Christopher Bradford was killed two days ago over at the Baker Building. He was involved in the murders of the five girls we found at Meadow Pond. We believe he's also responsible for the first abduction of Marty McMaster."

Doc attempted to sit a little higher in his bed. "What the hell. What do you mean the "first" abduction? What the Christ is goin' on here, anyway?"

"We believe Bradford was killed by Marty McMaster as she stood at the top of the cellar stairs in the Baker Building - where she was being held in a basement room. Looks like Bradford was bringing her upstairs when it happened. We theorize that she stuck a ball point pen into his head through the eyeball causing him to fall down the stairs. When we arrived we found Bradford dead at the bottom of the stairs but no Marty. Since she has not turned up anywhere, we believe Bradford's brother, Keith, took her prisoner and is hiding out with her somewhere in the area."

"You've got to be kidding me, Ron. Two killers? This is like a T.V. Movie, for God's sake"

"Yeah, right now we don't have too much to go on. We have a description of Keith Willingsby, Bradford's brother, but not enough information to give us any solid leads.

Kim and Derek are out at the state hospital in Westborough following a hunch. If they come up empty, we are right back at square one trying to find this guy. Hey, by the looks of those tubes and bandages, it looks like you just missed cashing in your ticket to see the guy at the Pearly Gates."

"At my age, who the hell would miss me?" doc replied.

"I would Dad." Doc's daughter Bonnie said as she walked into the room. "Hi, Chief Kosciak, it's nice to see you again. I don't think I've seen you since I moved out to California."

"You're right, Bonnie, it has been a long time. Nice to see you again, too. How have you been?"

"I'm good except for my father getting shot in a hospital morgue. Just goes to show you, you're not safe anywhere these days. I could understand getting shot during a robbery at a store or something, but in a freakin' morgue? Give me a break!" she said a little frustrated with the recent events.

"Bonnie, I know what you're saying. Believe me, I see a lot stranger things going on today than I saw ten years ago. The neighborhoods are changing a lot, and the people out there today don't play by any rules. Unfortunately, your dad met one of those people in his office the other day and ended up here."

"Hey, you two. I AM still here, ya know!" Doc said his stomach rumbling a little as he spoke.

"Believe me, Doc, we know you're still here. You won't let us forget it!" I laughed with Bonnie as we turned our attentions back to Doc.

The one thing I chose not to talk Doc about was Jerry's death. I thought it might be too soon for him to learn about Jerry being shot and killed. To my surprise, Doc was the one who broached the subject.

"Ron, it really bothers me Jerry was shot and killed the same day I was attacked in my office." He countered my expression with, "Yeah, I know, you didn't want me to know yet, but this is a hospital, and the staff let me know once I was moved up to this room. I'm thankful they did. Jerry was a good man, Ron. I'll miss him a lot. I understand his wake is tonight. Please, tell Michael and Jerry's family I send my regards to all of them."

"Don't worry, Doc." I'll pass on your sympathies to everyone. Listen, I have to get going. I want to stop out at the state hospital to check on Kim and Derek on my way home. I need to get cleaned up before Jerry's and Christine's services. Take care, ole' friend. I'm glad you're going to be alright. Bonnie, again, it was nice to see you. Take care of your old man, and I hope to see you before you return to California."

As I walked toward the door Doc yelled out, "Thanks for not tryin' to give me that kiss!"

I waved an acknowledgment to Doc's remark over my shoulder and, smiled knowing my friend would be O.K.

Kim and Derek arrived at the state hospital around two-thirty in the afternoon. It was below thirty degrees. The sky was an overcast, wintery, gray blanket allowing no sunshine through to warm the two police officers. Derek suggested that they stay together during their search just in case they did run into Willingsby. Kim agreed, remembering what each of the dead girls looked like after their ordeals, wanting every asset she could muster on her side should there be a confrontation.

They began their search in the main building. It was eight stories high, and most of the rooms and offices were vacant. This building was home to the three satellite programs providing services for mentally challenged patients living in adjacent communities. These were all outpatient programs, but today being a Saturday, no one was here. The building being vacant allowed Derek and Kim the opportunity to search uninterrupted. Deciding to start on the top floor and work their way down, they spent the next two hours methodically searching every room, closet, office, nook, cranny and cubby-hole before finding themselves in the basement.

Kim turned on every light switch as they entered each room, not leaving one shadow for a person to hide in and surprise them during their search. Derek was walking ahead of Kim in the cellar hallway. Kim turned to look back over her shoulder, making sure Keith was not sneaking up behind them. As she peered intently down the long, cellar hallway, Derek bumped a metal cleaning bucket sending it rolling down the floor. Kim, turning quickly, brought her 9 mm up and pointed it down the still unlit hallway to see Derek recovering from his tumble.

"What the hell, Derek! You wanna get yourself shot? You scared the shit outta me!"

Kim blared out as she pulled her 9mm upward against her shoulder, pointing the barrel at the ceiling.

"Jesus, Kim, I'm sorry. It's not like I planned to trip over the friggin' bucket! I scared myself, for Christ's sake! This isn't the nicest place I've ever been in. It gives me the creeps. Who knows what happened down here when this place was open? Do you believe in ghosts?"

"Okay, I'll let you off this time, but DON'T do that again! Let's get moving." she said taking the lead and turning on more lights as they went. "By the way, I do believe in ghosts, and this is definitely a place where we might run into a few!"

They spent the next half hour completing their search of the main building. Other than a few dead mice still caught in the springs and trip-wires of wooden traps, they did not see any other signs of occupancy, other than the three rooms on the first floor.

The next building on their list, and the second largest on the site, was one of the dormitories that used to house one hundred and fifty patients when it was at full capacity. The four floors each had exits and entrances from stairways on each end of the building as well as the entrance and exit in the front. Forty-five minutes later they were coming out of the building as I drove up to check on their progress. Driving up the road between the two structures, I opened my window as Kim walked over to the side of the Explorer.

"Hey, Chief."

"Any luck?" I asked.

"Not a damned thing: We found three dead mice and one cantankerous bucket," she replied, choosing not to explain the cantankerous bucket comment. I let the comment go, curious, but not wanting to press the issue.

"We've searched the main building and this dorm so far. We probably won't get to search all of the buildings today, unless you want to assign people round the clock."

I sat for a minute thinking about what I wanted to do.

"Tell you what Kim, you and Derek continue to search as many buildings as you can, and I'll be back after I stop at the services for Jerry and Christine. I should be back here about nine, nine thirty. I'll see if Ken Garber can send over a couple of his people to help us out before I come back. I'd like to keep this search going until we have searched every building on site."

"Can you do us one favor, Chief? Kim asked. "Could you bring us back a couple of coffees on your way back? We should have stopped on the way over here, but neither of us thought about it until we were half way through searching the first building."

"I'll do better than that, Kim. I'll go get coffees right now before I go to the services. The services don't begin for another hour and a half, and I don't want my officers telling people that I don't take care of them."

Kim looked at me like she had a smart reply, but decided to keep it to herself. Being the Chief does have its privileges - sometimes.

Before leaving to get the coffee, Kim, Derek and I spent a few minutes looking over the site plans for the facility. There were buildings located all over the grounds. Some were interconnected, while others were single structures standing alone on various parts of the property. As we reviewed the plans, I saw two buildings in a remote, back corner of the property with one access road coming in off a secondary town road. Looking at the plans more closely, I read that those buildings were used for storage and maintenance equipment. I told Kim and Derek to make sure these smaller buildings were searched.

Derek and Kim said that they would. They pointed to a row of garages and sheds by the dormitory, and said that is where they would be searching when I returned with their java.

63

"Kosciak was the only one Christopher didn't pay back before he got his ass killed," Keith was thinking as he sat watching the videos of the girls he and Christopher murdered over the years. Next to him, on a wall shelf, sat the glass jars with all of the children they had adopted. Until a week ago, he and Christopher were pretty much free to come and go as they pleased. Abducting young girls at their leisure, according to their schedule, no one ever questioned or glanced in their direction. Christopher was the one out in public sight every day while Keith stayed hidden in the shadows. The system worked flawlessly until the bodies were discovered out at the pond. Unfortunate, but the way life went. The brothers had just needed to adjust to the new situation, staying out of sight for a month or so before moving on to a new town to begin adopting all over again. For Christopher, the waiting was over, but before Keith would leave town he needed to finish what Christopher had started. Keith had to find Kosciak and make him pay for the events leading up to Christopher's death, for intruding on their family.

Keith entered the garage where the white van was parked. Knowing that every police officer within a couple hundred miles of Sutton was looking for it, he chose to his black SUV for this trip. He figured his best chance of finding Kosciak was at the police station. He would follow him and choose the right opportunity to kill him. The idea of killing Kosciak's entire family still lingered in his thoughts, and if the opportunity presented itself that is exactly what he would do.

Backing out of the garage, Keith noticed the overcast sky. The late afternoon hour made it look like night time. Being cautious, he waited until the SUV was almost on the secondary town road before turning on the headlights. After driving up the secondary road to the main road, Keith took a right, driving toward the police station in Sutton. He was not concerned about being spotted because the SUV was registered in the name of a person who had died three decades before. Keith created his double identity after getting a social security number using the dead man's information. After obtaining the new social security number the rest was easy. Next, Keith was able to get a driver's license using this dead man's name and his new social number. Credit cards and other purchases became easy once he possessed the right documents and identity. Keith could move around freely as Walter Simpson. No one was any the wiser and Keith loved the drama it created.

Driving up Route 9 toward Sutton, Keith decided to treat himself to a hot cup of coffee. He might even splurge and order a couple of those chocolate covered, crème filled doughnuts – that were his absolute favorites. He pulled into a parking space in front of the doughnut shop, got out of the SUV and walked in to order his coffee. The girl behind the counter was very pleasant and commented that the crème filled were her favorite, too. Keith smiled while looking past her at the drive-thru window. Another girl was handing her customer his bag of calories and three coffees. The customer paid and drove away, allowing the next customer to pull up to the take out window.

Keith could not believe his eyes. The next vehicle was a Explorer with Ron Kosciak sitting behind the wheel. Stepping back to his right, Keith hid behind a partition next to the register watching Kosciak. "How could I be this lucky? Chuckling to himself, he continued watching as Ron took his order from the girl at the window. When Keith saw Kosciak looking for the money in his pocket, he calmly walked out the front door and got into his SUV. Waiting for Ron to pull out, he started the engine and took a sip of his coffee, relishing the idea that destiny had put Ron Kosciak, the next victim of the brother's grim, right here, right now.

As Ron drove away from the window, Keith briefly looked the other way. Ron pulled out onto Route 9 with Keith following a few vehicles behind. Knowing the SUV was not a vehicle that would draw Kosciak's suspicion, he felt comfortable following a little closer without being seen. Hoping Kosciak was on his way back to Sutton, Keith presumed that the chief would be turn off this highway and take one of the dark, back roads to shorten the drive.

"This may be the perfect opportunity to get this son-of-a-bitch," Keith said out loud. Fate and destiny are working hand in hand to give me this chance to express my "dying" love for good, ole, Ronnie."

The two vehicles continued on Route 9 for the next five miles. Keith, keeping the same distance behind the Explorer, continued sipping on his coffee, enjoying the hot liquid as it rolled down his throat warming his stomach. Keith began to wonder why Kosciak was out this way buying three coffees. He was alone in the Explorer, and if he was driving to Sutton, the coffees would be cold by the time he arrived. No, there was something else going on here. Keith knew Route 9 was the road Kosciak would have taken to drive over to the Milford area, and was assuming Kosciak was doing just that. But when he saw the Explorer's right directional light start to blink he knew exactly where the Explorer was headed.

"Jesus Christ!" Keith shouted. "How the fuck did they think to look for me here?

There's no fucking way! NO FUCKING WAY!" he shouted again, his fist repeatedly pounding the dash board. Keith drove passed the exit for the hospital and watched the Explorer move up the main driveway to the facility. "Three coffees, three police officers," he thought to himself. That meant that they were searching the buildings, and would eventually find Marty. He had to make a quick decision as he continued up the highway a half mile, pulling into a strip mall parking lot to think this new problem through.

"If I go back and kill Marty right now, I can disappear without a trace. If I want to kill Kosciak, I can sit here and wait, killing him on his way back to Sutton." Keith finished his cup of coffee in silence. "No, I don't want Kosciak to get away with this. He, above anyone else, needs to pay for everything that has happened. I must kill him for Christopher. I'll wait until he drives by, then kill him between here and Sutton on one of the unlit back roads. No one will find him until it's too late. Then, I'll back track and see which building the police are searching. If they are still far enough away from my building, I may have time to take care of Marty before I leave." The plan made sense. Keith settled in the driver's seat waiting for Kosciak to drive by, on his way to meet fate and destiny.

After fifteen minutes, Kosciak's Explorer drove by with its ornamental police lights sitting on the roof waiting for the next time they would flash their red and blue authority. "Here we go, Kosciak! Here we go!"

Keith continued to follow the white Explorer, waiting for the vehicle to turn off of Route 9 and onto one of the back roads. In the dark of the winter evening, Keith knew Kosciak would not be able to see who was behind the wheel of the black SUV keeping pace with him on the highway.

"Here I come, Ronnie!" he thought to himself, eager for the exact second he would direct the police chief's last dying moments. "Ronnie, my boy, you need to take the next left up ahead. Don't be shy my man. Step right up and take a seat. You are center stage and the curtain is about to come down on you for your last mother fucking bow."

Keith saw the left directional on the Explorer start to blink.

"Well, I'll be damned. Now I'm a freakin' mind reader, too! You go, Ronnie. Go, Ronnie. Go!" he sang as he turned following his prey onto Crescent Street.

Crescent Street wound through the woods like a python through jungle swamps. The very sharp and erratic turns on hilly terrain were difficult enough to navigate during the day light hours, but at night, without any street lights, the roadway could be treacherous, if not deadly. More than a few people had been killed in accidents on this road over the years. The roadway abutted frequent wetlands and marshes with no guardrails to prevent vehicles from driving off of the pavement and into the muck and mire or even crashing head on into one of the large trees lining the road. In some areas, stone ledge ran parallel to the roadway only a couple of feet from the blacktop. The ledge sported many long, multi-colored marks from cars and trucks alike, that had scraped fenders and doors trying to regain control. The Blackstone River flowed through the middle of this forested area, its brown, muddy water rippling and churning under bridges and culverts. The fast moving current and visual impenetrability of the water, made the river a place where an object could stay hidden for years just beneath the surface without ever being discovered. Keith knew it was on one of the bridges crossing the river, that he wanted to deliver his death blow to Kosciak. Keith opened the arm rest between the two front seats. Taking out a Glock 9mm, he checked to make sure the clip was secure in the butt of the handgun. "This should get his attention, real fast," he thought, placing the weapon between his legs on the seat.

"If I remember correctly, the bridge I want is about a mile ahead of us. Calm yourself now - calm. THINK and BE calm. Control your emotions and you control your environment. He doesn't know what's coming. You will have the edge, the element of surprise. An unsuspecting small town police chief on a back country road? This is going to be FUCKING BEAUTIFUL!"

Keith knew by the turn and the slight down grade in the road that the bridge was just around the next right turn. This particular bridge did not go straight across the river, but instead crossed over the river at an angle making the bridge more diagonal and not perpendicular to the river's banks. Just before the bridge, the roadway narrowed until it was the same width as the one lane of the bridge. This meant Kosciak would have to slow down to make sure that here was no other vehicle or obstruction on the bridge as he approached. Like most back roads, the town had not spent the money to install blockades or safety railings on either side of the road leading up the bridge.

Keith began to tighten his grip on the steering wheel as both vehicles maneuvered around the last turn allowing his SUV to slow down, leaving a little more distance between the two. He watched as the entrance to the single lane bridge materialized in the headlights of the Explorer. Judging the distance to be about one hundred feet,

Keith pushed the gas pedal to the floor and heard the engine come to life. His SUV closed the gap to the Explorer with both vehicles twenty five feet from the bridge. Keith positioned the SUV so it would strike the Explorer on the driver' rear fender at the wheel well over the rear tire. As the SUV gained speed Keith saw the speedometer reading sixty-five miles per hour. By now, he knew Kosciak would see him barreling up on the back of the Explorer, but, it would be too late for him to react. As Keith had anticipated, the Explorer surged a little just before the two vehicles made contact. There was very little sound as the right, front bumper of Keith's SUV pushed into the Explorer, moving the rear of the vehicle sideways from the angle of the impact. Keith saw Kosciak in the front of the Explorer trying vainly to steer his vehicle out of the accident. There was nothing Kosciak could do to prevent what was going to happen. Kosciak would surmise this was a pre-planned attack by Keith and that his impending death was unavoidable. Keith could care less what Kosciak's thoughts were as his heart pounded excitedly, the two vehicles locked in combat moving toward the river's edge.

In the dark of the evening, their headlights lit up the bridge, the vehicles, and the river as it flowed away into the darkness. It was an eerie sight to behold as the Explorer, captured in this circle of light, was pushed sideways missing the entrance to the bridge by a few inches, then catapulting and spiraling into the air over the embankment. There was no sound at all as the Explorer fell the twenty feet down to the water below. Everything seemed to be moving in slow motion, as Keith watched with intent satisfaction as Kosciak's' Explorer entered the water, sending a spray of liquid ice in every direction almost as high as the bridge. Keith brought his SUV to a stop, jumped out, and ran over to the edge of the roadway with his Glock in hand.

The instant the Explorer hit the water the driver's door opened. The front of the vehicle was already underwater and it was being pulled along with the current away from the bridge. Only the headlights from Keith's SUV lit up the area as he watched Kosciak start to climb out of the vehicle before the river pulled it completely under claiming it as its own. With his Glock sighted on the shadowy figure struggling to get free of a surging, watery grave, Keith pulled off four quick shots. "Pop! Pop! Pop! Pop!" The gun sounded into the night stillness as two rounds found their mark and Keith watched Kosciak fall out of the vehicle limply into the water. There was no other sound after the Glock finished its death bark. Keith squinted, trying to focus more clearly on the lifeless figure floating away face down, being pulled into the night, most likely to snag on some fallen tree branch or rock formation downstream. It would be quite a while before anyone would find Ron Kosciak's water-soaked, bloated body.

"We, who have just killed your ass, salute you!" Keith announced to the quite, still night. He closed the door to his SUV and drove away from the bridge, already thinking about Marty McMaster, relishing this kill.

I held my breath for what seemed like five minutes before lifting my face out of the icy water to inhale lifesaving air. Trying not to move after falling into the water, I floated face down until the river's current carried me far enough downstream to a place where I could safely maneuver myself toward the shoreline. When I fell into the water off of the Explorer, the muddy water got into my eyes making it difficult for me to see clearly as I now fought to swim across currents that moved in many different directions at the same time. Where the bridge crossed the Blackstone, the river was about three hundred feet across. The river's depth averaged twenty-five to thirty feet with some stretches deeper, due to the water's speeds, currents, and downed trees or rock outcroppings along the shorelines. In some areas the river was smooth and almost calm. In other areas the water was treacherous and unpredictable with under currents that could pull you under never to be seen again.

Sitting in the Explorer as it spiraled off the road into the water, I thought that if it landed upside down I would not get out alive. The doors would have been held closed by the force of the turbulent waters and the vehicle would have submerged before I could escape. No, I was extremely fortunate it landed right side up and that I was able to get out into the open within seconds. I was not as lucky when I heard the sound of the gun and felt the bullet hit my left arm.

Although it was only a flesh wound that might need a few stitches, it hurt like hell as I moved my arm swimming sluggishly in the water. The cold water was already numbing the wound along with the rest of my body. If I did not reach the shoreline soon, hypothermia would deal the last blow.

A second bullet was firmly lodged in my Kevlar vest. Two other bullets missed their target and flew past me into the muddy river. I knew enough to fake being hit in a kill spot, letting myself go limp while falling away from the vehicle. The assailant, whom I presumed to be Keith Willingsby, must have thought I was dead otherwise he would have continued firing until he was certain. I was praying he was not following me down the river's edge to finish the job as I felt the muddy river bottom under my feet telling me I had reached the shoreline.

Figuring fifteen minutes since the accident and estimating the speed of the current, I figured I was about half a mile from the bridge into the woods. My clothing was soaked and the cold winter air was biting my fingers and my face as I pulled myself out of the river onto solid terra firma. My immediate concern was to find warm shelter where I could contact the station and let my people know what had happened. My cell phone would be useless after being submerged and my two way radio was missing, having separated from my belt during the attack and my escape.

My first steps where hesitant and unsure after my swim for survival. Keeping low while walking upstream toward the bridge, I kept my ears and hazy eyes attentive to any sound or motion that would indicate my attacker was still here hunting me in these woods. Without any streetlights on this road, I almost bumped into the bridge before I saw it. Struggling to pull myself up the embankment from the river onto the road, my thoughts were about Kim, Derek and their safety. If my attacker was Keith Willingsby, he was not here any longer. Believing I was dead he was most likely on his way back to the abandoned state hospital where I was sure he held Marty McMaster hostage. Keith must have seen us at the hospital and then followed me after I dropped off the coffees to Kim and Derek. If the shooter was Keith, then Kim and Derek were in very grave danger. He was now the hunter instead of the hunted. There had to be a way to warn them, but I knew as I became more lethargic that I was alone and would need a miracle in short order if I were going to get word to them about Willingsby. With each passing minute their situation became more life threatening and my life energies diminished, my body heat escaping through freezing muscles and soaked clothes. Even the blood oozing out of the bullet wound in my arm felt cold.

I was not sure I could walk any further and decided the best action was to take no action at all. Sitting down on the side of the road by the bridge, I thought about Peggy and how much I loved her. I thought about our kids, grand kids, and the blessed life I was allowed to live these past fifty some years. My eyes were burning from the river silt, my fingers and face numb and no longer feeling winter's sting. The one thing I wanted most was to lie down and sleep.

"Sleep," I thought, closing my eyes and leaning my head against the concrete at the end of the bridge. "Sleep. Then comes peace and quiet. Peace and quiet." The thought trailing off as something began to irritate me pulling me back to consciousness.

"Hey, Mister!" the voice said, sounding very distant. I did not want to pay attention to its nagging tone. I just wanted to be left alone in the quiet.

"Hey, Mister! Wake up, man. Come on, wake up!" the voice continued more insistently and urgently.

"What the hell happened to you? You've been in the river! Did you miss the bridge and drive over the edge?" The questions and statements rained down in my head like a thunderstorm pounding against my skull. I began to come around as hands lifted me up onto my feet and started to guide me to a waiting car.

"Shit, man!" one of the voices said. "This guys a cop! Look at his uniform. What's the badge say on his jacket?"

Another voice responding said, "Chief of Pol....He's the friggin' Chief of Police in Sutton! Oh man! This is big! This is really big! Let's get him out to the main road and call the Staties. They can meet us at Cumbies on Route 9."

The kid in the passenger's seat pulled out his cell phone and punched in 911.

I could feel the heat inside the car as they slid me onto the back seat, letting me fall onto my side. Hearing the excitement in their conversation but not understanding what they were saying, I managed to say Kim and Derek's names with the words…"need help." Somewhere between reality and the unbridled confusion in my head I was battling my way back. I had to help my officers – my friends.

66

Kim and Derek completed their search of the garages soon after I dropped off their coffees.

"No white van hidden in any of the spaces covered with a tarp like you read about in the crime novels," Derek thought to himself as they walked further down the road to search the next few buildings on their agenda.

"Won't be long 'til our replacements arrive," Kim said looking down at her watch and then at the map she was using as her guide. "That hot shower will feel good tonight after rummaging through these old buildings all evening."

"I wonder if the Chief will send some of our people, or if he was able to get through to Ken Garber for some extra help?" Derek replied. "Why don't you call the station and ask Todd what's goin' on?"

"I think I'll wait awhile before I do that. I don't want the Chief thinking I'm checkingup on him, even if that is exactly what I would be doing. We've got some time before they should be here anyway. Let's search these next three buildings, and if we haven't seen anyone by then, I'll give him a shout," Kim said folding the map and putting it into her jacket pocket.

The next three buildings contained doctor's offices and their quarters. Although closed for over two years, some efforts were being taken to maintain these buildings for someprobable use in the near future. The floors were being washed and waxed; furniture anditems in the rooms were being cleaned and dusted and the windows were clean as well. Curtains in the windows all looked recently washed and ironed. "Why spend the money now to keep these buildings clean?" Kim thought. "Why not clean them just before youuse them again? Doesn't make sense to me to spend money where you don't need to.What the hell do I know? I'm just a common sense mother of two." After another forty-five minutes, Kim and Derek checked these buildings off on their map as "clear."

There were four more buildings listed on the map that still needed to be searched. Three were on the west side of the property line and the fourth was on the north east end of the property. All four of these buildings were a considerable distance from the main facility and would require driving to get to them. Both Kim and Derek were hoping their replacements would arrive to take over the search, but as they walked back to their cruiser, no one was there to meet them.

"I'm going to give Todd that call no,." Kim said pulling out her cell phone and speed-dialing the police station.

"Hey, Todd. Kim here. Have you heard from the Chief? He was supposed to get in touch with Ken Garber in Auburn to ask if the Staties would send us some help here in Westborough to finish searching these buildings." Kim listened intently to Todd's response. "You haven't heard anything from him? When was the last time you talked with him?" she asked with a curious look on her face. Looking over at Derek, Kim shrugged her shoulders indicating that she had no idea what the hell was going on. "Okay, listen.

Try to raise him on the dispatch radio. If you can't get in touch with him, give Ken Garber a call to see if the Chief has been in touch with him. Derek and I will stay put until we hear back from you. Put a hustle on it Todd, my woman's intuition alarm is starting to go off."

"It's not like the Chief to just drop out like this," Kim said looking at Derek as they leaned against the cruiser, the chill of the winter's night creeping into their uniforms. "It should only have taken him twenty minutes to get back to the station after he left us. Even if he went home first to take a shower, he would have put that call into Garber over in Auburn."

"I think we're worrying too much, Kim. The Chief can take care of himself. He probably got caught up doing something else and hasn't had time to make the call. He has Christine's and Jerry's services on his mind, too; don't forget. He'll be calling us back in a few apologizing for screwing up."

"You're probably right. Well, how do you want to handle this? We have four buildings on this map left to search, and naturally, they are all located on the farthest ends of the property. What do you say? Let's drive over to that one on the northeast corner and check it out. By the time Todd calls us back, we can be over there and cross that one off of our list too."

"O.K.. Let's get it done."

Kim walked around to the passenger's door and they both got into the cruiser. Derek pulled out onto Route 9 and drove east about three quarters of a mile before cutting across traffic onto the secondary road leading to the northern boundary of the hospital's property.

It only took three or four minutes to drive to the access road leading to the lone building they needed to search. If they tried to walk across the property it would have taken them twenty to thirty minutes, not including time spent falling on the slippery, icy grass. Once they were onto the actual access road, Kim said, "Holy Shit Derek. Can you imagine being out here all the time? This place is scary as hell! There's no freakin' lights out here! Great place to go parkin' if you're a teenager though" she laughed a little, but still felt un- easy trying to see into the impenetrable darkness through the window of the cruiser's door.

The cruiser's headlights picked up the partially hidden doors of the garage as they pulled up in front of the subterranean building. Off to the left of the garage doors was the main door to the building proper. Derek used the probe light on the cruiser to look the area over before shutting off the engine and opening the door. Kim's door opened at the same time and both officers stood with one foot on the ground and one foot still inside the cruiser. Neither wanted to commit fully to searching this building, but both knew that this is exactly what they were there to do.

Kim was just about to tell Derek they needed to get a move on when her cell phone started to ring. Looking at the phone's screen she saw it was Todd returning her call.

"Todd, what's up, what did you find out?" Kim asked hoping for a positive response.

"The Chief never called Ken Garber. He said there was no request called in by anyone asking for help to search the hospital over in Westborough. I've tried calling him on his cell phone, on his two-way and on the dispatch radio. No response, Kim, nothing at all."

"Okay, Todd. Derek and I have to spend the next few minutes searching a building over here at the hospital. We really can't leave here until all of these buildings have been searched. If Marty McMaster is here, we have to try to find her before it's too late. Listen. Call the Chief's wife and ask her if she has heard anything from him. See if she can give us a lead on his whereabouts. This is getting strange, very strange. Call us back right away after you have talked with Peggy."

She put her phone in her pocket, looked at Derek, and motioned for him to use the master key to unlock the door so they could begin their search. The door made no sound as it rotated on its heavy duty hinges, hinges designed to prevent vandalism and break-ins.

Derek stepped into the building first, using his flashlight to locate the wall switch for the overhead lights. Finding the switch, he reached over and flipped it upward expecting the lights to go on and illuminate the building. The lights did not go on. Turning to Kim, he asked, "They did say there was electricity being used in this building, didn't they?"

"Yeah. The building is circled on the map as one of the nine using power. Must be a circuit breaker that popped," She replied. "Let's see if we can find the main box and get these damned lights on. It's creepy as hell in here."

Both Kim and Derek entered the first room of the underground building. Nothinglooked out of the ordinary, for a maintenance and storage building. An old, metal, graydesk was placed against one of the walls, with another one of those wooden oak chairs oncasters standing guard over its contents. A few filing cabinets lined the adjacent wall, anda cork board hung empty on the third wall opposite the entrance to the room. There wasno electrical box in this room. Kim, along with Derek, moved down a corridor to the nextroom, the only light being given off by the two flashlights. Everything else was pitch-black, and it seemed to Kim she could almost reach out and feel the darkness.

Perhaps it was the fact that neither Kim nor Derek really expected to find anything at the old, closed, state hospital. Having searched from building to building finding nothing, maybe it was the mundane nature of their search thus far that had worn down their awareness and dulled their responsiveness. Whatever it was that diminished their resolve, it would cost them dearly.

Kim entered the next room a few steps ahead of Derek. This room immediately stood out in stark difference to any of the other rooms they had searched that night. In one corner of the room was a neatly made twin bed with two white pillows sitting against a wooden head board. "That's not a hospital bed," Kim thought as her eyes scanned the rest of the room. There was a refrigerator, table and two chairs, counter top with a deep, kitchen sink, television set with disc player, and, the most intriguing item in the room, a surveillance monitor on the desk top. The screen was separated into eight different pictorials. Six of the pictorials monitored the outside approaches to this building, the main hallway, and the inside of the garage. The last two pictorials showed a young, naked girl sitting on a military type bed. Kim's heart pounded in her chest with the realization she was looking at Marty McMaster, still alive and in a room very close to where she and Derek now stood. Her excitement continued to grow as she turned toward the doorway to the room looking for Derek.

"Derek, get your ass in here!" Kim said in a whispering voice. The surveillance system: putting to put her on full alert. Whoever was living in this room could watch anyone or anything approach this building with plenty of time to be forewarned and therefore forearmed.

Derek, hearing Kim's whisper, never got the opportunity to respond to her request.

Kim caught the glint in her peripheal vision. The hunting knife appeared out of the darkness of the hallway, the light from her flashlight reflecting off of it's blade. In her mind, she knew that her friend was already dead. She watched in frantic helplessness as blood began to gush from Derek's neck, soaking his coat, and spraying onto the floor. As the knife finished its kill, Derek fell forward into the room. Kim saw the initial shock of the attack in his eyes change to the detached look of death. She instinctively reached out to her mortally wounded friend.

Kim knelt on the floor, holding onto Derek's arm. She braced herself for the attack that was sure to follow. She was distracted by the assault on Derek and had left herself vulver- able and exposed. A voice inside her head said, "You're dead." But, Derek's killer did not come through the doorway. There was only the silence of death hanging in the air, and the sound of Kim's heart pounding under her Kevlar vest.

Kim's training took over as her attention turned from Derek to Marty. Was Willingsby rushing to kill Marty, or had he taken these seconds to escape? The shock of Derek's death had momentarily crippled her, but the more she focused on Marty, the clearer her thoughts became. Kim moved to the doorway in a half-crouched position, and cautiously looked in each direction of the corridor. No sign of Willingsby. She eased herself into the hallway holding her Glock in one hand, while using her other hand as balance against the wall.

Moving deeper into the building, she listened intently for sounds that might lead her to Marty. With each step she took, she braced herself for that instant when Willingsby would jump out of the darkness and attempt to kill her, too.

The old, discolored, cast-iron piping attached to the ceiling took on an eerie, haunting look in the Shadowed corridor. Kim's eyes moved constantly, watching for movement, ears straining to hear the faintest sound. Thoughts in her mind swarmed like bees around a hive.

Thoughts of Derek, thoughts of Marty, and thoughts of her dying. Sweat beaded on her face. "Focus," she thought. "Come on girl. Focus."

Kim could see that the corridor ended about seventy-five feet ahead. Moving forward, she saw three doors, one directly in front of her at the end of the corridor, and two doors opposite each other on the adjacent walls. She paused on the left side of the corridor trying to decide which door to open first. She decided to open the door on her left, holding her Glock ready in her right hand, while keeping the remaining two doors in sight.

The door opened quietly into a room lined with lockers and benches. The room had no other exits. Kim opened each of the lockers, finding them empty. "One door down, two to go," she thought. Behind the door at the end of the corridor, Kim found an array of cleaning chemicals, mops, brooms, and a large utility sink. Her adrenalin level increased as she turned to the third door. She could feel an electrical energy entering her arms and legs. Sweat dripped off of her face onto the floor as a surreal excitement took control of her nervous system. If Willingsby had come this way, then he was most likely waiting for her on the other side of this last door.

Kim turned the doorknob, took a deep breath, said a quick prayer, and pushed the door open. She was totally focused, noticing immediately that the room was well lit, but empty. Kim backed out of the room into the corridor. She stood motionless, listening. The door closed against the jam, blocking out the light from the room, her flashlight dimly lighting the area. She sensed Willingsby's presence, could feel him. She remained still, unmoving, waiting as if suspended in time. "Here. He's here," she thought. "But where? Where the hell is he?"

The large paint chip, from the overhead pipe, fell onto her shoulder at the same time Keith Willingsby's full weight crashed on top of Kim, causing her knees to buckle, both falling to the floor. Kim's face slammed into the tiled floor, breaking her jaw and cheekbones, Willingsby landing on top. The pain was immediate, causing light headiness and confusion. Still, she rolled to the right attempting to gain the advantage. Willingsby, anticipating her counter-attack, shifted in the opposite direction allowing her to roll freely, maintaining his position and control. "Nice of you to drop in, officer," he said, bringing his right fist down into Kim's already shattered jaw. The impact almost made her lose consciousness. She felt herself floating, detached from the attack. Although her mind was foggy, her hands and legs reacted by instinct, hitting and gouging at his face, kicking him in the back with her knees. "Roll me over in the clover, roll me over in the clover and do it again," she heard him sing, his left fist punching her face.

The second blow ignited a fire in Kim's brain. Willingsby, an unspoken arrogance filling his chest, felt the fingers from Kim's left hand jab into his windpipe. It wasn't a particularly hard blow, but enough to interrupt his breathing and cause him to choke. In that split second, she reached between his legs and grabbed his testicles. Keith's grimacing scream echoed through the corridor. He fell off onto his side with Kim still crushing his jewels in her grasp. "Nice of You to drop by, scumbag." she slurred through her broken face. "Now, you sick fuck, where's the girl?" she demanded, squeezing harder.

Kim had lost her Glock during the struggle. She saw it about ten feet away on the floor. She knew she could not hold onto Willingsby indefinitely, and would have to release her grip to retrieve her weapon. Squeezing one last time with all of her strength, Kim let go and staggered toward her Glock. The one thing Kim had not thought of since Derek's death, came back to mind as it entered the small of her back. The hunting knife had entered just below her Kevlar vest. The impact of the knife propelled her past the Glock, onto the floor. She heard Willingsby struggling to stand as she reached for the knife. The Kevlar vest made it difficult for her to maneuver. She turned her head to look at Willingsby, saw that he already held the Glock, never hearing the shot.

As my rescuers pulled into the parking lot of the convenience store on Route 9, I was already beginning to thaw out and respond to what was being said. It only took five minutes to cover the distance from the bridge to the store. Pulling into the parking lot, I spotted a two-tone blue, State-Police cruiser waiting for us. Next to the cruiser stood two tall troopers who immediately came over to help me get out of the back seat as the young guys who helped me spoke without taking a breath, excited to be part of some evolving crime.

"Honest, Officers, he was just sitting there leaning against the bridge when we drove up. Whap! There he was in our headlights, barely breathing, with his head bent down onto his chest. We thought he was dead! When we saw his breath in the air, we knew he was still alive. We put him into the car, called you guys, and here we are!"

"Okay, you boys just sit tight here for a few minutes. We'll need to get more information from you both a soon as we talk to the Chief," one of the troopers said turning to assist the other trooper helping me into their cruiser.

"You have to call Ken Garber right away," I said huddling under the blanket. "He has to know what's happened. Keith Willingsby, the serial killer we are looking for, is in this area, and we have to act now before he kills another girl and escapes. He just tried to kill me over at the river" I said, feeling a little light headed.

"My partner is putting the call into Captain Garber right now. Sit back, Chief, and let me take a look at that arm," the trooper said pulling off my jacket and shirt. "You'll probably need some stitches to keep this closed. I'll wrap it in some Steri-Strips and gauze until we get you to the hospital in Worcester."

"Hospital, MY ASS!" I shouted. "I'm not going to any hospital! Let me talk with Captain Garber when you reach him. We need to get over to the abandoned state hospital. That has to be where Willingsby is hiding. It's the only thing that makes any sense. Two of my people are over there searching the grounds right now. We need to get there and back them up!"

"Okay, okay, Chief. I get the message. Ray, hurry up with that call to Captain Garber.

We need to get over to the state hospital and back up a couple of the Chief's people. If this guy would go after a police chief, he won't have second thoughts about taking out a couple of police officers."

I sat in the back of the cruiser while the trooper on the radio contacted Ken. A few minutes later the trooper in the front seat handed me a cell phone with Ken Garber waiting on the other end.

"Ken, that fucker Willingsby tried to take me out! Pushed my Explorer right off of the road into the Blackstone, and then tried to finish it up by shooting me!"

"Son-of-a-bitch, Ron. Did you see him?"

"No. It was too dark, and I was too busy trying to save my ass, but it's the only logical explanation. Listen, I have Kim and Derek over at the abandoned hospital searching those buildings that are still hooked up to the grid. I need to take your guys here and get over there right away. They're going to need all the help they can get if they run into that maniac!"

"Alright Ron, put Trooper Nelson back on. I'm going to send out the chopper and three more units to help you with the search. It will take about half an hour to get the other twounits out to you. You guys be careful."

"Thanks, Ken, I'll touch base later. This has become very, very personal. I really want a piece of this guy's ass!"

Two minutes later the state-police cruiser sped down Route 9 toward the state hospital, while I silently said a prayer hoping Kim and Derek would be waiting for us by the main building when we arrived. I borrowed Trooper Nelson's cell phone and put a call into Todd at the station in Sutton.

"Chief! What the hell! Where have you been? We're all looking for you. Kim and Derek are going out of their minds worrying about you!"

"Thanks for the concern, Todd, but I need you to contact Kim and Derek and tell them to meet us by the main building at the state hospital. I'm with two Staties and we're about five minutes out right now."

"Gottcha, Chief. By the way, you'd better call Peggy and let her know you're alright. We called her looking for you, and she is really upset."

"Listen, Todd. After you talk with Kim, call Peggy back and tell her I'm okay. Tell her I will call her later when all of this plays out. Have you got all of that?"

"I'm good, Chief. Kim first, Peggy second."

"Thanks Todd. Kosciak ou," I said sitting back. My strength was returning, but it seemed a very slow process. "So, this is what old age is all about," I thought as the cruiser pulled up the main drive to the hospital.

My heart sank when I did not see Kim or Derek's vehicle. This night was not over yet,and I did not like the way it had begun.

"What do you want us to do, chief?" Nelson asked looking over his shoulder into the back seat.

"Let me use your cell phone again."

Nelson handed me his phone, and I dialed in Kim's number. There was no answer. I left her a message asking her to call me right away with her location. I then dialed in Todd's number at the station again.

"Sutton Police, Officer Bentley, how may I help you?"

"It's me, Todd. I need you to put a call out to Derek Larson's phone and see if you can find out where he and Kim are located. I've tried Kim's phone, but there's no response."

"Chief, Kim said something about having four buildings left to search on their map.

There were three on the west side of the property and one on the northeast side of the property. I believe she said they were going to search the single building first."

"Okay, Todd. Make that call to Derek right away. We're going to find that building and see if we can catch up with them."

"Trooper Nelson," I said. I need you to get in touch with Captain Garber again and ask him to fax you over a copy of the layout for this facility. Tell him it's the one Kim and Derek are using that gives the details of the buildings still hooked up to electricity. There should be nine buildings marked off on the map. Tell him we need it ASAP. We don't have any time left. There could be three lives at stake."

Nelson got on the radio right away as I sat looking up into the night sky. My arm was beginning to throb. My clothes were half way between wet and dry. Totally uncomfortable, wrapped up in a blanket with two of my officers in jeopardy, I was beginning to get mad. I was beyond mad. I got angry back at the bridge when I sat like a human ice cube in, the road freezing my ass off. More than mad was just where I needed to be right now.

68

Within five minutes, Trooper Nelson handed me a faxed copy of the map. Quickly orienting myself to the map, I located the single building on the northeast side of the property, and we were on our way, covering the same route Kim and Derek had driven only forty-five minutes before. I would feel better once I caught up with Kim and Derek. We would then be a group of five with more re-enforcements on the way.

Kim's cruiser was parked out in front of the subterranean building. Both front doors were open, and Todd's voice from the radio echoed into the night trying to get in touch with Derek. After getting out of the cruiser, I stood listening as the radio in Kim's cruiser went silent. Within thirty seconds, Trooper Nelson's cell phone buzzed. Nelson handed it to me.

"Chief, I can't raise Derek either" Todd said sounding frustrated.

"Yeah, I heard you on the radio in Kim's cruiser. Okay, just hold tight there at the station. We're about ready to enter the building. I'll call you in a few minutes," I said, the pit of my stomach beginning to feel very uneasy. If neither Kim nor Derek were answering, they had to be in some sort of trouble. We needed to get in there fast.

I heard the rotor of the approaching State-Police chopper as the three of us entered the building. I signaled the other trooper to check out the garage while trooper Nelson and I entered the main building.

Walking slowly with our weapons drawn, we entered the same room Kim and Derek first inspected when they entered before us. Nodding to one another we moved silently into the hall and, taking a right, saw the door to the next room partially open. A dim light shown from the room. We approached the door on the opposite side of the corridor noticing splattered blood on the wall to the right of the door. The blood mark was curved and moved slightly upward away from the door. On the floor, more blood formed a tight circle about a foot in diameter next to the door jam. My apprehension peaked, dreading the thought that Kim or Derek were going to be on the other side of the door. Nelson and I raised our guns toward the doorway. Nelson went in first and signaled me over his shoulder to come in. His eyes were confirming my suspicions, as I pushed past him into the room looking at the body of one of my officers lying in a pool of his own blood, flashlight's beam illuminating his face.

"Chief, I'm sorry." Nelson said placing his hand on my shoulder. Turning away to let me have a minute with my friends, he took up a defensive stance at the doorway just in case Willingsby was still here waiting to ambush us as he had Kim and Derek.

Kneeling down next to derek, I gently reached over and touched his shoulder. Closing my eyes and clenching my teeth tightly, I felt myself tearing up, the first tears already falling onto the floor. I did not care if Nelson heard me crying. I did not care if God himself heard my sobs. One of my officers, my friend, lay dead on the floor and there was nothing I could do to bring him back. I thought of Derek's family and children. I thought about the vast, empty hole he would leave in this world. I had been lucky earlier tonight when Keith tried to kill me. Perhaps I had used up all of our luck when I survived the attack at the river. I knew in my head that that was not true, but in my heart I could not help but think this just might be the case. After a few minutes I stood up and looked at Nelson who turned to look back at me. Without saying a word, I knew by the expression on his face that he had experienced the loss of a fellow officer and friend, too. His look was empathetic, and whether or not he knew it at the time, his look helped me to re-focus on our present situation. I had progressed from anger at the river, to being mad.

Now, my emotions catapulted from being mad to seeking revenge. Keith Willingsby might be a serial killer, but, he had never dealt with me when I'd lost my temper. I hoped with every cell in my body that I would meet Keith Willingsby tonight, and that Nelson, or whoever elsemight be in the vicinity would turn a blinds eye to what I might do. I had one officer dead and Kim was missing. This was no longer by the book.

Walking over to Nelson, I turned one more time to look at my friend. That part of me that lives in reality knew that this was part of our job. Every law enforcement officer knew this possibility existed, but seldom spoke about it. We all knew we could lose our lives each day we put on our uniform. When you wear a police uniform, you sometimes found yourself in both the world of the hunter and the world of the hunted. Right now, I was determined to hunt down this bastard and make him pay. As Nelson and I stood there, I knew I had crossed the line. I was no longer Ron Kosciak, Chief of the Sutton Police department, I was Ron Kosciak, seeking total revenge for the people who Willingsby had killed during the last few years.

69

The State Police helicopter arrived shortly after we found Derek dead on the floor. Four additional troopers exited the chopper which had landed in a field close to the building. Two of the troopers joined Nelson and I inside the building, while the remaining two began a search of the outside perimeter. Nelson's partner had inspected the garage and found the white van as well as a black SUV with damage to the right front fender and bumper. The five of us continued searching the rest of the building in hopes of still finding Marty McMaster alive.

All of the troopers had been briefed on the situation before they landed. Everyone on the team knew that one officer was down, killed on the scene, and one officer was missing. Every person on the team who was familiar with Keith Willingsby's face, and the order had been given from the top echelon of the State Police to use any force necessary to apprehend and subdue this suspect.

Before leaving the room in which Derek had been killed, I looked around and found the video surveillance monitor on the desk. Views of the outside of the building were displayed as well as a room with an empty army bed. I figured this was the room Marty was being held in and was upset to see the room was empty. The thing I found peculiar, was that the van and SUV were still in the garage. That meant Keith was either still here, or had hidden a third vehicle with which he made good his escape. As our team of five began to move further down the hall, Nelson's phone began to vibrate. I raised my hand in the form of a fist and the team stopped without making any sounds. Nelson handed me the phone.

"Ron, Ken Garber. What is your status?"

"We're in the main hallway moving further into the building." I whispered.

"Listen, hold up for one minute. I have some information for you that might help your search."

"Ken, I'd like to stay and talk, but we don't have a minute. One of my officers is dead, one is missing, and Marty McMaster may still be alive. We have to move now!" this time an emphatic whisper.

"No. Ron. You don't understand," Ken was saying as I shut the phone off and handed it back to Nelson.

I gave the go signal and our group began its search once again. We had only moved twenty feet down the corridor when we heard the screams. Our instinct to run toward the screams at full gate was suppressed by the thought of Derek's bloodied body lying on the floor behind us. The screams could be a ruse to bring us running right into a trap. Instead of rushing toward the screams, I raised my hand in a fist once more, and the group stopped to listen.

"Nelson, take one of your people and stay against the right wall, one behind the other," I said very quietly. "The rest of us will stay single file on this side of the hall. Make sure you stay against the wall. Keep about six feet between you. We don't want to give this guy two targets for the price of one."

"Understood" Nelson replied. "What do we do if it is him, and we have a clean shot?" he asked.

"Shoot the mother-fucker right where he stands," was my reply. Still talking in a whisper, I followed, "We have the probability of a young woman being held hostage here. There is also the possibility she has been, or may be being tortured by this asshole right now. Marty McMaster is our mission. If every single one of us has to go down in order for her to be safe, that is exactly what I expect to happen. Are there any questions?"

There was no response. It was understood, and each man was willing to give his life so that Marty might survive.

Nelson and his partner moved to the opposite wall and the team began moving once again in the direction of the screams.

After killing the two police officers, Keith believed there would be ample time to "play" with Marty before killing her and making his escape. With Kosciak dead, Keith figured no one else would respond for at least a couple of hours. Needing only an hour to spend with Marty, he went to her room and dragged her by the hair, naked and screaming, down the hallway to his very special room: outfitted for just this type of party. Marty knew instantly as Keith entered her room that his intention was to kill her. He no longer wore the black mask to hide his face: a face with black eyes devoid of any emotion. No. This time, she faced a man fanatically determined to hurt her, and hurt her very badly.

Pulling Marty behind him down the corridor, Keith came to door of his special room. Opening the door, Keith pulled Marty violently into the room, releasing her hair. He pulled with such force, Marty's body did not stop sliding for about three feet, her skin squeaking as it slid over the tile flooring. Keith turned immediately, closing and locking the door.

Marty looking up from the floor could see the stainless steel table under the surgical light hanging from the ceiling. Instinctively she knew what Keith had on his mind and began to crawl across the floor away from Keith as sobs of hysteria began flowing uncontrollably out of her mouth filling the room.

"Go ahead and scream. Like they say in the movies; it won't do you no good," Keith said, walking over to a coat rack in the corner of the room selecting a white, surgical smock. "You are in my world now Miss Marty smart ass McMaster! This isn't Christopher's half way house. No. Indeed. This is MY house! In my house we play by my rules; which of course, do not exist! You were lucky the other day when you killed my brother. Usually he was very astute and aware. I know you surprised him, and, in fact, you even surprised me. But," Keith bowed like a knight of the realm in a theatrical gesture, "I'm sorry to inform you that tonight your life is going to end in a very painful and agonizing way. Let me just say I want to see what you look like from the inside out! Oh, don't worry yourself with a whole bunch of silly questions. This is going to hurt like nothing you have ever experienced before. You will feel everything as it happens. I would not think of holding anything back. It will be like Biology 101 when you dissect the frog in the lab! The only difference is this time you are the frog!"

Smirking and walking over to Marty, who now huddled in the corner of the room, Keith reached down and once again took Marty's hair in his hand. Pulling her up to her feet, he soundly punched Marty in the stomach holding her up as her legs went limp from the concussion of the blow. Marty lost her breath from the punch and gasped for air as Keith picked her up and roughly placed her on her back upon the surgical table. Marty, gasping to bring new air into her lungs, could not fight or resist Keith as he snapped the restraints onto her wrists, ankles and waist.

Marty was watching Keith's every move even though she was struggling to breath. Behind him she could see the shiny tools on the tray waiting for Keith to pick up and wield his carnivorous madness. Fear forcefully expelled itself out of Marty's mouth in shrilling screams of terror. Marty no longer had rational thoughts. There was no hope of escape. There was no hope at all. This asshole was going to torture her and cut her up. There was no ESACPE!

Keith pushed the tray over to the side of the table picking up a box cutter and Kelly Clamp. "Hmm," he said in a thoughtful manner while turning to Marty clamping her right nipple in the jaws of the Kelly Clamp. Within a millisecond, Marty's screams of unearthly agony filled the room. The pain, feeling like a white hot flame burning the end of her nipple, convulsed her body, every muscle tightening and writhing on the surgical table.

Smiling, Keith said. "I knew you had it in you girl! Now THAT is what I call a scream. No more of those namby-pamby screams for you. No, from now on, it's only big girl screams for you! Let's see now," he continued, placing the box cutter on Marty's stomach making a shallow six inch incision across her abdomen. Once again, Marty responded with agonizing screams from excruciating pain. Her body arched in resistance to the razor sharp blade cutting into her skin. Keith moved the blade to the inside of Marty's upper, right thigh beginning yet another shallow incision. Marty's screams intensified to an uncontrollable and deafening pitch.

"Well now, this is so much better than I thought it wou..." Keith was saying as the door to the surgical room blew inward from the plastic explosive precisely placed by Trooper Nelson seconds before the blast.

The force of the blast blew the instrument tray away from the table and picked Keith up off of his feet, throwing him upward against the far wall. If not for her restraints, Marty would have also been airborne from the force of the blast. Without the slightest hesitation, Keith rolled up onto one knee, pulled the 9mm out of the back of his belt and aimed at the doorway ready to kill the first person who was stupid enough to come into the room.

Without changing position, Keith pulled himself along the wall to a tall, metal, wall cabinet. Pushing quickly on the back of the cabinet, he moved it away from the wall exposing a three foot by three foot metal door. Turning the latch, Keith opened the door, allowing enough room to escape when it was time. But, not before killing one or two of his attackers. After all, this is what he lived for: this was his life!

Keith watched as the first uniform came through the doorway. He was about to squeeze the trigger sending the 9mm bullet on its mission when his finger froze in place as his mind recognized the man his eyes were looking at.

"YOU?" Keith shouted in disbelief. "How? YOU ARE DEAD!" he continued. Realizing Ron Kosciak had survived the attack at the river, Keith shot at him with a renewed frenzy watching the man lunge forward toward the surgical table.

I fired two rounds, landing against the bottom of the table watching and waited for Keith's response. Keith saw the second and third person rushing into the room with weapons drawn ready to fire. Knowing he only had seconds to escape, he ducked into the tunnel behind the metal cabinet firing three more times. He closed and latched the door, then scrambled along the tunnel. He could hear the shouting in his "play" room while running down the tunnel. The door would hold them for a couple of minutes. A couple of minutes head start was all he would need, to leave this place and start fresh in a new town, in a new state. This was the closest he had ever come to being caught, and the rush was exhilarating. He was still reeling after having seen Kosciak return from the dead, but looked at it realistically: "I can always come back and finish the job," he thought, coming to the end of the tunnel, his freedom only fifty feet away.

It only took a minute to cover the distance between the two buildings through the tunnel. Keith opened the door at the end of the tunnel, stepping into the smaller storage building. He had taken the time, when he first found this hideaway, to make, sure both doors at each end of the tunnel were in good working order. Right now he was very glad to have taken that time. It had just saved his life. This door, unlike the door in the other building, locked on the outside. This would help him gain a few more minutes when his hunters came rushing down the tunnel. Hurrying to the outside door of the building, Keith opened it slowly, making sure that the police were not outside waiting for him. He heard the police helicopter, but its light was shining over the building he had just escaped from. "These guys just don't get it, do they," he thought to himself, quietly stepping out of the building, walking toward a camouflaged tarp covering a second SUV hidden in the brush a short distance away.

Keith covered about half the distance from the building to the SUV before he heard a low, guttural, growling sound. "What the hell?" he thought. "What the hell is that?" Stopping dead in his tracks, Keith looked to his left and saw nothing except the rolling inclines of the hospital grounds. Looking to his right he saw the light from the police helicopter in the distance hovering over the crime scene. Turning his attention back to the SUV, he froze, paralyzed by the sight of the low, sleek, muscular body closing the distance between them. Keith tried running, but his legs did not immediately respond. When he was finally able to turn and run, the speed of his retreat was no match for the four legs about to bring a burning hell into his life!

After Willingsby made good his escape, I stood up and removed the Kelly clamp from Marty's breast. The dust still settling from the blast. I saw the blood on Marty's abdomen, and I covered her with my jacket, knowing just how far Keith Willingsby intended to go with his procedures. We loosened Marty's restraints and two of the troopers carried her out of the room to safety. Although one of my officers had died tonight, and Kim was missing, I was relieved that we were in time to save Marty from any further torture and her certain death.

Finding the escape door locked from the tunnel side, the Staties used more plastic explosives to blow the door and gain entrance to the tunnel. I believed Keith had once again managed to escape, probably having hidden another vehicle, and was already miles away. I was feeling depressed and angry. My only regret as I leaned against the cruiser, was that I did not get the opportunity to kill Keith and prevent him from killing someone else. Kicking myself in the ass, for not doing a better job, I felt embarrassed watching Ken Garber drive up beside me in his cruiser.

"Hey Ron," he said. "I'm sorry about Derek. I know he was more than just an officer to you."

"Thanks, Ken. I don't mean to be rude, but I'm just not in the mood to talk right now. Can I catch up with you in the morning?"

"Well, I think you will want to hear this, my friend," Ken said in such a way that I knew he had something important to tell me. "Our K-9 unit sniffed out a guy running across the property about thirty minutes ago. We weren't sure if he was our perp, so we pulled the dog off him to make a positive ID. Well, as luck would have it..."

"Chief! Chief Kosciak!" Nelson interrupted, obviously excited, running toward us from the building. "Chief. She's alive. We found her. Kim is alive. She's been badly wounded, but she's alive. Willingsby left her in the janitor's sink. Must have thought she was dead. They're bringing her out now."

I felt my knees weaken. Ken put his hand on my shoulder and said reassuringly, "She'll make it, my friend. I know she will."

"She's too damned stubborn not to." I replied, feeling thankful for Kim's survival, yet at the same time, saddened by Derek's death. I watched the paramedics wheel Kim's stretcher out of the building. She was unconscious, but the oxygen mask on her face gave me hope. I watched them put her into the ambulance and drive away before turning my attention back to Ken. "Finish telling me about Willingsby."

"The guy did turn out to be Keith Willingsby. The officer attempted to cuff him and bring him in. Unfortunately, we were not able to restrain Buster - that's the Sheppard's name - and Willingsby was attacked a second time." A smile grew on Ken's face, as he continued, "As fate would have it, Buster's partner, Trooper Davidson, fell and sprained his ankle while trying to get control of Buster. The trooper was unable to help Willingsby due to his injury until help arrived five minutes later. A dreadful situation, I know," he chuckled. "But, we were powerless to restrain the dog. Although Willingsby will probably survive to stand trial, he will have at least six months of re-hab, and a few hundred stitches to recover from, not to mention the rabies shots he will have to endure!"

"Thanks, Ken," I replied. "I wanted to kill this bastard myself. I was over the edge and I knew it. I honestly believe if I'd had the opportunity to put my 9mm to his head and pull the trigger, I would have done it."

"Don't think for one second that you're alone, Ron. There isn't one of us here who would have felt differently, or done the same thing if given the opportunity. I'm thankful Buster was able to meter out a little bit of revenge, and chew this guy's ass to bits in the process.

On the other side of the property, an ambulance was driving up another access road to pick up what was left of Keith Willingsby. A later report from the hospital would state Willingsby sustained over two hundred puncture wounds, but the compound fractures to his arms and legs were listed as "unknown origin".

The ambulance transporting Kim from the scene disappeared at the end of our access road. My thoughts turned to Doc Cavanaugh, Jerry Bickford, and all of the other victims, as I stood watching the EMT's care for Marty McMaster in the back of another ambulance.

I reached up to my shirt pocket for a cigarette that wasn't there.

EPILOGUE

Keith Willingsby, wearing a bright, orange-colored, prison coverall was led handcuffed and shackled from the state police SUV to the courthouse for his arraignment. His escort, six troopers, carrying automatic weapons and wearing body armor, watched the surrounding crowd and buildings intently as they walked the one hundred feet from the van to the courthouse steps. No one heard the single shot that blew the side of Willingsby's head off like an exploding melon hitting a concrete sidewalk. Willingsby died instantly and would never stand trial for any of the murders he was charged with committing.

Three quarters of a mile away, on the top floor of a ten story parking garage, Wayne Sawyer, retired Marine sniper, calmly closed the case containing his M40A1 rifle. Walking back to his wife, Bev, who was waiting patiently in their car, he stopped briefly, looked upward and said, "For you, my beautiful Christine, for you."

Printed in the United States
By Bookmasters